HONEYBEE

DAWN O'PORTER is a *Sunday Times* and *Irish Times* bestselling author, whose books have sold over a million copies worldwide. A full-time writer, Dawn is also well known for her TV work, journalism, podcasting, designs for Joanie Clothing, and as the co-founder of Choose Love.

After years living in LA, Dawn recently resettled in the UK with her husband Chris, her two boys Art and Valentine, and a whole menagerie of animals. Back on home soil, and feeling the pull for Guernsey where she was raised, Dawn was inspired to write a new chapter in the lives of island girls Renée and Flo – characters from her YA 'Paper Aeroplanes' series. A homecoming in more ways than one, her novel *Honeybee* came to life.

www.patreon.com/Dawnoporter
@hotpatooties
/DawnOPorter

Also by Dawn O'Porter

FICTION
The Cows
So Lucky
Cat Lady

PAPER AEROPLANES SERIES
Paper Aeroplanes
Goose

NON-FICTION
Life in Pieces

HONEYBEE

DAWN O'PORTER

HarperCollins*Publishers*

HarperCollins*Publishers* Ltd
1 London Bridge Street
London SE1 9GF
www.harpercollins.co.uk

HarperCollins*Publishers*
Macken House
39/40 Mayor Street Upper
Dublin 1
D01 C9W8
Ireland

First published by HarperCollins*Publishers* Ltd 2024
1

Copyright © Dawn O'Porter 2024

Dawn O'Porter asserts the moral right to
be identified as the author of this work

A catalogue record for this book is available from the British Library

ISBN: 978-0-00-869707-5 (HB)
ISBN: 978-0-00-869708-2 (TPB)

This novel is entirely a work of fiction.
The names, characters and incidents portrayed in it are
the work of the author's imagination. Any resemblance to
actual persons, living or dead, events or localities is
entirely coincidental.

Typeset in Berling LT Std by Palimpsest Book Production Ltd, Falkirk, Stirlingshire

Printed and Bound in the UK using 100% Renewable Electricity
at CPI Group (UK) Ltd

All rights reserved. No part of this publication may be
reproduced, stored in a retrieval system, or transmitted,
in any form or by any means, electronic, mechanical,
photocopying, recording or otherwise, without the prior
permission of the publishers.

This book contains FSC™ certified paper and other controlled sources
to ensure responsible forest management.

For more information visit: www.harpercollins.co.uk/green

Dedicated to Aunty Jane and all the bees
that worked so hard in our garden. Even the
one that stung me on the head that day
I skived off school. It was fair enough.

Part One

Drone

A note, disguised as a paper aeroplane, is launched by Renée in a biology class in May 1995. It lands directly in front of Flo.

> *Flo, I'm livid that we're stuck in this room while there is an entire world out there to discover. Like, do you know what stresses me out the most? That even if we bunked school, we'd still be stuck on this island. Think about it, there are about 69 (I think it's actually 63 but 69 is funnier) thousand people here, but there are about 6 billion people in the world. They probably don't even know we're here. I bet you can't even see Guernsey from space. We're so insignificant (oooh, good word!). I want to be SIGNIFICANT FLO.*
>
> *I dunno, I feel like we're stuck in here getting sex education from a teacher who coughs every time she says sperm and makes sex sound like you're buying a packet of ham from the supermarket. Is that diagram supposed to put us off cocks forever or what? It makes a man look like a watering can. It's so . . . functional. She hasn't even mentioned orgasms. Have you ever had one by the way?*
>
> *ANYWAY, don't you feel like everyone else is out there*

living actual life. With cool jobs and cool clothes and motorways that go for miles and miles. I feel like a prisoner. We are trapped. They are holding us hostage in this school. We could be more than this Flo. We could be out there making shit happen. Earning money, buying STUFF. But no, we're stuck in here being shown drawings of genitals in a blatant attempt to stop us ever having sex. IT IS MADNESS FLO! WE CAN BE MORE THAN THIS. We deserve to be out there in the big world, SPREADING OUR LEGS (I mean wings, calm down!)!!!!!!

Also, apparently, Gem is going on the pill. IMAGINE me telling Pop I was having sex and wanted to go on the pill. He'd sew my knees together.

Ewww weird image in my head. OK, see you at lunch. THIS IS SO BORING.

Friends Forever,
Renée x

Flo writes quickly on the wing of the plane and sends it back when the teacher isn't looking.

I like science. Stop throwing notes at me, I don't need another detention because of you.
FF, Flo x

Renée replies by writing on the other wing and sends it back.

You love me really. Can't wait for lunch, I've got a sausage roll x

AUGUST 2001

1

Renée

I worry constantly that I'm running out of time. When I'm lying on my deathbed, if I'm lucky enough to die in a bed, will I feel like I got it all done? Will I have succeeded in work and love? Will people have liked me? I really want people to have liked me. I want to have made an impact. I want people to remember my name. 'Renée Sargent, I loved her work,' is what I hope they will say, if I ever get round to creating any work. Will anyone care when I die? People get bored of me, or I get bored of them. It keeps happening. It's like the real thing, or the big thing, is always just around the corner. Nothing ever feels like enough. When I get there, to this deathbed, will I have done 'enough'?

I'm twenty-two and have no job, no home, no boyfriend, no real friends, and no idea what to do next. This was never my plan, and never who I thought I'd be at this age. Isn't something miraculous supposed to happen to us at this point? Like a less physical version of puberty that turns us into adults? How are we supposed to know when it's happened? There are things I have no idea how to do that adults just do instinctively. Like insurance claims, or mortgages. Or weekly shops with meal plans and clearing the room of naked feet when glasses get smashed, and always knowing where you put the dustpan and brush so you can sweep it away quickly. Receiving bottles of oils and vinegars as gifts and not being horribly disappointed that it isn't a Miss Selfridge voucher. Having one glass of wine in front of the TV to relax, instead of going on a bender. Knowing when to put what bins out and always having clean underwear in your drawer. Where do I learn how to do all that? How do I fit a career into all this, when just existing feels like a full-time job?

I've been in Spain for the last couple of years, staying with my dad. He lives there with his new wife and kids, and the less said about him the better – as it turns out, he has no interest in being Dad of the Year when it comes to me. And now here I am again, back in Guernsey. The tiny island where big things happen. It's been two weeks, and I've barely stepped out of Aunty Jo's house. I mean, why would I? She's so lovely it makes me wonder why I ever left. I haven't been in contact with anyone from school yet. Apparently my old friends Carla and Gem both work in banks and Carla is engaged. Who the hell gets engaged at twenty-two? I can't be bothered to meet up with them, hear about all their successes in life, and then have to tell them I have achieved nothing. I'm going to have to get out there at some point though, I need a job. I have zero money, and I want to save to move to London so I can start my inevitable career of being a world-famous writer.

It's weird to feel so alone in the place I grew up, but I do. I never thought I'd be back. Pride is keeping me inside the house. Except today, intrigue has dragged me out to catch up with another old school friend. I say friend, but we were never actually friends. Sally de Putron is dead. Her funeral isn't something I could miss.

As I look to the front of the crematorium and see her coffin, I wonder if in death there's truly any such thing as hate. It all seems so trivial now. We were in the same class at Tudor Falls School for Girls from age three to sixteen, and we never once, not even once, got along during that time. It's like we had a scrap over a toy in nursery and never made up. Destined to be arch enemies, always in combat, out to make each other feel awful. It makes me shudder, I'd never be arsed to be that way with anyone now: it feels so immature, so pointless. But we were kids, I suppose, can we blame it on that? I'm not a kid any more, apparently, so maybe.

There's a very old version of Sally's mum sitting at the front of the crematorium. Occasionally, her head bobs in time to the sound of her sobbing. There are only two other people on the pew with her: a lady, maybe her sister because when she turns to the side I notice she has a huge nose, like Sally; and a little boy, around five or six. That must be Sally's son. She got pregnant with him as a teen. He's just lost his mummy. I know how he feels. Maybe I should wait for him outside and whisper in his ear that his life is going to be OK regardless of this. Because despite my current dismal status, I think the thing that drives me forward the most is losing my mum when I was a kid. It gives me motivation to not just accept my disaster of a life. We are all running out of time. You can use it, or not. I choose to use it.

Sally's was a rare form of cancer apparently. It must have been really bad because the Sally I knew never lost a fight. But even her own body turned against her. Not that it's her fault, like my mum's cancer wasn't her fault either. Luck of the draw, I suppose. And not all deaths are bad. My nana died a few years ago, and I quite enjoyed the whole thing. Nana was old, she had dementia, and it was time. My aunty Jo had taken the best care of her and kept her comfortable, and then one night she went to sleep and didn't wake up. Apparently, that evening, she thought she was a professional dancer who worked on a cruise ship and was married to a younger man who refused to wear underpants, so she died on a high. I didn't cry when Aunty Jo called me. And I didn't cry at the funeral either, I haven't cried since. I was just so happy to finally experience a good death. It was more of a relief than anything else. Aspirational, even. She was so mad by the time she went, she didn't even have regrets.

HONEYBEE

There are about twenty people in the crematorium. Not much of a turnout for someone so young. Maybe Sally never changed, it's likely she remained unlikable her entire life. All twenty-two years of it. I feel that the Renée who went to Tudor Falls School for Girls is a million miles from the Renée I am now. But Sally never left Guernsey. She had a kid when she was a teenager. Maybe she was always a grumpy cow who couldn't hold down a true friendship. Judging by the poor turnout, I think that might be true. Although right now, if I died, who's to say I'd attract a bigger crowd?

The notice about Sally's death was in the Guernsey press a few weeks ago. It simply said, *Mr and Mrs de Putron sadly announce the death of their daughter, Sally, aged twenty-two, after a short battle with cancer. She leaves behind one son, Martin, five years.* It then listed the funeral details. I know her mum loved her but where were the words of affection? They could at least have thrown in a 'beloved'.

The vicar is giving a eulogy. He probably never even met Sally. When I die, I want Aunty Jo to do my eulogy, I know she'd make it funny. That's more important to me than anything else, that people think I'm fun.

'A loving mother to Martin, Sally was known to book his birthday parties weeks in advance to ensure the Wimpy, his favourite restaurant, could accommodate him and his friends.'

Christ, did he just list Sally's Wimpy bookings as one of the greatest things she ever did? I came here feeling like my life wasn't moving forward, but if the most redeeming feature anyone thought to mention at my funeral was that I was excellent at advance bookings in fast-food restaurants, I'd get out of my coffin and crawl into the furnace myself.

The service is coming to an end. The vicar begins to speak those infamous words: 'Ashes to ashes, dust to dust . . .'

There is a creak from the back of the room. The door is opening. A bolt of sunlight is thrust into the room and illuminates the coffin, as if God himself is shining a light on Sally's last few seconds on this earth. Everyone turns to see what angel created this moment. There is no angel. There is Flo.

Flo

I can't believe I'm late.

My journey to the church has been suitably symbolic, considering I'm coming to pay my respects to someone who made my life absolute hell for a huge chunk of my teenage years. I missed my alarm this morning. It was 8 a.m. and my flight from Gatwick was at 10.30. I knew I'd probably miss it if I got the Tube, so I called a cab. I didn't even have time to shower. The cab cost me nearly 100 quid, the traffic was awful because of a crash on the South Circular. I was so stressed in the car, and then got really sick because I was so hot and hungover and thirsty. I puked on the pavement at Gatwick Airport. When I got to the check-in desk, they said the flight was delayed by half an hour, but

I still somehow managed to miss the call. I had to run to the gate and got there just in time. I felt so self-conscious and then saw that someone I went to school with was on the same flight. I pulled my top over my face and kept my head down. That's the annoying thing about the Guernsey flights, there's always someone I know on it.

I tried to fall asleep on the plane, but the man next to me kept asking me where to go on the island after I stupidly said I grew up here. At one point I was holding the sick bag under my face, and he still didn't shut the fuck up. Once we landed, my suitcase took ages to come. Mum was supposed to be waiting for me but gave up when the flight was delayed: she texted me to say she had to go and meet a friend. I haven't replied yet. Why couldn't she just wait? Isn't me moving back to Guernsey a big enough deal for her? Some things never change.

There were no taxis, but I eventually got one. The old man driver was so slow I could have run here quicker, and then of course I had to walk through a graveyard and up a massive hill dragging a giant suitcase containing nearly all my worldly belongings. In my haste, I had to leave a few things behind. I'll have to go back to London to get them. I can't think about that right now, or what happened there. More pressingly, why did I make all this effort for Sally?

I open the door slowly, it creaks, everyone turns to look. I keep my head down and quickly slide into the back pew. There aren't many people here. I expected more. Why, I'm not sure. Sally was hardly Miss Guernsey. I daren't look up for fear of making eye contact with someone from school, or Sally's mum. I don't want to see people. I just, for some sick reason, want to see Sally's coffin. Not because I wanted her to die, I didn't. But because I've tried to shake off the shame she made me feel at school all those years ago, but can't. And I'm hoping that by actually watching her be rolled into a burning furnace, I will finally be able to find some closure.

As the coffin starts to move, the only other person on the pew slides closer to me. I notice my heart start to race, wondering who it might be. Someone from school? I don't want to explain why I am here. Or lie about caring. Or not caring.

'Hello,' the person whispers into my ear. I turn to look. 'JESUS CHRIST!' I shout, like she's a ghost who's jumped out at me in a dark hallway. 'Renée?' Of all the people in the world I'd expect to see here, it wouldn't be her. And now people are looking at me for the second time.

'What the hell are you doing here?' I whisper.

'That's blasphemy, Flo,' she says, facetiously.

I feel my face getting hot. Sweat is gathering on my top lip and running into my mouth. I'm disgusting. Why is it so hot in here? Oh God, the furnace. I might be sick.

I reach into my bag for a tissue. There is only a dirty one. The only other thing in there is a pair of period-stained knickers that I had to change on the plane. I wipe my face on my sleeve. Adding to the grossness. I might as well have used the knickers.

'Are you OK?' Renée whispers, possibly genuinely concerned, as I do look like I might have a heart attack.

'I'm fine,' I reply. 'Please stop talking.'

'You don't look fine,' she continues. Because that is what Renée does. She keeps pushing until she gets what she wants. 'You look a bit fucked, to be honest.'

'Renée, will you please,' I say, realising that people are starting to stand up. I look to the front, the coffin has gone. I didn't even see it go in. The entire reason I came was to watch that happen. I don't know why it was so important to me; it shouldn't be, but it was. And I missed it. Because Renée is here, and that is so bloody typical of her and exactly why I haven't spoken to her in almost three years.

Wow, is it three years?

'Flo, you came,' says a weeping Mrs de Putron, as she walks to the back of the crematorium. I didn't want this. I was going to get out before anyone saw me. Luckily though, the back door has been opened and a lovely gust of cool hair brushes over my face, calming me right down.

'I'm so sorry for your loss,' I say, hating myself for being so basic in my condolences. I wish I was better at thinking on my feet in awkward situations.

'Yes, I was so sorry to hear about Sally, Mrs de Putron,' Renée cuts in. 'Flo and I have thought about her a lot over the years. We wanted to laugh with her about the old days and let bygones be bygones. Sally was a huge part of our lives at school, and we are devastated by this. Aren't we Flo?'

How is she so articulate, it's infuriating. I turn back to Mrs de Putron and say, 'Absolutely.'

Mrs de Putron manages a small smile, before dropping

her head again and leaving the crematorium. Soon it's just Renée and me, alone.

'It's weird being here, isn't it?' she says. 'Have you been back . . . since?' I assume she's referring to my dad's funeral. He died, quite suddenly, when I was fifteen. It was one of the things that brought Renée and me together all those years ago: her mum dying, my dad. Two unlikely friends bonding over grief. Is that beautiful or horribly depressing, I have no idea.

'No. Luckily, no.' I just want to leave now, squashing down the memory of Dad's coffin disappearing. The overwhelming restraint it took me not to smash it open and drag him outside.

'I have. We did Nana's funeral here. She died a few years ago.'

'Yes, I heard,' I say, feeling guilty for never contacting her about it. I wanted to, I just couldn't. Not after everything that happened between us. 'Sorry to hear that, she was a lovely lady.'

'It's so strange that Sally, my mum, your dad, Nana and Pop all ended up in the same oven. Maybe us too, one day,' Renée says, staring aimlessly towards the front.

'Well, that's a morbid thought,' I say, turning and looking at her properly for the first time. She's still as pretty as she ever was. Her cheeks the perfect amount of chubby, her nose splattered with freckles. Her dark brown hair is scrunched up into a messy bun, with a multicoloured scrunchie holding it together. I know her well enough to understand that each bit of hair hanging down is meticulously chosen and separated from the rest, framing her face in a way that looks natural but is no accident. 'Organised chaos' is how Renée once described her appearance. It suits her perfectly.

'Depends how you look at it. It's only a morbid thought if we didn't live great lives,' she says. 'We can't fight the fact we are going to die; we just have to make sure we have the best time before we do.'

'I suppose.'

'Which is why we should probably go to the pub and get drunk,' she says, every bit the chancer she always was.

'Bloody hell, Renée. You think I'm just going to forgive you for everything you said?'

'Language, Flo. Your best friend Jesus won't like it,' she says, winking. 'Or did you ignore him for three years too?'

'Actually, Renée, I had an epiphany about faith all by myself. I moved on because of an educated decision that I made. It served me for a while and gave me what I needed, OK? Anyway, what are you doing here?' I ask, deflecting.

'Oh, you know. I can never miss a party. Can we leave? I'm a bit creeped out by Sally being behind that curtain.'

We head outside. The rest of the funeral guests start to disappear down the hill. My giant suitcase is still where I left it.

'What twat left that there?' Renée says, as I reach for its handle. 'Oh, sorry.'

'I flew in this morning. A bit last-minute, but looks like I'll be back in Guernsey for a while. I was in London, but it didn't work out.' I immediately regret saying that.

'London? When did you move there?'

'A couple of months ago, after uni finished.'

'And why didn't it work out?'

'It just didn't.' I walk away, my suitcase making a horribly loud noise as I drag it. 'I'll go back in a few weeks and . . .'

'And what? Why do you need to go back if it didn't work out?'

'I'll have to . . . God, do you know what, it's none of your business Renée.' I storm off down the hill, my suitcase filling the silent graveyard with an intolerable rumble. As the hill gets steeper it starts to overtake me, moving so fast I will have to let go or I'll fall. 'Shit, no!' I shout, running after it. Renée follows me.

'I'll get it,' she says, launching herself at the case. It falls flat with her on top and eventually grinds to a halt. She is laughing hysterically; I stand over her and the giggles make their way to me too.

'What have you got in here, a dead body?'

'Renée, not OK in a graveyard!' I tell her, laughing. 'Who throws themselves at a moving suitcase?' I want to add that I've really missed her, but I keep that to myself.

'This is quite a niche catastrophe. Splayed across a suitcase in a graveyard. That sounds like an indie song lyric. "I've been splaaayed across a suitcase in a gra-a-vyaaarrrd!"' she sings through giggles. I roll my eyes as she stands up and dusts herself off. 'Come for a drink?' she asks. 'I've got Aunty Jo's van. It smells like a goat's anus but it gets you from A to Pub. If we decide to get on it, I can just leave it in town overnight. It doesn't lock, but no one will nick it because of the whole anus thing.'

I don't want to go home, back to Mum's. She didn't even bother waiting for me at the airport, so she can get lost as far as I'm concerned. Who else doesn't see their mum right away after being away for months? Renée, I suppose. And now I am reminded of why we became friends in the first place. I pick up my suitcase. 'I'll come for a drink,' I say, walking away, hiding my smile.

It was easier to deny myself of Renée while I was on the mainland, but it seems like our friendship is growing out of the ground here. It's in the sky, it's in the sea, it's in this graveyard. Embers of our history are scattered all over the island. I suppose it's worth one last try to rekindle it.

'Goat's anus?' I say, my hangover tapping me on the shoulder again. 'I suppose hair of the dog won't hurt.'

Renée

Even parking on the Crown Pier with Flo gives me butterflies. It's like déjà vu, or something. Like we're following the tracks of our old lives, but observing ourselves from a distance. As we walk along the harbour wall, I look at her and it kind of takes my breath away. Same old Flo, but different. Her hair is long and brown. She's tall and slim. In fact, she hasn't really changed physically, except her black clothes look a lot nicer than the things she used to wear. She's lost the puppy fat on her cheeks that we all had when we lived on chippie chips and mayonnaise after school. She looks good, actually. Pretty. Maybe even beautiful, if she'd only believe it. That was always her problem.

There was a time Flo and I knew everything about each other. But she's been off, living in London, being so grown-up. I'm a bit intimidated by it, she's got this new self-assurance. I like it, I think. But it's weird.

We walk into the Ship and Crown, order two Bloody Marys and sit down at what used to be our table. 'It hasn't changed at all,' I say, as we both look around.

'You did that,' Flo says, pointing to a hole in the stool she's sitting on. 'You stabbed it with your tweezers because you wanted to pull out the stuffing and put it into your belly button to make some stupid joke about belly fluff. God you were weird. Do you still never leave the house without your tweezers?'

I pull my tweezers out of my bag and we both laugh.

'I remember doing it. We were chatting to that guy with the massive beer belly. Do you remember him, he was always in here, he sat over . . . oh my GOD!'

We both turn in the direction of the guy's old seat and there he is, still sitting there. Still drinking a pint of Breda, the local Guernsey beer. Still a huge beer belly. Still alone.

'Fuck me that's depressing,' I say, watching him gulp down his beer. 'I thought *my* life hadn't gone anywhere. He's been staring at that wall this whole time.'

'I swear he used to wear that actual T-shirt. Wow, that is really tragic,' says Flo. 'At least you've managed to get changed.'

'Yeah, go me! Do you still only wear black?' I ask, sipping my Bloody Mary. It's quite spicy and makes my nose itch.

'Mostly. Did you not get the memo about wearing black to a funeral?'

I look down at my navy jumper and dark denim jeans. 'I thought there would be more people and it would go unnoticed.'

'You thought being the only person not wearing black in a roomful of people wearing black would make you go unnoticed?'

I raise my shoulders.

'You never want to go unnoticed, Renée.'

I smirk. She's right. 'I turned up to pay my respects to someone who once gave me a dog poo wrapped in kitchen paper for my birthday. My presence was enough, she didn't quite warrant a new outfit.'

'What did you wear to Nana's funeral?'

'I wore one of her dresses from the Seventies. Aunty Jo did too. It was special, Sally didn't deserve it. Also, I can't get into it any more because I've been stress-eating since my best friend stopped answering my calls.'

There is a silence. Then some drinking. Then some more silence. There's a big conversation to have, possibly even a fight, and my guess is that we both feel like we need a drink before we go there.

'I'm sorry I wasn't there, I . . .'

'It's OK, I didn't need you to be there. It was for family, you know? Small. I had a few moments where I realised I'd lost almost everyone, either because they'd died, or they didn't want anything to do with me. I felt quite liberated, in a way. One less person to worry about. One less person to disappoint. After the funeral, we all went back to Aunty Jo's, I made polite chats with some of Nana's friends. She hadn't made a particular impact on anyone. She just sort of lived and then didn't. I went back to Spain, to Dad's, with a new energy after that, determined to make my mark on the world, you know?'

'Well, she created your mum and Aunty Jo, and that led to you. So I wouldn't say Nana didn't make an impact. That's a pretty good legacy, don't you think?'

That was a nice thing for Flo to say. I smile, to show my appreciation. She smiles back, because she loves me really, even if she might not want to admit it quite yet.

'How did your "new energy" work out for you in Spain?' she asks, finishing her drink. I'm barely three fingers into mine.

'I had loads of meaningless sex, drank over four million shots of sambuca and accepted that my dad doesn't love me. So great, it went fucking great,' I say, dealing with the spicy nose and downing my drink.

'I'm sorry Renée.'

'Yup. I went there to bond with him and left feeling like a total stranger. And if I mentioned Mum, he looked at me like I was trying to destroy his marriage to Maria. Like, to mention my dead mother was to bring a past so dark into his present happiness that it would shatter everything.' I stop talking to let the trauma run though me. 'What fucks with me the most is that he's such a good husband to

Maria, and a great dad to my stepbrothers. It's hard to see the person who has basically abandoned me emotionally be full of love for his other family. I have shame, but didn't do anything wrong. Like, with men I just automatically feel dirty and damaged. I really tried to fix it, but I was just this annoyance trying to tag onto their perfect lives. So, I fucked around instead. You know me, got an answer for everything.'

'What about Nell?' Flo asks, noticing her glass is empty.

Nell is my younger sister, we've never been that close. 'She needs love in a different way. She hates affection or intimacy, so her just being able to live with Dad is enough. Sometimes I'd watch him blatantly ignore her as he spent time with his other kids, and she'd not mention it. But I could see it hurt her. I think she's so scared of losing him that she just takes whatever she can. God, FAMILIES. It's so depressing.'

'Not as depressing as my dad being baked in the same oven as Sally de Putron.'

'You win,' I say. We raise our glasses and clink them together.

'How's Abi?' Abi is Flo's little sister. There's a fair age gap between Abi and Flo, but they get on really well.

'She's amazing; she seems to have got through Dad's death totally unscathed. And, well, Mum still treats her like the golden child, so she's a high-achiever at school and not wracked with self-loathing like the rest of us. She's an amazing kid, I'm really proud of her.'

'And I'm proud of you, Flo. Honestly, you've had a rough

relationship with your mum and look at you now. Back on the island in a pub with me, pretending she doesn't exist. Strong, healthy work.' We clink our glasses again. We always bonded over how broken we were, it's nice to know we still can.

'There aren't many people I can talk to about this, thank you,' I say, meaning it with all my heart.

'You're welcome,' Flo says. 'From one abandoned puppy to another. I guess there has to be a point in life where you stop hoping your parents will change and you just get on with things?'

'I agree. I feel like I could fight for Dad's love forever and then he'll just die, and it would all have been for nothing.'

'OK, well that's the most morbid thing I've ever heard,' Flo says, waving at a blonde girl behind the bar and asking for a bottle of wine. I watch her while she pours it into our glasses. She keeps going until it's almost to the rim.

'Flo, I'm sorry for everything I said in Nottingham. I've regretted it for years, and I've missed you.'

She looks at her glass and says nothing.

I'd gone to visit Flo at uni, gotten drunk, said some things I shouldn't. I remember calling her 'boring' and 'unadventurous' because she just stayed cooped up the whole time. I think, deep down, I was jealous of her newfound freedom. And it made me angry that she wasn't out, meeting people, seizing the day. It was one of those arguments that felt insignificant at the time. I hadn't known I was risking losing my best friend.

'I had no right to criticise you. And look, nothing about my life is how I want it to be. I'm back here living in Guernsey because I have nowhere else to go. I'm going to have to get some shitty job and see people who are thriving while I am floundering. I don't want to do any of it. I feel like a total drop-out and I can't tell you how good it feels to be with you right now. Please forgive me.'

She looks at me sternly at first, and then pitifully.

'You really hurt me. And not for the first time, I—'

I reach for her hand across the table. 'Please Flo, we're both back on the island. Great things ahead of us. Think of it as a sign from the universe.'

Eventually she reaches back, a small smile appearing. It's not quite forgiveness, but maybe we're close.

We both look up as a man appears at our table. He is staring at me and it's weird. 'Yeah, can I help you?' I ask him, in my toughest voice. I hate how men think they can interrupt two female friends who are talking, it's so rude.

'I'm sorry if this sounds strange,' he says. Flo and I roll our eyes and wait for whatever pathetic chat-up line he's come up with. Gross, he can't be less than fifty. 'But are you Helen Sargent's daughter?'

Immediately, Flo squeezes my hand. My face burns up, I can feel it turning red. My heart starts racing and it takes everything I have not to cry.

'Um, I am. Yes. Why?'

The man smiles so sweetly. 'I knew your mum. I knew her very well.' He blushes. They clearly dated. My heart stops pounding. 'You look so much like her. I saw you walk in and I knew right away that you must be her daughter, or at least related. It took my breath away. I was so fond of your mother, she was a wonderful woman. Beautiful and very funny. I'm John, by the way.'

He holds out his hand for me to shake, I put my sweaty palm in his. 'Renée. This is my best friend, Flo.'

'Hiya,' Flo says, also shaking his hand.

'I'll leave you to it, it was lovely meeting you, Renée. You are beautiful, just like your mum. I'll be happy all day having seen you. Goodbye.'

'Goodbye, John.'

I watch him walk away. A lump in my throat pushing tears up to my eyes. I am completely overcome; this island is haunted by my life, but not always in a bad way. I don't know what to do except run into the toilets and burst into tears. Mad thoughts running through my head. Why couldn't she have married him? That nice man could have been my dad. I look in the mirror, and I see her. He's right, I am so like her. I have her face, her hair, her blood. I could be sick from missing her. Flo bursts in.

'Renée, my God, are you OK? That was wild. Amazing, really. Beautiful, but my God, are you OK? If someone did that to me about my dad, I think I'd throw up on the spot.'

'I'm OK,' I say, both hands on the basin, trying to regulate my breath. Flo strokes my back. It takes a few minutes, but I get myself together. Long breaths out. A splash of water on my face. *I'm OK, I'm OK.*

Flo has gone quiet. 'Renée, look.' She points at the toilet door, and there, scratched by my tweezers are the words,

'*Renée and Flo 4ever.*' We just stand there, staring, until finally I can speak again.

'Come back to Aunty Jo's with me,' I say. 'We can sleep head to toe and pretend the last three years never happened. For old times' sake?'

'But my mum . . .'

'"I guess there has to be a point where you stop hoping your parents will change and you just get on with your life",' I say, quoting her, raising my eyebrows.

'OK, I'll come,' she says. 'But I'll sleep on the floor. I don't want to be anywhere near your feet. Are you sure you're OK?'

'Yeah, I'm fine. I mean, it was lovely, it just shocked me. You know? He recognised me, isn't that amazing?'

'It really is,' she says, linking arms with me. 'Come on, let's go. I can't wait to meet Aunty Jo's goats.'

2

Renée

It's 9 a.m. the next morning and I'm sitting in the kitchen with Aunty Jo. She's cooking Flo and me bacon and eggs. Flo is yet to appear. She was out for the count when I climbed over her in bed. It must have been the Bacardi I'd grabbed from Aunty Jo's drinks cupboard when we got back from the pub. Flo started doing shots of it when we'd run out of Coke. I couldn't face it.

'I knew you guys would work it out one day,' Aunty Jo says, over the sound of the kettle boiling and bacon sizzling in a pan. Being back here is heaven. She's the coolest, kindest, most loving person I've ever met in my life. She can't do enough for me; it's always been that way. I think, in many ways, she saved my life. After Mum died, Nell and

I lived with Nana and Pop, and things were so hard. They were too old to deal with teenage girls, it was exhausting for us all. And then Aunty Jo appeared, like a real-life angel. She moved back to Guernsey, and I went to live with her instead and it felt like a thousand tons had been taken off my shoulders. She's so like Mum, she even smells like her. I mean, Mum smelled mostly of Chanel No.5, but every now and then, before Aunty Jo has a shower and before she cleans out the chicken coop or mucks out the goats, I get this whiff of her. Her real, natural smell, so powerful that for one moment I can sense Mum's skin against my cheek. Her arms around me. Her gentle 'I love yous' in my ear. I'd do anything to feel that safe again.

I realise my life isn't exactly the greatest success story of all time, but I dread to think the state I'd be in if Aunty Jo hadn't taken me in. It's amazing how just one person loving you with all their heart can stop you from giving up on yourself. She isn't annoyed that I'm back here after all these years; she doesn't ask me how long I'll be staying. She just looks after me, offers solutions, tells me not to worry and that everything will work out. She's so good at being an adult and I want to be like her one day. Just another twenty-four years until I reach her age and have everything completely sorted. What scares me the most is that I can't rely on Aunty Jo to be this person forever. The quest to relieve her of that burden keeps me awake at night.

'FUCK!' she screams, making me jump and splash hot tea into my face. 'I burnt the twatting toast AGAIN.' She pulls it out of the toaster with her fingers, despite me getting her wooden tongs last Christmas. 'More for the geese, I suppose.' She puts another two slices in the toaster. 'Third time lucky.'

She places a massive fry-up down in front of me. 'I'll do Flo's eggs when she's up. I can't remember how she likes them.'

'Hard,' I tell her, remembering Flo's aversion to runny egg yolk. 'And you have to spread the yellow around with a fork so it's not all in one lump. But you're right, wait. Maybe Flo likes her eggs differently now. She's really changed.'

'She has? How?' Aunty Jo asks, sitting opposite me, eating a piece of discarded burnt toast without a plate.

'I'm not sure. Last night she seemed a bit . . . a bit wild. Like, she used to have this stop button that she'd press before she got out of control, and now it's more like an accelerator. It's kind of amazing, I just never imagined it. She's Flo, but different.'

'We all change, love. Thank goodness.'

Something suddenly catches my eye. 'Aunty Jo, get down, WASP!' I scream, throwing a sausage across the room and ducking underneath the table. She immediately jumps up and waves a tea towel around. Then she looks horrified with herself and drops the tea towel on the floor. 'God, I thought it was a man-eating bird the way you reacted. That's not a wasp, Renée. It's one of my bees.'

The bee settles on the corner of my plate. I still have suspicions that bees and wasps are in cahoots and plan to destroy us all. Aunty Jo can see that I'm scared. 'I don't get why you'd want them as pets, all three hundred thousand of them,' I say. The one negative thing about coming back to live with her is the five beehives she now keeps in the garden. I've hardly been out there for fear of being attacked by them. 'He might sting me,' I say, backing away.

'No, *she* won't. A bee will only hurt you if it feels threatened. You're right though, a wasp is quite different. They can sting you a hundred times and be OK. This little lady will die if she stings you, she knows that. She's just out and about working hard, aren't you my little worker bee?'

Aunty Jo lays her finger in front of the bee, and it hops on as if it's been waiting for a taxi and managed to wave one down. She walks slowly over to the back door, holds her finger up to the sky and the little bee flies away. I'm sure we'd have heard her say 'thank you' if we'd listened hard enough.

'There, no need to panic, just a little bee,' Aunty Jo says, picking up a frying pan and pouring the warm fat into the bin.

'See? That's what being a grown-up is,' I say, retrieving my sausage from under the table. 'Saving bees without hysteria. I'd have squashed it with my fork. I'm a terrible human.'

'I'd probably have done the same at your age, Renée. You learn these things, you realise not everything is out to get you. Come out with me to the hives, will you? They're nothing to be scared of, I promise.'

'OK, I will. But I'm taking the fly swat.'

HONEYBEE

We wander through the garden together, past Billy and Carol, the goats. Past Trudy and Tim, the geese. Past Brenda, Susan and Gloria, the chickens, and finally we reach the beehives. It's a sunny summer's day, the bees are busy. The collective sound of their wings flapping is creating a very loud buzz. Aunty Jo walks right up to the hives.

'Come on, Renée. Come closer. They won't hurt you, I promise. They're far too busy to worry about what you're doing.'

I take another brave step closer to the hives. I see hundreds of bees, thousands even. Some are flying out, some are returning. Aunty Jo is right, none of them seem bothered that we're here at all.

'You know, in the bee world, the only purpose of a male, a drone as they are called, is to mate with the queen. Other than that, he is totally useless. It's the females that collect the nectar and make the honey. It's not that different in the human world, the amount we women have to do and deal with to survive.'

She looks upset, for a second. Not something I notice very often.

'Is everything OK with you and James?'

'Oh yeah, we're fine. Fine, fine, fine. Just, you know, it seems a woman's work is never done. One thing after the other, bloody relentless. And it seems behind every busy woman who is trying to hold it together, there is a man in an armchair reading a newspaper with a hot cup of tea that he didn't make. I love coming down here and watching the bees get on with it. They're not bitter, they're not resentful, they're just getting on with what they have to do. They inspire me to keep busy.'

I'm not entirely sure what she's talking about, but there is definitely something on her mind. She walks up to one of the hives and gently lifts off the lid. 'Look inside,' she tells me, 'it's amazing, really.'

I crane my neck. Inside are what looks like thousands and thousands of bees, all scuttling over the honeycomb which is bursting and oozing in places.

'It's nearly time to extract the honey. You can help me, if you like, in the next few days. They've done this all by themselves. They've gone from being eggs, to larvae, to pupae then adults. And all through that process, they just knew what to do and what was needed from them. Imagine having that conditioning, born knowing exactly what your purpose is.'

'No, I can't imagine it. My "purpose" is like a mythological goblet that's totally out of reach. I hope the bees know how lucky they are.'

'They do, I'm sure of it. This is what happens when females stick together, look at what they can achieve. I swear, if the world were run by women it would be a better place. We know instinctively how to get the job done. Nature fires us with challenges and we power on regardless. Amazing, really.'

She wipes her forehead with the back of her hand; she looks very hot.

'I wish I felt that way. I don't know if I have any instinct, I'm like the bee that flew into the kitchen. Totally lost.'

She shuts the hive and loops her arm through mine. We start to walk back towards the house.

'What you don't realise, dear Renée, is that experience is as valuable as success. You've been through a lot. You lost your mum, your dad wasn't around. You've moved from home to home. I know it seems boring to you now, but Guernsey is an extraordinary place. All your life, when you tell people you grew up on an island that's six by three miles, they will think it's fascinating. On top of that, you spent years in Spain, battling for your dad's affection and being self-assured enough to leave. These are huge, interesting things. Without even realising it, you've added so much to the story of your life. Think about it, if someone was to sit down and read a book, would they choose the one about the kid who left school, went to uni and got a job? Or would they choose the one about the kid who flew by the seat of her pants, making maverick decisions in the quest of her true self? I know which one I'd choose. You're an interesting person, Renée. You have perspective and resilience and a shit-load of personality. You're doing great, OK?'

'I love you, thank you.'

'I love you too.'

'Are you where you want to be?' I ask her, sitting down to finish my cold fry-up. Aunty Jo puts some oil in a pan because the sound of footsteps upstairs tells us that Flo has finally woken up.

'It's an interesting question. I never landed where I thought I was going to land but I just went at things and gave them everything I had. And now, look at me, back on Guernsey, married to James, a lovely man who could do the washing up sometimes but seemingly accepts all of the strange things about me, and a farmyard of smelly animals who I love like the children I could never have. If you'd told me this would be me when I was your age, I'd have laughed in your face. I was certain I would marry a rock star and live a life on the road. What I have is the exact opposite, and honestly, other than missing my sister every single day, I'm really happy. And I have you.'

I stop eating and go over to her. I put my arms around her waist and rest my head on her shoulder.

'I'm so sorry your sister died,' I say, gently.

'I'm sorry your mummy died. But always remember: she'd be so proud of you.'

She pats my arm, and we stand still for a moment. She breaks the silence with another nugget of wisdom. 'And Renée, if you shroud yourself in negative, anxious thoughts, then they will eventually take over. You're healthy. You have this beautiful island to come back to whenever you want. You always have me, and now it looks like you have your best friend back too. Just don't fuck it up this time, OK?' She laughs and breaks an egg into the pan.

'I won't,' I say, sitting back down. 'I really, really won't.'

'I feel like someone shat in my mouth,' says Flo, coming into the kitchen then noticing Aunty Jo. 'Oh, sorry Jo, I . . .'

'Don't worry Flo, I've got two goats, two geese, three

chickens, two cats, three hundred thousand bees and a husband. I deal with an unprecedented amount of shit before nine a.m. You still like your eggs hard?'

'Yes please.' Flo sits down. She looks as if there is no blood in her head and her skin is made of paper.

'So what are you up to these days, Flo?' asks Aunty Jo.

'She's got a job in *marketing*,' I say, like she's all lah-di-dah.

'Ooooh, I used to work in marketing back in the day.'

I have no idea what they are talking about. Is marketing like advertising?

'It seems like a really nice company,' Flo says. 'I worked in their London office for a bit, and when I said I was from Guernsey they said they have a branch here and that there was a job here too, if I wanted it.'

'Wow, what chance,' Aunty Jo says. 'What kinds of brands do they look after?'

'All sorts. Some alcohol, a few clothing brands and Island Cheese.'

I burst out laughing. Flo shoots me a look.

'Cheese?' I gasp.

'Yes, cheese. They're working on a campaign to get Guernsey cheese to the mainland. Maybe even into the global market.'

'The global cheese market?' How is no one else finding this funny?

'Yes Renée, just because you don't know something doesn't mean it doesn't exist.'

'OK, you go market your cheese,' I say, sarcastically.

'I'll be office manager, actually,' she says, proudly. Her cheeks filling with more colour with every mouthful of her fry-up.

'Office manager? Check you out,' I say, totally intimidated by her success. We didn't actually get on to her job title yesterday. Or maybe we did; I have pockets of memory.

'This is wonderful, congratulations Flo.' Aunty Jo pours three glasses of orange juice and we all cheers. 'And where will you be living? With Mum?'

'Errr, no way. She's not made any gestures and I've certainly not asked. I'll be . . . I'll be living in Julian's flat, in Mill Street. He's gone to live in India for a year or two, with his wife.'

I spit my orange juice out across the table. 'Julian's *wife*?' I ask.

Julian is Flo's older brother. I lost my virginity to him when we were fifteen, then lied to her about it before Sally de Putron wrote it on the blackboard in front of the entire class and ruined our lives. Talking about Julian is not something Flo and I do with ease.

'Yes, Renée. He's in his mid-twenties now. Adults get married sometimes, it's not that weird.'

'Adult? Jesus.' Suddenly I feel way too young for any of this. 'Sorry, he never seemed like the marrying kind.'

'What? You mean when he was a seventeen-year-old boy?'

'Who is his wife?' I ask, unable to look Flo in the eye but needing details.

'He married a woman called India. She's five years older than him and they have moved to India.'

'She is called India, and she lives in India? Isn't that a bit awkward?'

'It's funny, isn't it? Apparently, her parents are very wealthy. Her dad does something to do with importing fabric. They conceived her in India, so that's why she is called that. They have a house out there too. She's cool, I like her. She's travelled loads, she's pretty. Julian did well for himself in the end.'

Ouch.

'Well look at you, all grown up with your own flat on Mill Street. Fair fucks to you,' I say, raising my glass again. I am so jealous. So horribly and desperately jealous.

'Thanks, I mean I'll have to get a flatmate, but I'll just put an ad in the Guernsey press. India has said I should find a "young professional".'

'Flo?' I say, downing my cutlery.

'Yeah?'

Surely, she isn't this stupid. I do a hard, forced smile and jazz hands.

'Eat your own,' she says, presuming I want some of her bacon because I've finished mine.

'No, Flo. Me?'

'You what?'

'Me, you massive dipshit. Why don't I come and live with you?'

Aunty Jo spins around and squeals like a fifteen-year-old from the Fifties who just got asked to dance by the boy she fancies.

'What?' says Flo, looking cornered.

'Come on, it's perfect. You need a flatmate, I need a flat. No offence, Aunty Jo.'

'None taken,' she says, leaving the room.

'It's perfect, no?'

'Renée, we haven't seen each other for three years; we can't just move in with each other.'

'Why not? It's us, Flo. It will be fine, and if it isn't, I'll move out. I can always come back to Aunty Jo's. But she and James don't want me crashing here forever; I'm twenty-two, for Christ's sake. Can't we at least try?'

'You told me you haven't got any money. You said last night, you've got about a hundred quid. That's it.'

'I can give you a loan!' shouts Aunty Jo from the next room. Flo stares firmly at her egg.

'Flo, come on. Don't make me beg you.'

'Renée, living with a friend can go really wrong. I've just been dealing with . . . what if it goes really wrong?'

'What if it doesn't?'

She gets up and walks over to the kitchen window. She gazes out of it like a forlorn wife waiting for her husband to come home. She doesn't move for ages. And then . . .

'OK.'

'OK, yes?'

'OK, YES, Jesus, not that you gave me a choice.'

I stand up and run into the middle of the kitchen where I do some sexy thrusty moves and scream, 'WE'RE ROOMIES!' I feel so happy. I refuse to stop moving until I get at least a little smile out of her. Eventually, she breaks.

'OK, I suppose if it goes wrong it doesn't have to be forever.'

'That's the spirit, Flo!'

Aunty Jo comes in too and we all, even Flo, start to laugh.

'We should have a drink to celebrate,' she says.

'Jesus, Flo. It's nine a.m.!'

This is going to be GREAT!

3

Flo

I hear Renée beep the horn outside. I'm all packed up, everything I currently own in two suitcases. One contains all the stuff I brought from London, the other is full of bits and bobs from Mum's house. A cushion, my favourite pillow. A couple of stuffed toys that I've held on to all these years, some bed sheets and a towel. I have also stolen a few pieces of crockery and cutlery that I like. I don't know if Mum will notice or not, but I've used them since I was tiny, and it feels right that they come with me as I start my new life here in Guernsey. I take comfort from the small things from my past. The big things are mostly awful.

My sister Abi comes to say goodbye to me; she looks sad that I'm leaving. As much as I don't want her to be upset, her sadness somehow validates my existence in this family because Mum has barely acknowledged my moving out at all. 'Will you sometimes come over to make me that Marmite-and-cheese-on-toast thingy for me?' Abi says, hugging me around my waist.

'Of course I will. That will always be our special dish and you will always be my special sister.' Of course we have lived apart before, but somehow living separately in Guernsey feels even more far apart than when I went to uni or lived in London. 'And you can come for sleepovers at the flat, OK? Now go tidy your room,' I say cheekily, not wanting her to be there as I drive away, because this isn't a huge deal even though it feels like it is.

Mum is upstairs when Renée arrives. She knows I'm leaving and would have heard the horn. I'm not going to tell her I'm off: a little test to see if she can step up to motherhood without being prompted. I head out to the van.

'Today is the day!' Renée says, jumping out. 'The first day of the rest of our lives.'

I want to match her excitement but I'm not quite there. I don't really get excited, I'm too used to disappointment. Also, I'm scared of this; I don't have the best history of living with friends. My last weeks in London were particularly bad. Also, Mum still hasn't come down to say goodbye and I don't even know why I'm surprised. She came into my room this morning and I thought she was going to offer to help, but she asked me to post something for her on the way to the flat. I have deliberately left the letter on the kitchen table. Oopsie.

'That big silver thing is to extract honey, apparently,' Renée says, pointing to a contraption and picking up one of my cases, wedging it next to hers in the back of Aunty Jo's van. She only has one case in there. We lift my other one together and balance it on top. She closes the van door and pushes it shut with her bum. 'It's happening, are you ready?'

'We're not Thelma and Louise, Renée. It's a seven-minute drive to the flat – hardly the journey of a lifetime.'

'Not literally, no. But figurately this is massive. Come on Flo, get in the spirit of things. This is such a big move for us. Adults, in Guernsey, you not living with your mum any more, me not relying on Aunty Jo. No more head to toe, our own rooms! We can do whatever we want, we're free! Let's see a smile, go on, show me ya teeth.'

I offer her a pathetic smile, which eventually turns into a bigger one. I am looking forward to it, I think. 'OK, OK, let's go!'

As we drive away, I see Mum running out of the house. She is waving the letter and looks mad. Not my problem any more.

'Shall we take a detour?' Renée says, turning left instead of right at the end of my road. 'Let's go see our old haunts, mark the occasion with a trip down memory lane.'

We set off, the windows down, the island breeze blowing in our hair. 'Come on slow coach,' I say. 'Crank it up a gear?'

'Sorry, I'm still nervous on the roads.'

I feel bad for pushing her. Renée had an accident a few

years ago. She let an underage boy drive her car while she was in the passenger seat. He crashed the car and died, it was awful and Renée was a mess, understandably. I give her knee a quick squeeze. 'Sorry,' I say, gently. 'I'm here, right beside you.'

Soon we pull into the car park of Tudor Falls School for Girls. It's pretty empty, being a Sunday.

'Wow, look at that. The caretaker's car. Like no time has passed,' I say, remembering it clearly. A green Toyota, always parked in the same spot. 'It's just occurred to me how much work he must do for the place, for his car to always be there. He arrives before anyone else, leaves late at night and comes in at the weekends. I never appreciated that at the time. Looking after a school with four hundred students might actually be hard work.'

'Yeah, and then throw in me messing around and cling-filming the toilet seats. He really had his work cut out. I wonder if there are any naughty students there now? Somehow it doesn't feel like there would be.'

'Sure, because you were the only naughty kid ever.'

'I don't mean it like that, I just mean things have changed, haven't they? Like, maybe we were the last generation of kids who were truly free. There was no internet, no mobile phones. We acted more in the moment. I'm glad we were kids when we were; the world feels scarier now, somehow. Come on, let's get out and explore.'

'We can't Renée, that's trespassing.'

'No, it's not, we went to school here. Our DNA is every-where, we practically own the place.'

We walk down the path by the side of the school and take a right to the sports pavilion.

'Think of all the times we did the knicker-trick in there,' she says, which really makes me laugh.

'Oh my God, so funny. The lengths we'd go to in trying to take our knickers off under our swimsuits without anyone seeing our fannies. We must have all looked ridiculous. Stretching the fabric down past our knees.'

'Unless you were Margaret. She didn't give a shit,' says Renée. 'She'd just take her clothes off and stand there naked, her hairy fanny staring at us all. We should all have been a bit more Margaret. I always thought she was mad, but maybe she was just the only one of us who didn't hate herself. I wonder what she's up to these days.'

'EVERYTHING! It drove me crazy. She was fun, though, my naughty partner-in-crime before I converted you to the dark side. Oh look, that weird stone bath. I did a séance in there once, trying to call the spirit of my dead mother. God, there are literally memories everywhere.'

I'm not listening any more. I've frozen. My feet won't move. I think the clouds even stop.

'Do you remember that day, Renée?' I say. She knows immediately what I mean.

'I do, like it was yesterday. When Miss Grut came to get you from French class and told you to go with her.'

'I was taken to the headmistress's office where she told me my dad had died. Mum didn't even tell me herself. I've still not forgiven her, maybe I never will.'

'You don't have to, it was shit.' Renée takes my hand in

hers. 'As soon as I found out, I knew I had to find you, like you were the only one who might understand me, and like I was the only one who would understand you. I was right.'

I've been holding something back from Renée since we met again just over a week ago. Like I have to protect myself from her. Like I can't fully admit how much I've missed her. But here, on school grounds, with memories hitting me like those hockey sticks used to smack our cold bare shins, it's hard to hold things back. I know that if she hadn't come after me when Dad died, I'd have totally fallen apart. I hug her as hard as I can. 'I love you,' I tell her. Because I really, really do.

'I love you too. Come on, let's get out of here. Let's go to our flat.'

'You betcha, roomie.'

We walk back to the van. As we're getting in, the caretaker storms over. 'Fuck, Renée, DRIVE!' I shout, my heart thumping. Being caught by the caretaker is even more terrifying than it used to be. She reverses and flings the car around. We fly out of the school gates, the caretaker shaking his fist behind us.

'See?' she says, laughing. 'We're just like Thelma and Louise!'

'Don't slam the front door,' I say in a loud whisper, making Renée squash herself into the wall.

'Why? Fuck, who's coming?'

'No one, it's just the old lady who lives on the ground floor,' I say whispering. 'Julian said you have to be really quiet coming in, probably because she complains or something. Just close the door gently and walk up the stairs quietly. Here, I'll take the front of your case. You hold the back.'

'Who are you?' a voice says from behind us. We both scream like we're about to be bludgeoned to death and drop the case, which goes crashing down the stairs. 'Who are you?' the person repeats.

It's the old lady. She is standing at her door. She's tall and skinny with a colourful top and Mary Jane shoes. She looks cross, and really stylish.

'Sorry, we didn't mean to disturb you,' Renée says. She's so good at talking to people. I think I swallowed my tongue. 'We're moving in today. This is Julian's sister, Flo, and I'm her friend, Renée.'

'He didn't tell me this. You'd think he'd let me know I could expect new people living above me.'

'I'll tell him you'd rather have known,' I say, pulling myself together.

'Well, I mean there's no point now, is there? You're here,' she says.

'I guess not,' I say.

'Well, like we said, sorry to disturb you. We have a few cases to bring up but will try to do it quietly,' Renée says.

The three of us stare at each other for what feels like ages, until the old lady goes back into her flat.

'Fucking hell, what a moody old bitch,' Renée says. 'She's like Mrs Mangel from *Neighbours*.' We head up to Flat 2, laughing at the cultural reference. 'This carpet is gross,' she says, looking down at the unvacuumed, crunchy fabric beneath our feet.

'I know, it's an ugly entrance but inside is great. And you can do what you want to your room, cover it in Dolly Parton posters if you like.' It takes me a minute to get the key to turn in the lock, but eventually, we're in.

'Flo, wow, this place is so cool,' Renée says, gesturing towards the Indian fabric throws, Mexican rug and Venetian paintings. Julian and India have travelled a lot, this place is like a museum of their adventures.

'Is it weird that we're living surrounded by other people's memories? We haven't been to any of these places,' I say.

'No, it's not weird, it's nice. We can go through it all and decide where we want to go. And look, a sombrero, I've been to Spain, so I feel right at home.'

She throws herself down on the low sofa. 'I could sleep for a month,' she says. 'Moving is exhausting. Wake me up when I have a job and can afford this place.' She pulls a large cushion over her face and screams into it.

'Don't you want to see your room?' I ask, and she jumps up with a sudden burst of energy. 'The bedrooms are upstairs.'

'The stairs are so creaky,' she says, noticing all the issues with the flat. 'Could do with a lick of paint.'

'All right Mary Poppins, stop complaining. You can moan about the walls when you can afford to have them painted. For now, be grateful, we're getting this place for next to nothing. We're part renting, part looking after it.'

My brother had initially told me to find a housemate

who could pay £400 a month, but when I said it was Renée and she could only pay £300, he just replied with 'don't fucking wreck the place', and I've hardly heard from him since.

'OK, this is your room.' I walk in slowly and Renée creeps in behind me, as if there might be someone in it already. 'Well, what do you think?' I ask her.

'It's cool. Big. I like the skylight,' she says, walking over to the bed and sitting on it. She bounces a few times, as if testing it. She seems happy enough with its firmness. 'It's so empty. I have nothing to fill it with.'

'That's OK, it will happen over time. You have a wardrobe, and a chest of drawers. We can find some cool bits and bobs, and in a few weeks, it will be your own little nest.'

'I don't know what I was expecting. I'm sorry, I don't mean to be ungrateful. I mean, I love it. I guess I've only lived in rooms in other people's houses where there were things on the walls already, or bed sheets, or a rug. Do I have to do all that myself?'

'Yes, but it can be fun. You can use my spare bed sheets for now. Hey, to celebrate moving day, how about we get the bus over to Cobo, get chips and sit on the wall? We can take drinks over in plastic cups from the pub. We can watch the sun go down. I've got my first day at work tomorrow, but I need a last hurrah. We need to remind ourselves why living on this island is so special. We're not going to realise that sitting here surrounded by stuff from the rest of the world, are we?'

'That might be a good idea,' says Renée. 'Especially the booze bit. I feel like I've just walked into a different world. I need that part of my personality that only alcohol seems to have access to.'

She's joking, but I know exactly what she means.

Renée

As the bus chugs happily across the island, from the depot in St Peter Port, to the small roadside stop in Cobo, we both sit quietly and look out of the window.

'Hey Flo, I basically carried you home along this road once, after one of Carla and Gem's parties,' I say.

Memories, everywhere. It seems like we have a story for every road. When you leave a place like Guernsey and move to the mainland, it can feel like life is just beginning. And yet, being back here, I'm reminded of how much we've lived. I've learned since leaving and meeting people who weren't raised on a tiny island that we had more freedom than most kids our age. We never realised that at the time. I suppose the trick now is keeping hold of that sense of freedom and bringing it into adulthood. Rather than seeing Guernsey as restrictive, we need to see it as extraordinary. This strange little bubble with its dramatic coastlines and sandy beaches. A speed limit of 35 mph and nowhere to buy booze on a Sunday unless you order food. There are local beers and Silk Cut Red, the island's very own brand of cigarette. We grow great tomatoes, make jumpers for fishermen and produce the best cheese in Europe. Our butter is bright yellow, our milk thick with cream. We get spring four weeks earlier than England, the tidal system is so dramatic that the coastline changes every six hours, right before your eyes. You can earn £200k a year and surf every day before work on this cheeky little tax haven, if that's what you want to do. A grand total of 24 square miles and you're never more than ten minutes from the sea. This island that once felt like it wouldn't let us go, is now welcoming us again with open arms. Maybe it has a lot to offer two twenty-two-year-olds. It's idyllic, really, when you break it down. Mine and Flo's happiness depends on us embracing all of these things, seeing ourselves as lucky as opposed to trapped. We can do that, if we let go of where we thought we would be and just accept where we are.

Chips in hand, the smell of vinegar wafting from the bag, we walk along the wall to the German bunker that overlooks the beach. We didn't bother with pints from the pub and just got two bottles of cold white wine and some plastic cups from the Co-op instead. I threw a bottle of red in there too, a third bottle of white would be warm by the time we get to it. We settle down, tear open our chips and pour the wine into plastic cups.

'Cheers. This is the life,' I say, holding my cup up to Flo's.

'Cheers.'

'I don't know if I ever appreciated how beautiful

Guernsey was when we were growing up,' I say. 'Not that we've finished growing up, but you know what I mean.'

'I do. You were too busy trying to get off with everyone.'

'True. Hard to take in a sea view when your face is buried in someone's pants. Bleurgh, blow jobs. They're only fun when you're in the mood, aren't they? When you're not in the mood, the idea of them is awful.'

'Yeah, can we talk about something else?'

We sit quietly for a while. Eating, sipping, looking at the horizon, taking long, deep breaths.

'Is something on your mind, Flo?'

'It's just a lot, isn't it?' she says, putting down a chip that was about to pass her lips.

'Oh don't get all boring about portion size. You used to want seconds.'

'Not the chips, Renée. Growing up. Being an adult. There's so much to think about, isn't there?'

'So much. Like, at least at school if you were shit at something you'd just go into the lower set. It felt so hard at the time, but all you really have to do at school is get through.'

'Exactly. Now if you aren't good enough, you get paid shit, or even lose your job. And then you have no choice but to find another one because if you don't, you can't afford your home, car, food. Being a grown-up means you have to stay good at things. You can't just be shit for a bit, because if you drop the ball then it will all fall apart and you'll lose everything and maybe even die.'

Flo's chest is rising and falling. She's staring at her lap as if looking out to sea, at the unknown, is all too painful.

'What happened to your dad won't happen to you, Flo.'

Her dad was going through a really rough time before he died; it's clear she still bears the scars of it all.

'It might.'

She's right, it might. 'It won't,' I say, anyway.

She finishes the wine that's in her cup, then fills it all the way to the top and gulps down half of that too. 'Need a top-up?' she says, waving the bottle over my cup. I hold it out for her. 'Do you ever want to do something mad, just to prove you're alive?' she says, making me spit my wine out all over my chips.

'Excuse me?'

'What?'

'I just . . . I don't know. That's the kind of thing *I'd* say, not you.'

'Yeah, well, maybe I've changed. And anyway, do you?'

'Always, what do you have in mind?'

'I dunno, jump in the sea, flash our tits at cars as they drive by, knock on doors and run away.'

I can't stop myself laughing. I spent most of our teenage years trying to get Flo to do crazy things, and now she's the one instigating it.

'OK, let's flash our tits. But I bet you don't.'

'Oh yeah?' She stands up and faces the road. 'Here comes a car, you with me or not?'

'Oh Flo, sit down. I'm not drunk enough for that.'

She bends down, filling my cup as close to the top as she can, and then drinks more of hers. 'Come on, here comes another one.'

Reluctantly, I stand next to her. My hands gripping the bottom of my top, though I'm sure she'll inevitably chicken out and sit back down. But before I know it, she's pulled her top up and her boobs are bouncing up and down as she screams with pure delight. The driver of the car presses down on their horn until they've passed us. I'm too stunned to do anything.

'That was fun!' she says, sitting back down. 'We should do that kind of thing more often.'

Flo's like a totally different person after a few wines. I stand above her, words struggling to form in my mouth.

The next morning, I wake up freezing at 8 a.m. I'm lying on the bed in my new room with leggings, socks and a jumper. I have another jumper over me, and I've used more clothes as a pillow. I didn't like the idea of using someone else's mattress, duvet and pillow without covers on them, and Flo was too drunk to get me her spare sheets when we got back last night. She passed out on the sofa.

I hear clanging in the kitchen. She's up. I get off the bed and take a second to look around my new room. It's so empty, apart from my pink suitcase that has now exploded with clothes on the floor. I rummage through the pile and find my slippers.

'Oh, you're up,' says Flo, cheerily, when I walk into the kitchen. 'Tea?'

'Yeah, tea. I think I might puke. My head is banging. How come you're so chipper?'

'I feel fine. Great, actually. First day in the new office and I'm raring to go!'

I notice a bottle of vodka on the kitchen counter. Did we get into that when we got home? That's probably why I feel like I'm going to die. The washing machine kicks into spin cycle and creates too much noise for us to keep talking in the kitchen. I can't believe Flo's already done laundry this morning. She walks past me into the living room and quickly throws a cushion onto the couch.

'Sorry I didn't give you my spare sheets, were you comfy enough?'

'Yes, I managed. Are you sure you're OK? It's quite a big deal to start a new job, especially after what we drank yesterday.'

'Totally fine. I mean, I've got the shakes a bit, but that could be nerves or the booze, who knows? Who cares? Shakes are shakes, right?'

'Right.' She's being weird and hyper, which means she isn't really 'fine'.

'How do I look?' she asks. She's wearing black trousers and a black shirt. She has showered and put on some basic make-up. Her hair is dry but the ends are still a little wet.

'You look great, good luck. I hope it goes well.'

'Thanks, me too. OK, byeeee.'

'Byeeee.'

She leaves.

When her footsteps disappear, I take a deep breath. It feels good to be alone for a minute. I go into the living room, my head throbbing. I lie down on the sofa and pull a cushion out from under my legs so I can be perfectly flat. Maybe I'll sleep again, just for an hour or so. Then I'll get up and plan my life. As my eyes fall shut, I become aware of my upper thighs getting wet. I roll to the side and have a feel. The sofa is drenched, Flo must have spilt the glass of water there when we got back. I get up. I probably should do something constructive anyway. Like tidy my room and make my bed.

As I walk up the creaky stairs back to my room, the door to Flo's bedroom opens. I haven't even seen it yet, so I go inside. There is a large bed, maybe king size. The sheets are a paisley pattern and there are a couple of scatter cushions. It's so weird that this is her brother's bed. To this day Julian remains the most beautiful human I have ever touched, even if my memory of having sex with him creeps me out and makes me want to scrub myself with bleach.

There is a photo of Flo's mum and her younger sister, Abi, next to the bed. Why have a photo of someone who drives you mad there? If I put a picture of Dad by my bed, I'd end up in therapy. It's either really forgiving or tragically self-destructive to be reminded of how a parent let you down every time you wake up in the morning. Surely Guernsey itself is enough of a kick in the face?

There is a make-up bag on a chest of drawers. I look in, it's very basic. Old brushes, a dried-out mascara, some cheap foundation, a bronzer, some tweezers and some nude lipstick. I wonder if Flo will personalise the room a bit. She arrived back in Guernsey with her life's belongings stuffed in one suitcase. A bit like me. Is that all we have to show for ourselves? I need to buy things for my room, and I'm going to start with a full-length mirror.

I spot a calendar on Flo's wall. She's written 'WORK' on almost every weekday, as if she needs to be reminded to go. That's the kind of thing I do when I'm drunk and determined to wake up the next day with a better grip on my life. She's such a funny fish.

I leave Flo's room and pick up the sheets she left outside mine. I make my bed, and already the room looks a little better. In the wardrobe there are ten wire hangers, so I get as many of my clothes on those as I can and fold the rest into drawers. I push the pink suitcase under the bed, open the skylight to let in some air, and lie down. I have an odd feeling of motivation, despite the hangover, and remember my laptop is downstairs. I'll write something, maybe a book about my life. A young girl who lost her mother, then lost herself, only to find herself again by going back to where it all began. But what happens next? I don't know yet. I have to get up and work on the plotline of my life. Everything is a story; everything can be written about. Aunty Jo was right, no one can take away the experiences I have. But I won't get any inspiration lying on the bed in my bleak bedroom, will I? I have to get up, write something. I have to make my life happen.

Downstairs, I get my laptop out of my bag. It's the one good thing I own. Even the bag is a shitty old tote I got for free from someone who was handing them out at the airport. One day I'm going to buy an expensive handbag. Not because I particularly care about bags or designers, but

I reckon that's a real rite of passage in a woman's life, to go and blow an unnecessary amount of money on a handbag. That will be the day I'll feel like I've made it.

Dad got me the laptop for my twenty-first birthday. It screams of guilt for not giving me his love, but I was so happy I didn't care. A brand-new Mac, they cost nearly two grand. It's brilliant and beautiful and I love it with all my heart. Falling onto the sofa, I rest it on my thighs and open it. Right, here we go. A job, a paragraph and a . . . DAMN IT! The sofa is soaking wet and now my bum is too.

I must just be imagining this, but it really smells of piss.

Part Two

Worker Bee

A letter arrives for Renée in Spain, November 1998. It's from Flo in Nottingham.

Hey, I hope everything is OK in Spain and that you and Nell are getting on better. How are things with your dad?

I'm really stressing about money. Mum has said that she can't keep giving me pocket money now I'm at uni. She said my rent is OK and she will pay that, but I need to earn my spending money. Why is she telling me this now, two months into term starting? I could have saved more over the summer. Ugh, she's being really annoying again. I don't know why I thought things could be different between us.

I have to get a job. A fucking job! My course already takes up so much time and there is all this coursework. And now I'm going to have to work on Saturdays and maybe Sundays too if I want to be able to eat anything other than Kwik Save pasta and tuna. There are some jobs going in the campus bar, but I don't know if I can do that. It's too . . . I dunno, I'd feel like everyone would be looking at me.

Someone in town gave me a flyer about selling

photography sessions. I did a shift today, you can pick your hours. For every session you sell you get 2 quid. You have to sell so many to make decent money, but I came out with 20 yesterday. I hate it though, it's a massive scam. I basically cold call people and say they have won a free session with a really great photographer and that the photo costs only 10 quid. But then what happens is they come for the photo and get handed a print that is deliberately horrible so then they want to buy the others. I'm trying not to think about it morally because it's their fault for being so gullible, right?

I can't get this thought out of my head, that life is just hard work now. No more long summers of kicking around Guernsey doing nothing, I'll have to work forever. It's scary Renée. I feel like I've been chucked into adulting, and I wasn't ready. Mum said that's what being a grown-up feels like all the time. She even said she still feels that way. I asked her if that's why she keeps trying to marry rich men, so she doesn't have to work any more. She hung up and we haven't spoken since. At least my rent money went into my account yesterday, so that's something.

How are you? Are you still working in that pub? Did your dad buy you the laptop you were hoping for, for writing? I'd love a laptop but I can't afford it. I can't afford anything. Sigh.

You still planning to come stay with me next month? I'd love that. I'll have loads of work to do but we can do nice things. How do people still have fun around jobs? I'm knackered all the time.

HONEYBEE

Do you remember at Tudor Falls we'd joke around about the amazing careers we'd chase, the people we'd become? I'd be the hot-shot lawyer, you'd be the glamorous magazine editor in the big smoke. But what if that was just fantasy? And more than that, why do we have to BE a fancy professional in something? Why can't we just be happy, you know?

Do you ever think about it Renée? The fact that we're not kids any more, that any money we have is money we have to earn? Until we're like, NINETY!

Urgh, love you.
Friends forever,
Flo x

4

Renée

'Look, if he still works there who cares,' says Aunty Jo. 'He should help you get a job after the way he treated you. And if he's horrible, I'll put bees in his pants and let my little darlings go to town on his nuts, deal?' She pulls up in the van and puts the handbrake on.

'Deal,' I say, gagging at the thought of Dean's nuts. They hung really low and were extraordinarily hairy, if I remember right. Dean is an ex of mine who works at the *Guernsey Globe*. We broke up when I walked in on him having sex with another girl from my class.

'What do I even say when I go in?' I ask Aunty Jo, regretting this idea. Flo's gone for her first day at Magic Marketing, and I enlisted Aunty Jo's help. We drove here all fired up, hoping I can bag a job myself, but now the whole idea seems utterly ridiculous.

'You say you want to work at the paper, are there any jobs going and can you have an application form. And then you come out with the form and we fill it in, lying about how much experience you have, and you get the job. Easy. Go on!'

'OK. OK, I'll just go in, and say that. They'd be lucky to have me, right?'

'That's the spirit. My God, is it just me or is it really hot in here?' She turns the aircon up as high as it will go and sits back as the cold air spreads over her face. 'Oh look, Renée, you're dressed like a bee,' she says, as I get out the van. I'm wearing a long mustard jumper with black skinny jeans and DM's. Aunty Jo said people who work in media don't wear smart clothes, so I look nice, but casual. Cool, I think. Like a writer. 'How funny that we didn't realise,' she says. 'My little worker bee, off to start her career. I could cry.'

She doesn't cry, she makes a shooing motion with her hand, as if I *am* a bee and she wants me to get out of her van. 'Go on, time to be brave. I'll be right here hoping it snows.'

I look at my reflection in the glass of the door before I walk in. I look good, I am good. They *would* be lucky to have me. It doesn't matter that I have no experience, this is just the beginning. And also, it's the *Guernsey Globe* for fuck's sake, hardly the *Sunday Times*. I push the door and go in.

'Hello, I was wondering if there are any jobs going at the moment?'

A male receptionist stops typing and looks up at me.

'Um . . . not that I know of.' He continues to type. I find this really rude; isn't the entire purpose of a receptionist to greet people politely? I might be his boss one day, and then he'll wish he looked me in the eye. Nonetheless, this is the person I am faced with, so I need to pull out the big guns.

'Is Dean here?' I ask, confidently. Half hoping he says yes, half hoping he says no.

'Dean? Yes, he's always here. Who shall I say is looking for him?'

Damn it. Damn it. Urgh. Why did I do this?

'Renée. Renée Sargent.' I want to end that with, 'You'd better remember the name, bitch.' But I keep it classy. I wait patiently while he calls Dean's phone.

'He's not at his desk, I'll go and find him.' He disappears into the office. I could run and pretend this never happened. What will I even say? Soon afterwards, Dean walks into reception looking very confused. He looks at me quizzically for around two seconds, but it feels like twenty minutes.

'Oh,' he says, as if he just found an answer in a crossword that's been bothering him for hours. 'Renée Sargent, of course. Wow, it's been . . .'

'About four years, I guess. Hi Dean, how are you?' I say, trying to be a more grown-up version of the girl he cheated on.

'I'm OK, yeah, good. Why um . . . why are you here?'

He looks really old. So much older than me, with some grey hair, which is weird. I don't remember him being that much older than me, but he's aged about ten years since I last saw him. And I swear he used to wear that exact same Led Zeppelin T-shirt.

'I've just moved back to Guernsey and I'm looking for a job. You might remember I wanted to be a writer?'

He clearly does not recall my aspirational goals.

'Well, I wondered if there's a job I could have here?'

'Um, right. A bit weird, you just turning up and asking for a job, but OK. Um, I've got to go out on a story now – they're talking about dropping the speed limit on the coast roads, can you believe it?'

'Wow, big news,' I say, trying to sound interested in local journalism opportunities.

'But I could meet you after work, go for a pint? Talk about what it is you want to do?'

'OK, great. Yeah, that would be brilliant. Ship and Crown? Six p.m.?'

'Cool, yeah. Good to see you, Renée. You're looking really good. Bigger.'

'Bigger?'

'Older I mean, you look older.'

'Well, I am. Four years older. As are you.'

We allow the strangeness of this reunion to settle in the air. The receptionist is looking at me with eyes that scream, 'It's so obvious you fucked.'

'Great, I'll see you then,' I say, putting an end to this madness. I head back out to the van and get in.

'Well, how did it go?' Aunty Jo asks.

'They'd be lucky to have me,' I say, confidently. 'Very lucky.'

At 5.55 p.m. I walk into the Ship and Crown. The man with the big belly is in his usual spot. There is a barmaid I don't recognise. I order a vodka and Coke. Dean is sitting at a table at the far end of the room. He looks like a sad person drinking on his own. When he sees me, his face lights up.

'I thought you'd changed your mind,' he says. 'Things have been coming back to me all afternoon. We were seeing each other for a while, if I remember rightly?'

'A few months. You were also seeing Meg Lloyd, if you remember rightly.'

It takes him a second, then he remembers. Probably because there were multiple women besides me and Meg and he's trying to work out who's who.

'Meg, yeah, I remember Meg. What happened to Meg?'

'I don't know. We didn't really stay in touch, partly because I walked in on her being done from behind by my boyfriend.'

'Fair enough. So, you been at uni?'

'No, Spain. I'm back for a while, not sure how long. I want to write, and I thought maybe I could work at the *Globe*, get some experience.'

'Right, and you thought you'd tap up an old flame to see if he could boost you up the career ladder?'

How humiliating. 'Yes, basically.'

'Well, I can't help you, I'm afraid. The *Globe* is on its way out, I'll be out of a job in six months.'

Damn it. An entirely pointless drink with an old flame I never wanted to rekindle. 'You couldn't have told me that this afternoon?'

'That dipshit on reception doesn't know. I couldn't tell you there. And this meeting doesn't have to be pointless.' He drinks his lager, whilst raising his eyebrows. He slides a hand onto my leg. 'You loved me licking you, if I remember rightly.'

Oh wow, oh God. This is horrible. What the hell did I think was going to happen? I pick up his hand and drop it on his leg.

'That's not why I'm here, Dean. I wanted to talk about a job at the *Globe*, and if that can't happen that's OK, but I'm not interested in anything else.'

'I do know people. There's talk of an independent magazine starting on the island. I could connect you with the team, but you don't think I'd do it for free, do you?'

'You mean you'll introduce me to them if I have sex with you?'

'Doesn't need to be sex.'

'How often does this approach work with women, just out of interest?'

'I've done pretty well out of it.' He looks proud of himself. He's giving absolutely no hint of shame for being a sex pest. 'Lots of wannabe journalists on the island.'

'How old are you?' I ask. He told me he was in his early

twenties when he had a stream of sixth-formers in his bed just four years ago.

'Thirty-three.'

Some sick shoots up my throat and pools in the back of my mouth.

'Bye Dean. I hope that with losing this job you lose all access to women and that your dick falls off. Good luck.' He doesn't even stand up, like he's had similar speeches thrown at him a few times. He shrugs his shoulders and drinks his drink.

What a creep. To think he once felt so mature and exciting. Maybe one thing about being a grown-up is being able to spot a pervert when you meet one. Teenage me didn't have a clue. This is why parents are so protective; they can spot wrong'uns like Dean way before their kids do.

At least it's a huge relief to realise so early in my career that I'm not willing to sleep with anyone to get to the top, especially with someone whose balls are probably down to his knees by now. The *Guernsey Globe* is not where I'm meant to be, I'm already above it. I'll get another job that pays properly, save up, and get the hell to London to become a writer there.

I've got way more self-respect than Dean and his droopy bollocks ever will.

Flo

'Flo, isn't it?' One of my new colleagues comes over to my desk. I stand up, which is weird.

'Yes, can I help with anything, do you need some coffee? Is the printer out of paper?'

'Nope, all good. I just wanted to say hi. I'm Phil, by the way. Welcome. It's not a big office but if you need any help while you settle in, just let me know. I'm on line 239.'

'239 sounds just fine,' I say like a cowboy, hating myself.

'Are you local?' he asks, still talking to me, which is promising.

'Yes, born and bred. But I've been away for a few years. Uni, then a little stint in London. I worked in the Magic Marketing offices there for a bit, actually. Back here for the foreseeable though. This island has claws, it always grabs you back.'

'Maybe that's true. I never left. I wonder why anyone would, to be honest. And I could never leave my mum.'

'Oh, wow. That's so nice of you. My mum's a fucking arsehole so I do not relate.'

I can't believe I just said that. With a big smile on my face too. I sounded horrible. Who says that to a stranger about their own mother? At work. On their first day. Oh God. What must he think of me?

'Sorry to hear that,' he says. There's an awkward pause. 'Anyway, line 239 if you need anything.'

I watch him walk away. Was he just being nice or was

he flirting with me? Either way, he probably won't bother again after I just slagged off my own mother.

The rest of the day, thankfully, goes off without a hitch. The office is nice. Nestled in a little side street just off Trinity Square. It's quite small, and up three floors in a lift. The reception area is stylish with a big purple sofa and a coffee table covered in magazines; it's my job to keep them up to date. I'm to arrange the newspapers on it every morning so that people who come in for meetings have something to read. They're looking for a new receptionist who will take on these smaller roles, but I'm happy to do them until then. I have no issue with the more menial jobs, they all keep this office running smoothly and that's the main point of my role. To keep it all ticking along. I can't deny I'd rather be in the London office but I do love this job. It's good for me on so many levels. I get to be busy, impress people with my organisational skills and feel like I have a plan to follow. I like plans. Making lists. Being on top of things. I'm a good office manager as I have no interest in sitting in rooms with my colleagues with the pressure to come up with ideas. I'd much rather make sure they all have notepads to brainstorm on. You wouldn't know it, but for people like me, who live with chaos inside their head, being organised and helping other people stay organised is very therapeutic. The rat sleeps while I'm at work. Not even a scratch. Nothing to drown. I'd come here seven days a week if I could.

In the main area, it's all open-plan apart from Ben's office. He's the boss. He seems like a really nice guy, very calm and charming. Everyone has a lot of respect for Ben, and I suspect that the three women who work here, one of whom is me, have a crush on him. He's married, though, so it's a look-but-don't-touch situation for us all. It's lovely to be around him, though, he has the kind of manner that makes you want to adjust yourself to be more like him. He started the company in London, apparently, then when they saw an opportunity to open an office in Guernsey, he brought his whole family over because he liked the idea of his kids growing up with beaches instead of underground trains. I bet he's an amazing father and husband. His wife is so lucky. I can't deny though, that when I first saw him, I was taken aback. Having been in Nottingham and London I've been around a lot more black people than I ever did living in Guernsey, so I feel much more worldly than I used to. But I wonder what it's been like for Ben here. Not just as the only black person in the office, but one of the few black people on the entire island.

As for the other men in the office, there is Matt, a big guy, plays rugby I think, or maybe he just watches and talks about it a lot. He's a few years older than me I think, but I don't recognise him from when we were kids. He definitely wasn't at the boys' school, so maybe he went to the grammar before Renée and I went there for sixth form. And there is Phil. We've spoken a little more now and he seems really nice. Polite. He is skinny and wears patterned shirts buttoned all the way up. Tidy, more than smart. His job title is 'brand manager', which makes him sound very sexy and creative. I don't think creative people like uncreative people like me. I'm sure we seem so boring in comparison to them, and the way their minds are constantly in action. Dad was creative, it's what I loved about him. But I think he died before it rubbed off on me. These days I tell myself that creatives need non-creatives to organise everything for them so that their minds are free to conjure amazing ideas. And that is why my role in this office is so important. I facilitate their imaginations. I'm here to go unnoticed, to make things easy, and to ensure they are not distracted. It's why I am the perfect person for my job. Everything in this office, from the coffee they drink to the chairs they sit on, is under my control.

The other two women who work at Magic Marketing are Georgina, second in command to Ben, and Chloe, the 'senior brand manager'. Chloe is tall, blonde, and attractive because she has made a lot of effort to be. Her clothes are perfectly curated. She is very thin and apparently goes to the gym most days before work which absolutely baffles me. How can anyone be bothered to do that? She's cold, almost chilling in her demeanour. Sometimes I shudder when she walks past me, like I imagine I would if a Disney baddie walked into the room. It isn't that she's horrible, or mean, just stoic and hard. I can't imagine she'd be very nice to cuddle.

I overheard Matt talking about her this morning. He and Phil were in the kitchen, and I came in as he was saying she would be like 'fucking a tree'. And that she 'looks pretty but would hurt your dick because of the friction'. I had to pretend not to hear him, it was such a gross thing to say. I was pleased Phil just seemed to listen and not join in. But it did make me wonder what Chloe would be like in bed. Could someone like her be as useless at sex as someone like me? Maybe. It also made me wonder if the guys in the office will start gossiping about me. Will they make jokes about what I would be like in bed? I hope they don't. The idea of anyone imagining me in bed terrifies me nearly as much as the sex itself.

And then there is Georgina. She is about five feet six, size 16 if I were to guess. Her clothes are basic: black trousers and a simple, shapeless shirt. She isn't very pretty, which I hate myself for thinking because women shouldn't have to be pretty, but you can't not notice when you're faced with it. Her hair is curly and could do with a wash. She doesn't wear any make-up at all despite having quite a few blemishes and spots. Compared to the other women in this office, including me, her appearance seems to be the last thing she worries about. And what is most surprising about that is that from the second you meet her, you can tell she is the most confident out of all of us.

There is something I envy about Georgina. The way she seems so open about who she is. How her flaws are played out for all to see. It's like she's freed her mind of them, so she has brain space to think about other things. Like being extraordinarily nice, which she really has been towards me. She has asked me if I'm OK and if there's anything I need about six times today. And she just seems so un-anxious. Whereas almost everyone else seems self-aware and worried about something, Georgina doesn't, she's so calm. Her demeanour almost makes her attractive.

I wonder if maybe I should let myself go. I could stop shaving my legs and my armpits. I could drop down to two showers a week, instead of every day. Wash my clothes once a fortnight instead of once a week, stop bothering with trying to wear matching clothes and just put on whatever is clean. I'm hardly high maintenance, but what if I was to do nothing? Would I feel liberated, or gross? There really is something about Georgina that I admire.

At lunchtime, I have a big baguette full of salami and cheese, with a packet of Wotsits and a can of Fanta. While sitting at my desk, feeling repulsive because I overate, Chloe comes over to talk me through the stationery orders. I hold my breath for almost the entire time so my cheesy Wotsit breath doesn't waft over her bony frame. And yet—

'Ew, what's that smell?' she says, fanning the air. 'Do you smell that, Flo?'

Maybe tomorrow I'll have a salad and water for lunch. The idea of letting myself go is suddenly totally out of the question.

Renée

Full steam ahead in finding a job that pays well, saving up, and moving to London. That is my plan. That is all I have to do. And so today I have booked an appointment at a recruitment agency for office work, even though I've never done anything but work in pubs, and the very thought of me working in an office is hilarious. But I'm feeling very grown-up about this, I'm doing what needs to be done, not what I want to do. How reassuring it is to know I can make mature and sensible decisions to secure myself a better future. Let's not worry about the fact that I am late because I went back three times to change my outfit.

I had on a pair of Flo's black trousers and a navy jumper but felt boring, so I put on a gingham polo neck with the trousers instead. Then I worried the person interviewing me would think I was a raver, because of the gingham. I used to wear it with velvet hotpants. An outfit I can't imagine wearing here in Guernsey because, along with McDonald's, fashion has never made its way to the island. In the end I wore the gingham polo under the jumper for a pop of personality. I plan to take it off if the interviewer seems fun.

On the phone, I was told to bring a notepad and a copy of my CV. I haven't got a notepad, but I do have a pen. Not sure if it works though. I haven't got any copies of my CV either – mainly because I haven't created one. It's too depressing to see my pathetic professional life on paper. I'm winging it, because that's who I am. I intend to smash this interview by relying on my electrifying personality and natural charm.

Forgetting myself and distracted by my efforts to be dazzling, I slam the front door shut behind me. It's so loud it even makes me jump. I stop and scrunch up my face, waiting for drama.

HONEYBEE

'Please, will you try a little harder not to slam the door! It scares me and I could slip?' the old lady downstairs shouts. Today she's wearing a bright green cashmere jumper with a chunky necklace and high-waisted, wide-legged trousers with pleats on the front. It's the nicest outfit I've seen since I got back to Guernsey – why on earth is she wearing it? She looks cross again. All I did was slam a door, hardly the crime of the century.

'I'm sorry,' I say, as nicely as I can. 'I forgot that I have to close the door gently behind me. I'm on my way to a job interview.' She looks me up and down disapprovingly.

'Where is the job?'

'Oh, it's an agency. I need a job. I have never really worked anywhere other than pubs and bars so I'm not sure how it will go, but you have to try, right?'

'You're wearing that?'

'Um, yes.' We both take a minute to scan my outfit. 'I'm sorry, I'm going to be late.'

She huffs and goes back inside. Who the hell does she think she is? I never want to end up like that. An angry, bitter old lady who lives alone and feels angry with the world around her for not being just as she wants it. What a depressing way to live.

I walk down Mill Street, past the market and through the arcade. The feeling of familiarity is almost overwhelming. There are memories on every corner. After-school chips, mayonnaise and hot chocolates in Dix Neuf, countless baskets of strong-smelling toiletries topped with tight cellophane from the Body Shop for almost anyone who had a birthday. I got my ears pierced in a little place that's now selling digital cameras and got fingered by a twenty-year-old in the doorway of the tobacco shop at around 2.30 a.m. one Sunday morning. Memories everywhere.

The recruitment place is on Smith Street at the top of a hill. By the time I reach the office, I have broken the sort of sweat that tells me I need to sort my life out. And then I have to climb to the fifth floor for 'Pink Apple Recruitment'.

'Hello, I'm Renée. I have a three o'clock appointment,' I say to the girl behind the reception desk. When she raises her head, I want the ground to eat me alive. Why can't this island swallow my past and stop chewing it up and spitting it in my face?

'Renée, I thought it must be you. Not many Renée Sargents about!'

'Hi Nancy, what chance.'

I went to school with Nancy at Tudor Falls. She was a bit of a hippie, I think. Always smelled of incense. She wanted to move to Peru and live in a forest, or some shit like that. I suppose her dreams didn't come true either.

'I wasn't a hundred per cent, though, because the Renée I knew would never want an office job, but I suppose we all change, don't we?'

'Oh no I haven't changed,' I say, feeling aggressively defensive of my personality. 'I just need to make some cash; I'm moving to London to be a writer. Just back on the island as a little stopgap and I don't want to work in pubs any more.'

'OK, well maybe pretend to want the job when you meet Mel? Just an idea. You look the same.'

'I am the same. I mean, I'm the same, but different. You know? You must be too? Same old us, lots more experience. I have a lot of experience, Nancy. Not in offices, but of life. My dad doesn't love me, that teaches you a lot.'

She stares blankly at me, and with sympathy. 'Yeah, I remember that.'

Ouch, she remembers my dad didn't love me? Was it always that obvious?

'Here, take a seat and fill in the first three pages of this then give it back to me. Mel will be ready for you soon. It's good to see you, I'm sure Pink Apple can help you get back on your feet.'

'I'm on my feet, Nancy. I just need to get paid.'

'I get it. Hope we can help. If you don't have an answer for one of the questions, just leave it blank.'

This is one of those terrible situations where I don't understand what's happening. Am I being defensive or is she being mean? I sit down with the forms. I hate forms. Especially ones with questions asking about my work experience. I have no experience other than using tills in pubs, there's no way I can fill this form in and sound qualified for anything. Aunty Jo always told me that if I showed off my personality instead of my brains, I'll win. She thinks that, ultimately, even when it comes to employment, people want to be around people they like. This comes from a woman who describes herself as 'allergic' to office culture and who now runs a garden centre. But right now, it's the best advice I have. It's time to let my personality shine through because, in this instance, my brains won't get me anywhere.

* *What office experience have you got?* – This is a very personal question! But if you must know, I've only ever done it in one office. Cars on the other hand . . . and don't get me started on bike sheds . . .

* *List the Microsoft programmes you have experience with* – I don't really watch Microsoft programmes, I'm more of an *EastEnders* girl.

* *List your qualifications* – Costa del Sol Beach Karaoke winner, 2003. Puerto Banús Yard of Beer Champion two weeks running. I mean, I could go on . . . ?

* *Where do you want to be in five years?* – Not unemployed and with a regular and satisfying sex life (I'd also like a successful writing career and to move to London).

I worry that one was going too far. I've made quite a few references to my sex life. I'm about to rub it out when—

'Renée?' says Nancy. I get a whiff of incense; maybe she hasn't changed that much after all, she's the same her, in the wrong place. 'Mel is ready for you. Just take your forms with you, second door on the left.'

No time for edits.

Mel is about five feet nine, size 12, with big boobs and long brown hair. She looks similar in age to Aunty Jo, but the version who's had to present herself well every day for the last twenty-five years, as opposed to Aunty Jo who has a clean pair of wellies that she wears to the shops. Mel's nails are purple, her skin bronze, and she is wearing a tailored suit. I notice a wedding ring and a picture of

HONEYBEE

two girls around my age on her desk. She looks at me as if I've taken her breath away. I look nice but not that nice.

'Are they your daughters?' I ask, referring to the picture.

'Yes, both at uni now. I don't know where the time went. Do you have any?' she asks, casually. I laugh. I have never been asked if I have kids before. I would say it's screamingly obvious that I don't.

'Absolutely not,' I say, sitting down, shuddering at the thought of adding a child to the list of things that makes my life complicated. She clocks my shudder and smiles, before looking at the forms I just handed her. Her eyebrows keep shooting up and down, as if she's an actor playing out the direction 'respond to surprising content'. I feel like a total dick for trying to be funny, then all of a sudden, she bursts out laughing.

'I mean, the one about the bike sheds is my favourite, what the hell?'

Phew.

'So, the truth is I have sod-all office experience. I thought I'd make you laugh instead of impress you.'

'Well, you made me laugh, that's for sure. What is it you want to do? You know this is an agency for receptionist, office manager and other non-creative roles? I presume you don't want to be a banker?'

'No, I want to move to London and be a writer. But I'm back here because I've got no money and no idea where to start. I thought I'd better temp while I get myself together. I've probably blown it, though. Does this go down in history as the most unimpressive interview of all time?'

'Kind of. In one way. Most people come in here sounding like they have a degree in spreadsheeting. Do you even know what a spreadsheet is?'

'Of course, I do. It's a flat sheet. You have to do hospital corners to make it stay on the mattress?' I say, pleased that some of my best material is coming out in this interview.

She laughs again. And I feel proud of myself for sticking with it. I'm being myself. If I get a job out of it, great. If I don't, it's back behind a bar for me.

'I want to write. That's what I want to be doing in five years. I have no idea how to achieve this dream, but that's what I am hoping will happen. I just need money in the meantime, and if I'm honest, I'm sick of working in bars. Drunk people are so annoying.'

'Well, that sounds fair. OK, look, your options are quite limited because there isn't much you can do. And don't tell anyone I said this, but it sounds like you'd be suited to a job that allows you to use your personality, but gives you a bit of spare time to do some writing? My husband is a writer. What that actually means is that he's never really worked because he refuses to do anything but write and I'm not sure he's very good at it. It was useful when the kids were small, I could build the business and he sorted them out, but still, I wonder if this dream of his will ever happen. I'd quite like to be the one at home one day.' She stops, as if surprised by how much she's revealed. 'Anyway, sorry, not sure why I told you that.'

'It's OK, it's interesting. You don't hear that very often.

The guy at home with the kids, the woman at work. I love that. I think I'd want it to be that way round too.'

'Well, it worked for us – it worked for me. I think my husband wishes he had more going on, but I suppose that's how generations of women have always felt, isn't it? I still feel guilty. So, let me deal with my guilt by helping out another artist, shall I?'

'Wow, thanks,' I say, genuinely baffled by how nice she is being. I was expecting to be laughed at.

'I have a position that's just come in. It's a receptionist job at a little marketing company. They need someone right away, the office is in Trinity Square. What do you think?'

'That sounds great. Thank you. My flatmate works in marketing. She can give me the low-down because if I'm totally honest I don't really understand what it is.'

'You're funny. But maybe lose the honesty when you turn up on Monday morning, OK? You'll be representing me and my agency when you're there, so at least pretend to be interested?'

'OK,' I say, remembering that jobs are serious.

'They're looking for a receptionist indefinitely until they find someone full-time for the role. If you're good, that won't happen anytime soon. You'll be meeting and greeting, setting up the meeting rooms and a few other bits and bobs, but you'll also get some time to sit at a computer on reception when it's quiet and write a few words, if you promise to do it discreetly, and not give me a bad name?'

'Of course. Wow, thanks so much!'

'And they have a London office, so you never know, prove yourself and you might even get a transfer one day.'

'Great.'

'Here's the address,' she says, handing me a form. 'It's called Magic Marketing. You'll be reporting to Flo Parrot. She's the . . .'

I make a very strange noise that could mean anything from shock to trapped wind.

'Is there a problem?' Mel asks, frowning, and I see a firmer side to her. 'You know Renée, I'm sorry it's not a more exciting role, but I've really tried to help you out here.'

'No. No, it's a brilliant role and I'd love to do it. I just wasn't expecting it to happen so quickly. I'm stunned, that's all. Thank you, really that's great.'

'OK good. Well good luck, keep me posted on how it goes.'

'I will,' I say, getting up to leave.

She stands up suddenly and calls me back in. 'Renée, when I saw your name on my calendar, I wondered if it could be you. And as soon as I saw you, I knew. I was friends with your mum at school. Really good friends. You're hilarious, just like she was. She'd be really proud of you, I'm sure.'

It's like stubbing your toe or hitting your funny bone. A reaction that you have no power over. My eyes overflow with tears.

'Oh, I'm sorry. I didn't mean to upset you,' Mel says. 'I shouldn't have said anything.'

'No, no, not at all. It's just so nice. Almost feels like she just helped me out.'

'Maybe she did. Good luck with the job. Please be punctual and look smart, you're representing my agency, OK?'

'Of course,' I say, drying my eyes on my sleeve. 'I'm honestly so grateful and I won't fuck it up.'

Mel smiles and sits back down. That's twice in just a week that I've met someone who knew Mum. Her entire life was here, all thirty-six years of it. If I move away, one thing I'll never get more of are all the memories of her.

'All good?' Nancy asks as I come out of Mel's office.

'All great. Hey, did you ever get to Peru? I know that was your dream.'

'I did, yeah. I went straight out of school. I spent a year there, I hiked the Inca Trail and worked as a teaching assistant for a language school. It was amazing.'

'Wow, are you going to go back?'

'No, that box is ticked. I'm back here now. I want to buy a house, find a husband, start a family. You can't just wander around forever, can you?'

'I guess not.' It's never occurred to me that an ambition could be achieved so young; you can relax and just get on with living a normal life having fulfilled the thing you always wanted to do. How liberating for her. She's done. Marriage and babies from now on.

'Nice to see you, Nancy.' I go to leave.

'Oh, Renée, did you hear that Sally died? Cancer, apparently.'

'Yeah, I did. I went to the funeral.'

'You went to Sally de Putron's funeral? You did? Did you two become friends in the end?'

'No, never. I just, I dunno, I felt sorry for her. She had a kid, you know? I lost my mum at that age, I felt weirdly connected to it.'

'Fair enough. I'm sorry about your mum, by the way. I'm not sure we ever said things like that to each other at school. It must have been really hard for you.'

'It was, thank you.'

I leave, feeling more empowered than when I arrived. I hurry down the stairs and back into the fresh air. I can't wait for Flo to get home so I can tell her we'll be roomies and colleagues. She'll be so happy. Maybe.

I think of Nancy, aged twenty-two, having lived the dream she always wanted to live. Just the great expanse of life sitting in front of her. And for me, the big stuff is yet to come. My real adventures are just around the corner.

5

Flo

'Why are you being weird?' I say to Renée as I walk into the kitchen after work. She's standing by the sink and looks tense.

'Something happened.'

'Oh God, what? You broke something? What was it? My happy cup?'

'Your what?'

'My happy cup. I read an article once about how you should nominate things to make you happy, so you associate them with feeling good. I have a happy cup, a happy spoon, a happy wine glass.'

'You have a happy spoon?'

I've never told anyone about my happy spoon before.

I might make that the last time I try to explain it. 'So, what then, what happened?'

'I got a job.'

'That's so great! Wow, that was quick. When do you start?'

'Monday.'

'OK, well this is good, right? Why do you look like this isn't good?'

'Well, don't be mad, but it's . . . it's at your office. I just got the job as your receptionist. Ta-*dah!*'

She is doing jazz hands. You always know when Renée is nervous because she does jazz hands. I feel some scratching in my belly. I put my hand to it and rub gently. I breathe in, breathe out. Breathe in, breathe out. My work is my place. My zone. I want to keep it that way. This clearly shows on my face.

'Flo, I knew you'd react like this, but maybe it's not that bad? And I don't have to stay for long. We can see how it goes, and I can tell Mel at Pink Apple that I need to find something else, but at least I'll be working in the meantime?'

'I suppose so.'

'Flo, it might even be fun?'

It won't be fun. It will be stressful. The receptionist at Magic Marketing works under me. I'll essentially be Renée's boss. Does she really think she'll like me telling her to clean meeting rooms and check the toilets?

'You realise I'll have to tell you what to do, right?'

'Flo, you are applying stress and pressure to this situation before it has even arisen. Can we just presume it won't be awful, see how it goes, and if it doesn't work out, I'll just leave? I don't want to work in a bloody marketing office anyway, I don't even know what marketing is.'

I exhale a huge, defeated breath. I choose not to take offence at her suggestion that working in a marketing office is rubbish. 'OK, but Renée, my job is important to me, OK? I don't want to get put into a situation where I'm having to stick up for you, or where you're not doing the job, and it's showing me up, OK?'

'Jesus, have some faith.'

'Fine, but you working in an office makes about as much sense as Madonna working in a bookshop.'

'I'm not an idiot, Flo. I think I'll manage answering some phones and putting on a smiley face to greet visitors. It might not be what I want to do forever, but it doesn't mean I can't do it.'

She looks genuinely hurt, and now I just feel awful.

'OK, I'm sorry. Congratulations, it's great you got a job. And we can play it by ear, I suppose, if living together and working together feels like too much.'

'Sure, let's play it by ear. Whatever you need. I thought you'd be happy.'

'I am happy, of course I am. How about I cook spag bol and we watch *Dirty Dancing* on the sofa tonight?'

'That sounds great,' she says, as I pour two glasses of red wine. She sits down at the kitchen table, and I get all the ingredients together.

'Sorry, I didn't mean to be negative.'

'I'm sad,' she says. 'Maybe I can use your happy spoon to cheer me up?'

I tell her to sod off.

'How do I look?' says Renée, coming into the kitchen. It's 7.45 a.m. the following Monday. She looks smart with a pair of my black trousers on, and a red shirt of hers. She usually wears the top four buttons undone on everything, but she's buttoned up at least two. This is good, it suggests she is taking this seriously and won't humiliate me with raunchy outfits and raucous behaviour. I don't mean to be so pessimistic of how this will all go. But I know Renée. She's hardly a wallflower who avoids trouble.

'You look great,' I say, convincingly. She doesn't really look like Renée. Quite serious. I could laugh, but I won't.

'I'll go shopping when I get paid,' she says, obviously uncomfortable but not wanting to offend me as she's in my clothes.

It occurs to me she can't be entirely herself at work, she has to find a version of Renée that works in the office. That's what we all do; we all have our work persona that gets the job done and keeps everyone happy. It's why it will never not be weird to bump into colleagues outside of work. Seeing them in their casual clothes, relaxed, with people who don't pay them to be there. I panic about bumping into someone from work in town. All I'd know to talk to them about is stationery.

Renée fidgets with the red shirt. She seems really nervous,

which I suppose is understandable. 'It's OK, Renée,' I say, reassuringly. 'I'm here to help, you can ask me anything.'

She takes a few more moments to express her concerns.

'Are any of the guys in your office fit?' she says, winking at me. 'I've always loved the idea of a shag in a boardroom.'

This is going to be awful.

Renée

'This is it,' says Flo, as we stand outside a modern building with a large glass door in Trinity Square. It's the kind of Guernsey I've never known personally but always knew was here. The island is a tax haven, apparently. That means lots of businesses are based here, and the headquarters of lots of banks and financial things. It's another world. The business world. I suddenly feel fifteen again. I see my reflection in the glass. I look unimpressive, in an unimpressive outfit. I wish I'd worn my jeans, but for some reason you're not allowed to wear comfortable clothes when you have to sit down all day in one room.

'Ready?' Flo says, like we are about to burst on stage and sing for the queen. She takes a big breath and opens the door with her fob. We go inside.

As the lift doors open, we step into a small hallway that quickly merges into a reception area. It's nice, smart, without much character. A purple sofa and the front of the reception desk is lit nicely, with 'Magic Marketing' across the front. It's surprisingly exciting seeing it. A proper reception in a proper office. I'm going to sit there and be all receptionisty. It already kicks arse over pulling pints.

'This is your desk,' says Flo, as if I haven't already worked that out. I make my way behind it, taking my jacket off and hanging it on the back of my chair. I feel confident and excited, just as a very skinny and extremely stylish blonde woman walks up to the desk and makes me feel like a dorky child who has no place with the cool kids in the working world. I gulp down my insecurities and put on my best me.

'Hello, I'm Renée,' I say to the woman who has identified herself as Chloe. She kind of smiles, I think. Her blonde bob is short and perfect, her jade eye shadow is the exact shade of her cropped, stripy jumper that sits perfectly on top of a floral shirt with a pussy-bow collar. A bold clashing of prints which takes a certain self-confidence to pull off. Her skintight trousers show the kind of thigh gap supermodels have, and she walked in here like she was floating on a cloud, despite her four-inch heels. I hate her and want to be her all in the first three seconds of meeting her.

'We walked here,' I say, like a thirteen-year-old girl talking about the first time she wears a bra.

Chloe replies with a strained smile. 'Do you two know each other then?' she says to Flo.

'Yes, by chance Renée and I live together. We . . .'

'Don't worry, we're not lesbians or anything,' my mouth spurts before my brain has the chance to stop it. Both

Chloe and Flo's heads bounce in my direction, but neither of them is quite sure what to say. 'Sorry,' I add. 'I'm a little nervous. I lose control of what I say when I am nervous. We are not lesbians. And I won't say lesbians again.'

Flo drops her head and shakes it. This may have been what she was talking about when she expressed concerns about me working in her office.

'I'm a lesbian,' says Chloe, proudly. The three of us stand staring at each other in one of the most surreal silences I've ever experienced.

'I did not know that,' Flo says, sounding like Stephen Hawking.

'Why would you?' Chloe says, her nose still aimed at the roof. 'I'm not wearing an "I am a lesbian" T-shirt. It's quite hard for people in Guernsey to comprehend when they find out. It would be easier for you all if I strapped down my chest, shaved off half my hair and wore heavy boots.'

I find myself looking at her chest, and wondering what the point would be in strapping down her very small boobs.

'I comprehend it,' I say, politely. She seems pleased about that.

'I actually remember you, Renée, from Tudor Falls. I was a prefect when you were in Junior Remove. I once caught you eating the phone book. You were standing on a desk with a swarm of girls cheering you on.'

'Oh wow, that was you? You reported me to the headmistress, I got my first detention.'

'Of course I did. You were destroying school property.

Tearing out pages, stuffing them into your mouth and chewing them. It was extraordinary.'

'Yes, well, no one was more sorry than me. I didn't poo for a week after that. Who knew surnames beginning with P were so un-fibrous.' I think that's quite funny; Chloe looks as if she might be sick.

'I remember that day too,' Flo says.

'Oh, you were at Tudor Falls as well?' Chloe asks. Flo looks like she's trying not to be upset about how unmemorable she must be.

'Yup, but I kept a low profile.'

'Strange, I never forget a face,' she says, rubbing it in.

'Well, I have a very forgettable face. Shall we move on?'

'OK, well this is where you will be based,' Chloe says, turning back to me. 'The switchboard is very simple, Flo will explain it all to you. You can take an hour for lunch, but please no eating at your desk; you are representing us all while you sit here. Are you OK to walk Renée through everything, Flo? I have a meeting at nine fifteen.'

'Of course,' says Flo, efficiently.

'Great. Well, welcome to the team, Renée. And Flo, if we can get coffees and pastries for the nine fifteen, that would be great,' she says with a small, unfriendly smile. 'Good to see again, Renée. Please don't eat the directory. It's laminated. Can't be good for you.'

'No need, I packed a sandwich,' I say, as she struts away. I brace myself for a bollocking. 'There is no way she eats pastries,' I say, hoping to distract Flo.

'Are you serious?' Flo says, turning to me. 'We are not

lesbians? LESBIANS? Why would you say that? That was the first thing you said after hello?' She goes behind the reception desk and starts moving things around, turning things on and opening and shutting drawers.

'I'm sorry, I got nervous,' I say. A little annoyed that there is no sympathy for me. I got tongue-tied and said something stupid, it's not that bad. 'Got the conversation going though, didn't it? Did you know she was gay?'

'No, I didn't. It's not the kind of thing you talk about in an office.'

'Well, she seemed keen to tell us.'

'Only because you . . .' She is talking quietly but clearly wishes she was shouting, 'Just please watch it, Renée. Please?'

I nod. 'OK, I'm sorry. She's just so uptight-looking, it threw me off-guard. Is she nice? She doesn't seem nice. I remember her now, proper snooty.'

'She's nice. I mean, she's fine. Come here.'

I join Flo behind the desk and sit on the chair.

'Oooomph, its comfy,' I say as I pull a lever that adjusts the height up and down. I suddenly slam down so that my face is below the desk and an unpredicted bolt of giggles bellows out of my mouth.

'Renée, seriously. Stop it. Just be serious, please.' She is speaking in a loud aggressive whisper. I release the lever again and I rise slowly back up to the correct height. Flo picks up the phone receiver.

'So, you answer the phone, ask who it is and who they want to speak to, and then you put them through. You always ask who it is, OK? When the person here answers, you say who is on the call and they will either take it or ask you to take a message. Here is a list of extensions.'

While she is talking, I slowly lift my hand and put it on her bottom. She screeches and then pulls back, mortified. As she looks around reception and cranes her neck behind the desk to make sure no one is coming, she angrily pushes my hand away.

'For fuck's sake, Renée. Enough. Seriously, I can call Mel at Pink Apple and have her send someone else if you don't pack it in.'

'Woah, did you just threaten to fire me?'

'No, I . . .' She did, and now she can't believe she said it. But she did. 'Please, can we just focus? I'm not like that here.' This sends me over the edge.

'Not like *what* here?'

She looks around again. 'I don't know, fun.'

I choose not to wind her up by asking her if she's ever fun. I'm really annoying her now and, funny as it is, I don't actually want to annoy her, so I stop messing around and listen. She pulls out a laminated sheet of A4 listing names and numbers and puts it on the desk.

'You answer, ask who it's for and who it is, press hold, introduce the call and either press release to put it through, or return to take a message from the caller. OK?'

I nod but can't remember anything she just said.

'Do you need me to show you again?' she asks, sincerely. I tell her there is no need. 'OK, I need to go and set the meeting room up. That will actually be your job too, but

I'll do it today to ease you in slowly. Do you think you'll be OK with the phones for ten minutes? I'll talk you through the rest when I'm done.'

'Yeah, I think I'm good. I mean, it's just answering phones, isn't it?'

'OK, cool. And please, if anyone comes up to you, try not to talk about lesbians.'

She smiles as she walks away. More a smile of resilience than affection, but a smile nonetheless. The whole word-vomit thing was terrible and embarrassing, but even Flo can't deny that it was a little bit funny.

I feel a little high up, so I pull the lever on the side of the chair, and I get slammed back towards the ground again. This gives me a real fright, so I could do without the phone ringing at that exact moment. I stand up and look at it, like it's the first and only phone in the entire world and I have no idea what it is. Why is answering it so terrifying? What did Flo tell me to do? Pick it up. Just pick it up.

'Hello,' I say. Shit, I've forgotten the name of the company. 'Hello?' I say again, but the person on the other end of the phone seems to expect more. 'Hello, the Magic Place,' I say, to which they say, 'The what?'

They don't laugh.

'Can I speak to Ben, please?' says a male voice.

'Ben who?' I ask.

'Did we recently employ another Ben? It's Jordan from the London office. Who is this?'

Why is someone from the London office so scary?

'My name is Renée, it's my first day. Ben . . .' I pick up

the laminated sheet of A4 but drop it. It wafts somewhere under my desk. 'Hang on please,' I say politely as I get down on all fours to retrieve it.

'He's extension number four,' says Jordan, impatiently.

'OK, great,' I say, getting up and whacking my head on the desk. 'FUCK!' I yell down the phone, which is greeted by a 'Bloody hell, I'll just call his mobile' and a dial tone. I remain under the desk for a few seconds while I rub my head. How did just answering a phone go so badly?

As I come back up, I jump again when a man's voice says, 'Hello.'

I say hello back, before I look up. 'It's her first day,' he continues. I realise that he's on his mobile, and not actually saying hello to me, which I find really embarrassing.

'All right, I'll get it straight over,' the man says, hanging up his call. 'Well, that went well,' he says, smiling at me.

'Yup, Flo told me to swear and hang up on everyone who calls. Just doing my job.'

He smiles. I smile. I hope the phone doesn't ring again while he is still standing here. He's tall, slim, handsome and black. He's wearing a nice blue suit. He has the kindest eyes.

'I'm Ben.'

'Hi, I'm Renée. First day, obviously.'

'You'll get the hang of it. Maybe try not to swear, though. And personally, I find sitting on my chair helps, rather than the floor. I dunno, that might be just me.'

I sit on my chair and feel infinitely less stressed than I was thirty seconds ago.

'I'm going to suggest that you press that red button there. That is your out-of-office, it means that if you're not at your desk, the phones ring in the main office and one of us will pick it up.'

As my finger is heading towards it, the phone rings again. My heart bursts through my shirt. 'Fuck. Shit, no sorry. I'll just answer it.'

Ben leans over the desk and presses the red button. Instantly I hear the phone ringing in the office behind me. My relief manifests itself physically, and I sit back into my chair with a large exhalation.

'Thank you,' I say, noticing a wedding ring, and feeling disappointed.

'No problem. Ah, Flo,' he says, looking behind me as Flo walks back over. 'I suggested Renée puts the phones on her out-of-office while she gets acquainted. It's a lot to take in, I'm sure.' Flo looks at me nervously, wondering what mess I've created, but relaxes when she sees how calm and happy Ben seems. 'OK, good luck,' he says. 'I'm on line four if you need anything. See you later.'

'See you later,' I say, like a child staring at a lollipop. He is delicious.

'No,' says Flo, firmly.

'No what?'

'1) He is the boss and 2) he is married. Stop thinking that right now.'

'He's the boss? Wow, that just made him one hundred per cent sexier,' I say.

Flo presses the red button again. The phones are back

under my control. She runs through the procedure one more time. 'Got it?' she says, firmly.

'Got it,' I say.

'I'm nearly done in the meeting room. Hang here for five and I'll come get you for a walk-through. OK?'

'OK.'

As she walks away, I call her back. 'Flo?'

'Yes Renée?'

'How married is he?'

'Renée, no!'

The phone rings again. I stare at it for a few seconds, then slam my finger on the red button. The sound of it ringing in the main office is a relief. I will master this, I just need a moment to settle in.

I look at the list of extensions. My gaze hovers over 'Ben Jackson #4'.

I hope he gets a lot of calls.

Over the next few hours, I notice that Flo is very serious at work. She's very formal with people and, even though I get that it's her job, it all seems very silly. She sends lots of emails with stunted subject lines, telling us things she thinks are important. Stuff like: *To all concerned, there is plenty of printer paper in the back room if you need a top-up. Just reply to this email to let me know if I can get it for you. Thanks, Flo.* Or: *To all concerned, I have noticed a distinct lack of uptake on the decaffeinated coffee in the kitchen. I am considering disposing of it to make space. If anyone has an issue, please come to me directly. Thanks, Flo.*

This one makes me laugh out loud at my desk. Like, seriously Flo, WHO FUCKING CARES. I can't help myself and have to wind her up a bit on email. I respond: *You sound so sexy in emails. All this talk of decaf coffee is getting me aroused.*

Next thing I know, Flo is standing up and shouting, 'WE ARE NOT LESBIANS!' across the office. No one knows where to look. I see that an email has popped up from me, how is that possible? Is there someone else called Renée Sargent here? Flo storms over, steam coming out of her head.

'You REPLIED ALL you absolute twat-basket,' she hisses.

'Eh? I what?'

'When you get sent a group email, you click Reply to respond to the person who sent it to you and Reply All to respond to everyone on the chain. You just told the entire office you think decaf coffee is erotic!'

'Ohhh, that's what that means!'

I turn and look around the office. All the men are laughing, and Chloe looks cross. I stand up, face them all and shout, 'I'M ONLY JOKING!'

'There, all OK now,' I say, sitting back down, trying to avoid eye contact with Flo.

'Just TRY to *not be you* here, OK? Just TRY!'

God, professional Flo is so uptight.

6

Flo

We make it to Friday without Renée talking more about lesbians, or her making fun of me in front of my colleagues. She finally mastered the phones yesterday afternoon after three days of calls being put through to the wrong people, clients getting hung up on, and Renée having breakdowns about how much she hates technology. Things are OK, but the office is a very different place.

It's rare that I don't see at least one of the guys going to her desk to ask unnecessary questions – especially Matt, he can't get enough of her. I watch him looking to make sure there's no one else there, then go up himself to make crap chitchat. Renée is chatty back, because that is what she does. He fancies the pants off her, and it's so obvious.

Even Phil hasn't stopped smiling since Monday. There is a new energy in the air, a more flirtatious vibe. It's a bit like when Georgina brings in doughnuts for everyone. Renée is the doughnuts.

At the flat last night, Renée said, 'The guys in the office are quite lechy, aren't they?' And I had to admit that I hadn't noticed until she started. 'It's probably because I'm a temp. I'm novelty. They know I won't be there long, so flirting with me isn't going to create a long-term issue,' she said, noticing that I hadn't been subject to their advances. But it isn't that, it's simply because Renée is sexual. She is confident and sociable and guys have, and always will, love that. She's not one of those women who flaunts her body, but she's pretty. And even though she isn't skinny, a size 12 with normal-sized boobs, she radiates something that guys respond to. I don't. It's that simple. You either have it or you don't. Men are nice to me, they flirt with her.

'Yes,' I said, agreeing with her comment about her being a temp. 'I'm sure that's it.' But of course I know it's because I have no sex appeal. I've been wondering if Chloe's lack of sexuality is deliberate, to stop men hitting on her. That's quite clever if it is.

Renée walks purposefully over to my desk. This is good. She is focusing on work and obviously needs me to organise something important. 'My armpits smell of onions, do you ever get that?' she says, sniffing her pits and looking at me as if replying would be normal.

'Renée, what? Are you . . . ? You can't just . . . did you want anything else? Anything work-related?'

'Oh yeah, Matt says everyone is going for drinks tonight, shall we?'

'Renée, you can't just put your out-of-office on to come and ask me about social plans,' I say, trying to look unbothered that I don't know about these drinks that 'everyone' is going to.

'I didn't, I'm going for a wee. I just came to see you on the way. So, shall we go? He just emailed me.' I look over at Matt, he is straight up staring at Renée's bottom. I pretend not to notice. 'Well, shall we?'

'No, I don't think so. I don't know if socialising with colleagues is a good idea.'

'Oh no, nope, not having it. There is no way the old Flo is creeping back.' She leans down to me, her elbows are on my desk, her face is very close to mine. 'Flo, stop acting like this job is everything. We're twenty-two years old, this is our first true summer of being adults. Look at us. We have a flat, an income. We're flying, Flo. This should be the summer that sets the tone for the rest of our lives. We are young, we are professional, and we are fun. We can be all of those things at the same time. Or, you can be boring. Up to you.'

I don't know how it's happened, but by the end of her speech our faces are almost touching. She appears to not be moving until I respond.

'Fine. Let's go,' I say. 'I've never been for "work drinks" before, it sounds very grown-up.'

'Great,' says Renée. Matt has now got up and slides over.

'Hey honey,' he says to Renée. 'What's this mothers'

meeting all about?' Renée doesn't seem to buckle at being called 'honey'. Also, 'mothers' meeting'? Rude. I find him so gross.

'We'll come after work, for the drinks. Fun!' Renée says, as she walks off towards the toilet. Matt watches her the whole way. He's so animal in the way that he is towards women. It must take a lot of control for him to keep his tongue in his mouth. It gives me the creeps. Renée seems entirely comfortable with it.

After work, we gather in reception. Matt arrives on the dot of five o'clock, asking Renée questions about Spain and what the social scene was like down there. Every time she mentions going clubbing, he raises his eyelids repeatedly and very quickly, as if instead of 'clubbing' she'd said 'shagging'. I'd tell him to go away if I was her; it must be annoying to have someone hover around you in that way. Not that I'd know.

'Can you come, Ben?' Matt asks when everyone is assembled and ready to leave.

'I can't, I'm sorry. I need to get back for Penny.'

'Oh, come on, mate. She won't mind you having a quick pint, surely?' Matt pushes.

'If he needs to go, he needs to go,' Georgina says, putting a comforting hand on Ben's arm. 'Send our love to Penny,' she says, to which Ben smiles back. I pick up on something weird that makes me wonder why Penny needs 'our love'.

'Have a pint for me!' Ben says, leaving. Everyone is clearly disappointed. If Ben is this lovely at work, I can only imagine what great company he is on a night out.

Chloe isn't asked directly but tells us she is on a cleanse and not drinking, and Georgina says she has a ritual of fish and chips with her sister on Fridays and wouldn't miss it for the world. I love that about her.

'OK, let's go,' says Matt, who is acting like our group leader. Renée links arms with me and rushes to the lift. She used to do this when we were at school, always walking in front of the boys so they could see her bum. Renée likes being watched. I don't. It feels very odd to be going out with the boys from work. I suddenly feel like they're all total strangers. Without the security of talking about office supplies, I have absolutely no idea how to make conversation.

In the pub, Matt offers to get the first round in. Everyone orders pints of lager and he makes a joke about how he never thought I was the kind of girl to drink pints. 'Flo drinks like a man,' Renée says, nudging me as if that was a nice thing to say. 'Clearly office Flo and out-of-office Flo are quite different then,' Matt says, winking at Phil.

Why did he wink at Phil? What did that mean? I think Phil moves a little closer to me, or maybe he just moved out of someone else's way. Does Phil fancy me? If so, do I fancy him? We've never really said much to each other. He's kind of quiet, like Matt's sidekick. He always does the top button of his shirts up, I always thought that was quite square. Maybe it's not, maybe it's actually sexy. Why did Matt wink at him? I suck my belly in and down my pint. The rat just woke up, I won't let it ruin this for me. 'Anyone want a Blow Job?' I ask, immediately regretting it.

'Get in there, Phil!' Matt says, and I want to die.

'I mean the drink,' I splutter. 'Amaretto and Baileys. Not . . .'

'We know, Flo. Jeez!' says Matt, making me feel so stupid. Why didn't I just say shots? Idiot. Regardless, everyone says yes, so I go to the bar and order everyone a Blow Job. But rather than humiliate myself again I say, 'Can I get six of those shots where you put the Baileys on the Amaretto, sorry I can't remember what they're called.'

The barman looks at me straight-faced and says, 'Blow Jobs?' as if I was being such a prude to not just say it. I feel even more stupid so down an extra one while I wait for my change.

A few rounds in and we're all sitting in a booth. Matt is next to Renée; he is openly flirting with her, and turning absolutely anything she says into an innuendo. 'I used to work in the Ship and Crown' is met with, 'I bet pints weren't the only thing you pulled'. And 'growing up on a tiny island without much to do' gets, 'I bet you found something to do, eh?' and more of those super-fast eyebrow raises. He must think she had loads of sex to pass the time. Which isn't a million miles from the truth. Both Matt and Phil are from Guernsey, but we've never met them before. They went to schools on the north of the island, very different from Tudor Falls. Matt went to the same sixth form as us but he's a few years older, so we never met. And Phil left school at sixteen and went to the College of Further Education to study business. Neither of them went to uni, both getting jobs right out of studying. It makes them seem so experienced compared to us. It's weird how people go to university when the people who don't bother seem to come out of school and get the same jobs anyway. I wonder what I actually learned at university. How to cook pasta with pesto and battle through a drunken blow job, mostly. There weren't seminars in either.

I can't imagine giving someone a blow job on Guernsey. I'll always assume that everything I do here will be spread around the island in five minutes. It was very liberating being in England with no history. Here, even with people I didn't know growing up, my shame seems to hang off the walls. I can feel the old me putting the barriers back up. There's only one way to break them back down again. I finish my pint.

'We should dance,' says Matt suddenly, raising his eyebrows at Renée again, as if he just said, 'I think we should all have sex.' I've never seen this twitch-like face manoeuvre he now keeps doing. What is it? It's horrible. How does Renée not want to punch him in the face? She lets out a high-pitched 'Wooooo' and waves her arms around in the air, making her boobs bounce up and down like basketballs. This almost pushes Matt's eyebrows off his face.

Phil turns to me and says, 'You up for a dance, Flo?' He nudges me with his elbow and Matt makes an annoying 'Oooooh' noise. What is happening? Is Renée going to dance with Matt? Am I going to dance with Phil? Is it the 1950s?

I should probably just go home. I like my relationship with people at work. I don't want to dance or kiss or do anything with Phil, as Matt and Renée are implying. Damn my anxiety around men. The rat inside me wriggles and squirms around. When it wakes up it feels like it's nibbling and scratching at my insides, making me uncomfortable, reminding me I'm not good enough. I can kill it though, by drowning it. I visualise each drink increasing the fluid level around its head. Each one filling me up more and more until its ugly little nose is poking out of the top. I drink until I'm sure it's fully submerged. And only then can I forget that it's there.

'I should get home, really,' I say, feeling there is still time to get out of this and resume normal office life on Monday without too much damage.

'What?' asks Renée, obviously not feeling the same way. 'Flo, I need a wee, come with me,' she says, dragging me up from the booth. In the toilets, she pretty much pushes me against the sink.

'Flo, stop being weird. We are going dancing,' she says, firmly.

'I don't want to go dancing with people from work. Matt obviously really fancies you. It's going to go one of two ways. You'll dance and get off with him, or ditch him at the end of the night. Either way, Monday will be awful.'

'You need to get laid, Flo,' she says, putting her hands on my shoulders and talking to me like a dad encouraging a son to go onto a football pitch and play the best game of his life.

'I do not,' I reply. The drunk half of my brain not disagreeing with her. The sober half still thinking sensibly.

'We are going. What do you need to make this happen?' she asks me.

'Two shots of tequila?' I say, seeing as she asked. So we go to the bar, she orders me two shots, I drink them, and the four of us head off to Follies.

Back in the day, Renée and I always went to the Monkey. It was messy and cheap with a young crowd. They played the same music every night, and if you wanted a snog, it was pretty much guaranteed. Follies was the more grown-up nightclub on the island. Other than Saturday nights, people queued up in their work clothes. The men were in suits, the women in office clothes. It felt so sophisticated to us, like a place we would never go. But now here we are, in our work clothes, with our colleagues, joining a few hundred other drunk office workers who may or may not be able to look each other in the eye on Monday morning.

The club is split into two levels: on the top mezzanine there are three bars, down below is the dance floor with a stripper's pole in the middle of it. I look down from the balcony, Renée is already spinning around the pole driving all the men wild. 'Show Me Love' is playing, proving Guernsey is a cultural time warp that doesn't fix anything that ain't broke – we used to dance to this in the Monkey. Why play new music when people respond so well to the old? A swarm of people head to the dance floor, all with their arms in the air, all hammered, knowing every word. Matt joins Renée at the pole and they do some weird, sexy version of pole dancing together that will surely end in a broken bone. Phil goes to the bar, I follow him.

'What do you want?' he asks me.

'What are you having?' I shout back, annoyed at myself for not being assertive. Renée used to get so cross with me for following all the time and never leading; she'd say it isn't sexy to guys and irritating for other girls. Phil says he's having a beer. I don't want a beer. 'A double gin and tonic,' I tell him. 'And a shot of tequila.' He smiles, I think he liked that. He orders our drinks. I drink them quickly. Finally, the rat is drowned. Here comes Flo.

'You're different out of work,' Phil yells in my ear.

'You haven't seen anything yet,' I reply. I drag him to the stripper's pole.

I wake up on my bedroom floor wearing just my knickers and bra. My duvet is on top of me, and my pillow is under my head. Why did I make a bed on the floor? As I lift my head, I realise that it is throbbing. I need water. I settle on all fours for a minute while I allow my body to calibrate to a new position. I put my hands on the bed and pull myself up. I see a huge purple stain across my mattress, and an empty wine glass where my pillow should be. Gross.

My alarm clock says its 6.07 a.m. I can't remember getting home, it can't have been long ago. I feel like I'm sucking sandpaper.

As I reach the bottom of the stairs, the smell of stale

booze and cigarettes hits me. The living room door is slightly open, the air is cold. Is a window open? I push the door open and see Matt passed out on the armchair. He is naked, other than his underpants. He is snoring, his mouth wide open, around four rolls under his chin. He is a big guy, his chest is moderately hairy, his thighs are thick. I can see the outline of his penis through his red underpants. It looks big. He looks like a disgusting oaf. There are empty alcohol bottles all over the floor and a number of overflowing ashtrays. How many of us were here last night? Where is Renée? Did they have sex? Why else would he have no clothes on?

Too many questions for my head to handle. I stumble into the kitchen and pour water into a pint glass. I down it. Then another. I stand for a minute, both hands on the sink. What happened? How long was I asleep on my bedroom floor? I realise I'm still in my underwear and would die if Matt woke up and saw me. I notice a half-empty glass on the kitchen table. I pick it up and smell it. Whisky and Coke. I finish it and creep back up to my room to fall asleep on the floor.

Renée

There is not enough Berocca in the world to take today's pain away. I stand next to the kitchen sink and drop two tablets into a pint glass full of water. I have three tablets of ibuprofen in my hand; I get everything inside me as quickly as I can, holding my breath to stop me puking it all back up. Hurry pills, please hurry.

'Did you have sex with Matt?' Flo appears at the door, making me jump. The orange liquid slops in my belly. I need to eat so badly.

'Urgh. Morning. No. I let him go down on me for a bit, I think I sucked him off, but I fell asleep. When I woke up, he was passed out in his pants, so I went to bed. He wasn't here when I got up.' I burp and expel a thick and poisonous breath into the air. 'How you feeling?'

'I'm all right. I woke up at six a.m. and drank loads of water.' She is holding her sheets and kneels down to put them in the washing machine.

'What happened?' I ask her.

'Red wine. I must have spilled it when I went to bed. Not sure why I was taking red wine to bed, but hey ho.' She laughs.

'Yup, you insisted Phil took a glass too. So funny.'

'What?' she says, standing up.

'What, what?'

'What do you mean I insisted Phil took one? Was he here?' she says, looking worried.

'Yeah, Phil and Matt both came back. You were quite insistent that they didn't go home after the club. Don't you remember?'

'No.'

'OK, well we all came back here and drank almost everything we had in the cupboards. You passed out on the sofa and Phil said he'd carry you up to bed. As he was lifting you—'

'As he was *lifting* me?'

'Yeah, you woke up and poured yourself another glass of wine. I'm surprised it made it as far as your bed.'

She looks horrified and sits at the kitchen table with a slump. 'Wait, if I had passed out why didn't you take me to bed? Why did you let Phil do it? Oh God, he tried to lift me? That is horrible. Renée, I woke up in my underwear on my floor.'

I sit down on the other chair. 'Don't worry, Flo, we were all really drunk.'

'You should have told them to leave. Not watched as one of my colleagues tried to pick me up and take me to bed. Jesus, Renée, that is so embarrassing. I can't remember anything. Did he take my clothes off?'

'Flo, I don't know, I wasn't there.'

'Why weren't you there? Why was I alone in my bedroom with a guy from work? You should have taken care of me.'

'Why would I have gone with you? We're not twelve, Flo. You'd pulled. You seemed pretty sure of what you wanted, don't blame me.'

Christ, she's the one who's always saying we're adults now.

'Flo, I'm sorry. I was drunk too and . . .'

'And thinking about yourself?'

I don't say anything. She's right, I was. But I really thought she was doing what she wanted to do.

'Renée, I have to go to work on Monday with no idea if I had sex with a colleague or not. That is horrible.'

'Well, what I do know is that he wasn't up there with you for more than five minutes. OK? I can't imagine much happened in that time. I'm sure he just got you into bed, OK?'

'On the floor. FUCK. Did he take my clothes off? Did I? What did he see?'

'Flo, calm down. Phil is a really nice guy. He likes you, it's obvious. I'm almost certain he took you upstairs, made sure you were OK and then went home.'

She looks genuinely devastated. I go over and put my hand on her shoulder. 'Flo, really, don't worry. We were all drunk. People get up to things, work will be fine, you weren't that bad.'

I am lying. She was pretty full on. She was never a good drunk, always a real lightweight. If she got drunk when we were at school, it was always by accident. Most of the time she was so self-controlled it never happened anyway. Like she always knew booze made her crazy, so she'd drink with caution. But that caution has gone, she's the one who orders the shots now, who downs her drinks and wants to play drinking games. It's fun, I think. But it's a lot. And it's very different. I just thought she'd gained confidence during her time at uni, but what if I'm wrong?

'Who knows what he will say about me to people,' Flo says, pathetically.

'Oh Flo, who cares? If he says anything, which he won't,

we'll spread even worse rumours about him.' I can tell something else is really bothering her. 'Flo, what is it?'

She puts her face into both of her hands and sighs. 'I had this really horrible experience at uni. Not long after you came to stay. I was still a virgin, and I just wanted to get it over and done with. So, I went out with this guy from my course. I thought maybe he'd teach me a few things, so I'd be better the next time I had sex. I really didn't expect much from the first time.'

I'm nervous. I'm worried she's going to tell me he hurt her. 'OK, and what happened?'

'Well, it was fine. We got really drunk but I think I was OK. We were in my room, kissing, it was nice. But when he put his hand into my pants, he pulled it out again. I asked him what was wrong, but he didn't say anything at first. We carried on, then he went down on me, we had sex, and then when we were finished he said, 'Your vag is so flappy.'

I splutter. 'He said WHAT?'

I roar with laughter. I can't stop.

'Renée, please. It was awful.' I hold it in when I see the look on her face. She does not think this is funny, of course she doesn't. 'I've been too embarrassed to do anything with anyone since, unless I've been really drunk. And even then, I don't really go through with it. I'm good at blow jobs though, and just pretend that I love them and don't need anything else.'

'How many blow jobs have you given?'

'I honestly don't know. A lot. Oh God, what if Phil saw my vagina and tells everyone at work it hangs down too far?'

'OK, firstly that guy sounds like a dick. No guy who has a vagina in front of him says that unless they are evil or gay. So, get him out of your head. As for Phil, he isn't like that. He just isn't. And who would he tell, Chloe? Georgina? No. And finally Flo, it's normal for vaginas to hang down a bit. They all do.'

'Not all. Not the ones I've seen.'

'Which ones have you seen?'

'The ones in porn?'

'YOU watch PORN?' This morning has been so revealing, I've totally forgotten about my hangover.

'Yes, sometimes. It's not like I get sex anywhere else, is it?'

'OK, Flo. Porn stars are paid to look like teenage girls, they are not a true representation of what women really look like. Have you ever seen a real vagina?'

She thinks for a minute, then shakes her head.

'OK,' I say, standing up and taking off my pyjama bottoms.

'Renée, what are you doing?'

'I'm going to show you mine.'

'Renée, no, please, you don't have to do that.'

But she's too late. I put one foot up on the chair, and with two fingers I uncurl my labia so they hang down in their natural position.

'See?' I say. 'Mine hang down too. And according to quite a lot of men, I have a gorgeous pussy. OK?'

She stares at it, long enough that I start feeling uncomfortable. 'Flo, OK?'

'Yes, I see,' she says, softly. 'Please put it away now.'

I put my foot back on the floor and pull my pyjamas back up.

'Flo, you're normal. He was likely a homosexual who was terrified of vaginas. I'm sorry he was your first, but he cannot be your last. Now, if seeing my vagina hasn't put you off bacon for life, can we go and spend way too much money on a fancy fry-up from Dix Neuf, I'm starving.'

'I can't believe you just showed me your flaps,' she says, possibly a little stunned.

'It was an act of sistership, Florence. You're very welcome!'

7

Renée

Later that day, I decide to walk to Aunty Jo's instead of getting the bus. It's quite hard to get a moment to myself now I'm living and working with Flo, and it's especially claustrophobic when she's got the fear about her drunken antics. I'm starting to really appreciate the medicinal qualities of island life. When it all gets too much, I can walk to see my aunty with the sea next to me almost the entire way.

I roll with the ups and downs of the cliff path, the other Channel Islands hovering in my periphery. Jersey sits confidently to the right, with Herm and Sark hogging the foreground with all their tiny might. Alderney sits quietly in the distance, and on a clear day like today, the outlines of French shores wink cheekily back at me, reminding me that my little island is a mere blob in the grander scheme of the planet. I wonder if anywhere else could offer me the moments of reprieve that Guernsey does. I never thought I'd admit this to myself, but I love the moments of calm I can find here. They are restorative. I feel a bit sorry for people who can't come here and take deep breaths of island air.

Aunty Jo flops down into a kitchen chair. 'Oh God, it's just relentless, Renée.' She's just been outside tending to her menagerie of animals.

'What is, shovelling poo?' I ask her.

'No Renée, being a woman. Never-ending.' She pulls off her muddy wellies and unbuttons the denim shirt she's wearing over a pair of corduroy dungarees. She takes the shirt off and exhales, as if she's just hiked up Kilimanjaro in a ski suit and finally got to take it off. 'Oh, for the love of bees, that's better.'

'Are you OK, Aunty Jo?' I ask gently.

'Am I OK? Good question. Let me think about that. You know, I suffered from terrible period cramps in my teens and all through my twenties. Deep, painful throbs tried their darndest to stop me living my life, but I did. I powered on. In that way women do. We crack on in pain and pretend to be fine. Then I spent ten years trying to have a baby, realising that every second of that pain was pointless. A reproductive system that caused me nothing but agony only to be defective when it really counted. Years of torture for nothing. And now, after three harrowing decades, the periods come like rivers of red blood pouring from me when I least expect it. It's like being a teenager again. My body is changing, and I have no idea what it's going to do next.'

She closes her eyes and inhales deeply, then breathes out to the count of ten. 'I'm sorry, love. I don't mean to rant.'

'Well, what is it?' I ask, my heart rate rising. 'Are you ill?'

'No, Renée. I'm not ill, I'm just a woman. It's the menopause, darling. The Change. Or "perimenopause", as my doctor called it. I'm one of the lucky ones who got it really early. I could be stuck in this purgatory for ten years. I thought the hardest bit was done. And if I'm anything like my mother, I'll get through this then lose my fucking mind. Will it ever end!'

The front door slams. Aunty Jo jumps up and brushes herself off both literally and mentally. 'James love, you're home.' She kisses him. 'Would you like a cup of tea?'

'No, I'd better shower. Just did a ten-k run, beautiful day on the island.'

'Beautiful day!' Aunty Jo says in a very high-pitched voice.

'How are you, Renée? Taking the island by storm?' James asks me, sweat running down his thin face and bursting through sections of his Lycra outfit. He hasn't aged at all in the past few years, unlike Aunty Jo, who has quite a lot of grey hair now and the definite onset of middle-age spread. I say that lovingly; she's always gorgeous to me. But I can't deny the changes.

'I'm doing my best,' I tell him as he pours himself a glass of water and heads upstairs.

'I'll bring up the tea,' Aunty Jo calls after him as he heads upstairs to the bathroom. When he is out of earshot, the real her pipes up. 'Fucking men have no idea what we go through.'

'Do you talk to him about it, about the premi, primit . . . what was it again?'

'The perimenopause? No, I don't. It's bad enough that sex feels I'm being rogered with a toilet brush, without him needing to hear about how my engine is drying up. I'm trying to stay just a little bit sexy for the guy.'

'Oh come on, Aunty Jo, that's not you. You're always so open. James is cool, he'd understand.'

'Honestly Renée, I feel like my body is being taken over by an alien lifeforce and I just need to get my head around it first. It kicks you sideways, it really does. Thank God for the animals, the perfect distraction. Speaking of which, the hives are bursting and I need to extract the honey. James and I are planning to do it this afternoon, you can help us if you like?'

'Oh, no thanks. I got my first pay-cheque and thought I'd go into town to get some new clothes. The summer sales are on, I'm hoping to grab a bargain because paying rent sucks, doesn't it?'

'It all sucks, Renée. To think we spend our childhoods so desperate to grow up. Kids are idiots. You sure you want to choose new clothes over watching the slow drip of the bees' hard work plop into a jar?'

'Yes. You two have a romantic afternoon making sweet honey. It sounds like you could do with getting sticky together. Talk to him, Aunty Jo. You shouldn't feel like this on your own.'

'Hey, who is the grown-up here?' she says, hugging me.

I have to admit, she does feel quite clammy.

All the good stuff in the sales has gone. The best thing I've found so far is a pair of dark green skinny trousers for £18 and a cute shirt with little tortoises on it for £9. The green of their shells matches the green of the trousers perfectly. It's not your standard office wear, but I'm wearing it until someone tells me the office is no place for a tortoise motif. I'm desperate to express myself through my clothes, but the shops are rubbish if you have zero budget.

I remember there's a posh new shop on the high street that sells women's clothes. It's surprisingly fashionable for Guernsey and way out of my price range, but there is a '30 per cent off' sale on, so I go in anyway. A KOOKAÏ dress catches my eye. It's strappy and short with a floral print. Not my usual style, but I'm bored to death of my normal style so I take it off the rail. The sale price is £30, which translates to almost three hours of sitting on reception. Three hours for one dress. And I have to save, or I'll never get to London. Can I justify it if it's for work? I could wear it with tights and a shirt over the top so it's not too revealing, then if we go out after work I can take the shirt off and slide up and down the stripper's pole in Follies looking sexy as hell. I take it into the changing room; it can't hurt to just try it on. There are three cubicles, two are taken, so I go in the third. Just as I zip the dress up, I hear a familiar voice.

'Oh my God, I love it. Quick, Gem, come see.'

There is a screeching sound of a curtain against a metal pole. And then another very familiar voice.

'You have to get that. Look at your waist, you look teeny. It's perfect for the rehearsal dinner.'

'It really is,' says the first familiar voice. It's Carla. I suddenly don't want to move in case they recognise the sound of me breathing. I went to school with Carla and Gem. They were sort of my best friends before I met Flo, but really I was just the third wheel in their friendship. They were inseparable. Lovely, but nauseatingly nice. I tried so hard to be in their gang, but looking back I don't know why I wanted to be so much. We're different kinds of people.

I turn quietly to look at my reflection. The dress looks nice, but my waist does not look tiny. I'm immediately catapulted back to the past, and how inferior I felt in their presence. They never did anything mean, but being around perfection when you are flawed is never good for the soul. I can't afford this dress, I just want to get out of here. I pull the zip down and step out of it. But my foot gets caught and I trip. I fall through the curtain and land in front of Carla's feet.

'Renée? Oh my God, Renée!' They squeal and jump, just as they did when we were teenagers. They'd make me feel so special, so happy to see me, and then they'd always go off together when they'd had enough.

I get myself to standing. I'm just wearing my bra and pants, my tummy feels so flabby. They're still both so thin. I use my big personality to hide my insecurity.

'Oh my God, Carla, Gem? What the hell?'

We all hug. My body slaps against their bony frames. I want to be confident, one of the girls, not care. But I do care, I care so much. I duck back into the changing room to put my top on. They would never have done that; they'd just stand there in their bra because they don't know what belly fat feels like. Thank God we're not friends any more, so I don't have to feel like this every day.

'We thought you'd moved to Spain?' says Gem. She looks even thinner than she used to, gaunt, even. I heard she was on a £60k salary. If I earned that much, I'd be massive.

'I did, but I'm back now. Flo and I have got a flat on Mill Street and we work at Magic Marketing.'

'What? Wow. That's so cool,' Carla says, clearly stunned. 'I know Magic Marketing, they're a great company. They did a campaign for us when we were promoting the finance sector in schools. What brands are you on?'

'What brands am I on?' I ask, unsure of what she means.

'Yeah, what accounts do you look after?'

'Most of them. It's not for long though, I'm just saving up some money because I'm moving to London to work as a writer.'

'No way!' says Gem, with very excited eyes. 'That is so

cool, we always knew you'd make it. Who will you be writing for, *The Times*? Oh my God, the *Observer* magazine?'

They both look at me with utter conviction, like they wouldn't for a minute think I'd be capable of anything less.

'Oh, I don't know yet,' I say, as confidently as I can. 'I've had quite a few offers so I'm just back here getting together a deposit to buy a flat in London so I can go and pick the job.'

'Wow, I'm so proud of you,' Carla says. 'Buying a property is no joke at our age, but look at us all. Who'd have thought we'd all do so well?' She admires herself proudly in the mirror. I don't understand how anyone who enjoys life can be skinny, do they just not eat chips?

'Well, anyway. I'd better pay for this and go back to the flat,' I say. 'I've got a few articles to work on.'

'Amazing to see you, Renée.' They both step forward and hug me at the same time. It's an awkward embrace between the three of us.

'Great to see you both. Congrats on everything.' I walk out of the changing room, but Carla comes running after me.

'Hey Renée, wait! I wanted to tell you, I'm getting married.'

'Oh Carla, that's amazing, congrats!' I pretend I don't already know. 'Wow, so cool. Married, wow, yay!'

'Thanks. My fiancé Will is so great. His dad is CEO of a trust fund. They only moved here five years ago. He suits Guernsey so much you'd think he was from here, and luckily he never wants to leave. He's blond, he surfs, he'll probably take over the business one day. He's . . .'

'He's perfect,' Gemma says, finishing her best friend's sentence just like she used to. They both look smitten with Will. I could throw up with jealousy.

'Would you come to the hen do?' Carla says, excited. 'I'll send you an invite. What's your address? And Flo too, it would be so nice to have you both there. It's a bus party, remember those? The wedding is at St Pierre Park Hotel, in December. I could definitely squeeze you and Flo in.'

I shout 'Christ' but manage to make it sound like a cough. That's the only five-star hotel on the island – getting married there must cost a fortune.

'Um, yeah, that would be lovely. Thanks. The address is 14c Mill Street. Honestly, I'm so happy for you. Honestly, I am. I really, really am.'

'You're still funny, Renée. You haven't changed. See you there.'

They both disappear into the changing rooms to try on more nice things that will fit perfectly and cost a fortune. For a few seconds I just stare at the curtains. They act so grown-up, but it feels silly somehow. Don't they feel awkward with their nice handbags, their credit cards and talk of marriage? Like they're little girls playing dress-up, pretending to be ladies. How can they be so comfortable with those things when we were just kids five minutes ago? Or do some people just wake up one day all sorted? I feel like I'm being dialled in slowly. Like if I went full throttle into adulthood, I'd crash and die.

I hang the dress on a rail and stuff the tortoise shirt into my bag. No one wanted it anyway.

8

Renée

Flo left the house and ran back upstairs three times this morning. Each time pretending to have forgotten something when I know she was just stalling. I offered to make her a coffee but when she lifted her hand, it was shaking so much we both agreed that a hot drink, especially one with caffeine, probably wasn't a good idea. In the end, I snatched her keys out of her hand and pushed her down the stairs just hard enough that she didn't fall but had to go down. I swear I could see her chest moving, her heart was beating so fast.

Mrs Mangel obviously came out to see what all the noise was about. She said we 'sounded like a herd of elephants going up and down the stairs'. That she was 'trying to concentrate', and she couldn't 'hear herself think'. What the hell does she have to concentrate on: the crossword? I stood and apologised while Flo faffed about. To be fair, Mrs Mangel was wearing another amazing outfit. A purple jumper with a high-waisted A-line skirt. A gold chain belt, navy tights and green Mary Janes. Her nails painted red, her hair neat. Where on earth does she go that it means she has to dress up like that?

Eventually, Flo builds up the courage to leave for work. 'OK, let's go. I mean, I have no choice, do I?'

'You've got nothing to be embarrassed about,' I say as we walk towards Trinity Square, her nerves creating a force field so powerful that I wonder if I can catch her anxiety. When we reach the Magic Marketing office, Flo starts to visibly shake and hyperventilate. I feel bad for her, but she needs to get over it. I drag her into the toilets and give her a proper talking-to.

'Flo, as far as we know, Phil didn't see anything, and you didn't even kiss. What about me? Matt went down on me, and I fell asleep, I should be the embarrassed one. Get over yourself. Life is to be enjoyed. We are in our twenties, we are single, occasionally men see our vaginas, it is not the end of the world. Own it, like the adult that you are.'

'Aren't you embarrassed? Nervous to see Matt?' she says, panting.

'No. I mean, I kind of wish I hadn't gone that far with him because he wasn't very good at it, but I'm not embarrassed for getting drunk and getting it on with someone. *He* might be embarrassed. Well, he should be. He'd have woken up naked and alone in our living room. If anyone should be dreading work today, it's Matt, not you. OK?'

'OK,' she says, unconvincingly. She knows she has no choice but to walk into the office, no matter how much she wants to run away. When we get in, Matt is sitting in reception reading a newspaper. It's Friday's paper, I haven't laid out today's yet. He's blatantly waiting for me. The way men and women handle the day after the night before is wild.

'Morning,' he says, jumping up. Flo slams her eyes to the floor and runs off like a frightened penguin into the office. At least she's in.

'Morning,' I say, smiling politely and getting quickly behind my desk. I don't fancy him, I don't want a repeat performance, but I'll try not to be mean because this is work.

'You went to bed,' he says, obviously full of further questions.

'You passed out,' I say, stating a fact.

'Honey, you could have woken me up.'

I buckle at being called honey, why is that so annoying? Does he call all women honey? Or did he just claim me as his honey? Either way, I hate it. And why am I responsible for everyone passing out now? First Flo, then Matt. What the hell is this?

'I tried, but you were out cold.' This is a lie; as soon as I saw that he was asleep, I pegged it up to bed and locked the door, presuming he'd wake up and sort himself out.

'OK, well, Friday was fun. Maybe we can meet up at

lunch?' He raises his eyebrows repeatedly while staring me directly in the eye. I think that means he wants to get it on at lunchtime?

I don't.

I offer a forced smile but say nothing. I don't want to have to dump someone I got off with when I was drunk. I just won't reciprocate any flirting; he'll get the message. I'm saved by the phone ringing. Luckily, it's for Matt. I gesture that he should hurry back to his desk to take it, and he does. Flo immediately enters and begins whispering in a highly paranoid way, 'He isn't here, do you think he quit because of me?'

'Who?'

''ill,' she says, mouth barely moving, as if no one will know who ''ill' is if they overhear.

'He's probably just late,' I say. 'Go back to your desk. Google "fluffy kittens", stop worrying.' She puts her tail back between her legs and disappears into the office.

Chloe arrives, her usual uptight self, looking incredible in a mini dungaree dress and a white blouse with a large collar and lots of bangles, the playfulness of her outfit not reflecting her personality at all. She makes her way past me, managing to muster a Mona Lisa-style smile.

Next, I see Ben coming out of the lift. He's holding his phone, frowning, clearly having a difficult conversation with someone via text. Maybe a client has pulled out of a deal, or Jordan is being difficult as I imagine he often is from my short interactions with him on the phone. Ben looks stressed, and unusually tired. He puts his phone in his pocket and stands for a moment, rubbing his head with his hands. I could be imagining it, but I swear he wipes away a tear. He notices me watching him, and I quickly pretend to look away but it's too late, I was clearly staring. He comes through the door after a quick and deliberate change of mood.

'Morning, Renée,' he says, with fake cheer.

'Good morning, Ben, all OK?'

'Of course. Everything's fine. The sun is shining, and I got the last almond croissant at the coffee shop. What more does a man need?'

He's joking, of course. But I want to suggest that maybe he needs the sweet loving of his hot new receptionist to really top off his day.

'You're nailing life, Ben. Look at you!'

We smile at each other. Our eyes linger a fraction longer than what would be normal. He knows I know he's not OK, having seen him in the hallway, but of course there is no need for him to share anything with me. He heads toward his desk, then turns back quickly.

'Oh, Renée.' I stand up, which is weird. 'I've got a meeting here with some of the London team at one p.m.'

'Yes, I saw that in the diary,' I say, like a brilliant receptionist.

'Can we get lunch in, something nice? I was thinking sushi. From that new little Japanese place in the market.'

'Sushi, on Guernsey? Are you sure?'

'I know, mad right. Sushi and a black man, it's like a boat from the rest of the world actually made it to the island.' I laugh, but I'm not sure if it's OK to laugh. I wonder what it's been like for Ben here. He seems very happy, so I hope people have been kind and welcoming. I'm not sure how you could be anything but kind and welcoming to Ben. He's so wonderful it's overwhelming.

'Do you mind ordering and picking it up? I don't trust sushi delivery. Last time we got it, half the fish had come off the rice.'

'Of course, what's it called? I'll do it now,' I say, reaching for a file that's full of local menus. When I find it, he obviously notices the worry on my face as I read the menu.

'Oh God, what? You've eaten there? Was it awful?'

'No. Um . . .' I just have to tell him. 'I've never eaten sushi. I have no idea what any of this means.'

He laughs – nicely, not patronisingly – and comes behind my desk. He very innocently leans over my shoulder and looks at the menu. I want to lick him. I bet he tastes as good as he smells. I feel a swirling in my knickers. A heavy thud as moisture gathers, ready to receive him.

'Salmon rolls, tuna sashimi, California rolls,' he says, among other jargon that I don't understand. He's so close to me that the smell of his aftershave wafts up my nose. It's gentle, citrus. He smells so clean. 'Basically ten from that menu, four from that menu, some edamame and a couple of miso soups should be plenty. If you phone and order, you can pay when you pick up at 12.15. That's enough time to get the meeting room set up but it will still be nice and fresh. Thanks Renée.'

'No worries, Ben,' I say, inhaling his smell as he walks

away. Lost in a sensory fantasy, I nearly leap a thousand feet in the air when Flo appears in front of me again, looking like someone who just got mugged.

'Have you seen him yet?' she says. 'Has he quit?' She means Phil.

'Flo, he's at a meeting. It's in the diary. He'll be back after lunch, which gives you plenty of time to pull your shit together.' It's weird that she hasn't even looked at the diary. She's usually so on it with who is where.

'What did Matt say? Was he laughing about me?'

'Flo, all Matt can think about is my fanny. He didn't even mention you, so stop it. Let's go out for lunch, we can get sushi?' I suggest, aware she'll need to get out of here for a bit for a breather.

'Sushi, on Guernsey?'

'I know right?'

'I can't,' she says, abruptly. 'I better stay here, wait for Phil.'

And off she goes again. I google 'fluffy kittens' and send her the link. If there was ever a need for cat therapy, I think it's now.

A lady yells 'MAGIC MARKETTIIIING' across the market, and plops two huge plastic platters with clear lids onto a table. I'm the only person waiting for takeaway, so the volume of her screech was completely unnecessary. The 'market' is inside a huge building at the tail end of town. There are lots of stalls selling everything from local jams to giant marrows. The new sushi stall is tiny with a little table in front of it. The smell of raw fish does not make me want to eat it. I pay with the money from the petty-cash tin and take the boxes outside. Walking back to the office, I peer into the sushi. Is that it? Lumps of raw fish on white rice? What's all the fuss about?

I manage to get all the way into the lift without a single piece of fish falling off the rice, which I'm pretty pleased about. As the doors are closing, a huge hand appears between them making me jump. I make a really embarrassing screech and the two trays start tumbling towards the floor.

'Oh, I . . . I got them,' says Ben, intercepting the trays and bringing them back up to waist level almost unscathed.

'You made me jump,' I say, feeling so silly. 'You've got big hands.'

'Sorry, I saw the doors closing and I had told myself that if I missed it, I had to take the stairs. I did legs in the gym this morning so really couldn't be bothered,' he says, smiling. 'Sorry if I startled you.'

I nod. Who cares about me almost dropping the sushi, not when all I can think about are his thighs. He presses the button for level 4.

We stand for a split-second looking at the doors as the lift starts to go up. He's so nice, so relaxed. The most relaxed person in the office, but he is the boss. I wait for him to speak because I don't want to say anything stupid.

'So, you've never had sushi, huh?'

'No, I . . .' Suddenly there's a loud bang, and the lift jolts. 'Woah, has it stopped?' I say, a bit freaked out. Then the lights go off and it's pitch black.

'Shit,' I say, 'will it fall down the shaft?'

'No, Renée. We're safe, don't worry.'

We are quiet for a moment. I am trying so hard not to laugh but I just can't keep it in.

'What?' he asks. 'What are you laughing at?'

'"Shaft". I'm sorry, it's just such a funny word. I'm not sure I've ever used it in a serious sentence before.'

Ben doesn't respond, which makes me worry I have massively overstepped the professional boundaries that we probably still need to maintain in this lift. Why did I say that? And why did I laugh? Why can't I just shut up and not make a total tit out of myself at every given opportunity?

And then he starts to laugh too.

'Sorry. Shouldn't laugh, but shaft is really funny.'

We giggle awkwardly. This is so weird. There is something so easy about him, so casual. But he is my boss, and we are stuck in a small, dark place. I need to watch what I say.

'Try not to worry,' Ben says, in a confident voice. 'When the power comes back on, everything will be fine. It shouldn't be long, we might just have to sit it out. Are you OK?'

'Yeah, yeah I'm fine.' He presses the alarm button.

'It might take them a minute, but they'll get it working again. Sit down. Just in case it jolts when it comes back on. Annoyingly I left my phone on my desk, I'd only nipped out to get a Diet Coke.'

I realise my phone is in my bag but choose not to mention it.

We both make it down to the floor. It's weird, being in the dark with someone you don't know. You realise how much of conversation is inspired by what you can see; I can't think of anything to say.

'Well, this seems as good a time as any to try sushi, don't you think?' he says. And I hear him reaching for one of the boxes.

'Don't you need it for your meeting?'

'We'll have to think of a contingency plan. It's hot in here, this fish becomes a health hazard in about ten minutes. We need to do what we have to, to survive, right? And besides, you haven't tried sushi.'

'OK,' I say, excited by this bizarre experience and trying something new at the hand of someone who I think gets better and better with every word he says.

I hear him fumble about and the tiny tear of some sort of utensil being unwrapped. 'What the hell am I doing?' he says, and I assume he realises how ridiculous this is and is aborting the whole idea.

'OK, ready,' he says. 'Lay out your hand.'

I do as he says, he finds it with his, then puts a piece of something on it. I eat it.

'Your thoughts?' he asks as I chew, massively underwhelmed by the flavour.

'Um, honestly, it's warm and soft and doesn't taste of anything. I don't get it?'

'OK, hang on.' He rustles around in the bag, and I listen to him opening things and preparing another mouthful. 'Hold out your hand again,' he says, and I do. 'I found a little bottle of soy sauce so hopefully I aimed that right. See what you think now.'

I put it into my mouth because he told me to. 'It tastes like . . . Um . . . I mean, it tastes like salt.'

'That's the soy sauce. But sushi is really about the texture; it's buttery, right? Melt-in-your-mouth?'

'I suppose so,' I say, unconvinced. 'I should have some more.'

'OK, you're not put off yet, that's good.' He gets to organising me another taster.

I never want him to stop feeding me in the dark. I want to be stuck in this lift for hours. For the next six to eight minutes, he continues to place various pieces of Japanese cuisine into the palm of my hand. These offerings are followed by little lessons about how it is supposed to taste. It's the sexiest meal I have ever eaten in my life.

'OK, no more,' I eventually say, defeated. 'I'm so full.' We sit for a minute. Almost as if we remember where we are. Wondering what to do next. It's getting hot, and the darkness is becoming oppressive.

'I'll buzz again,' says Ben. 'It can't be too much longer.' He does, and we wait in silence for a minute or so, but nothing happens.

'So how long have you worked here?' I ask, feeling like polite chitchat is the best next move.

'Ten years, I started the company with Jordan in London. But, two years ago, we saw an opportunity to bring half of the business here, so I said I'd head it up. I loved the idea of the kids growing up near a beach.'

My body tenses with jealousy at the thought of his family. What would his wife say if she knew he'd just fed me in a dark lift? Nothing probably, because nothing has happened. We're just passing time. This is not a date, I remind myself. When those doors open, he will be my boss and none of this will have happened.

'Did Jordan not want to come?'

'He came over, but it was far too white for him.'

'Too white?' There are very few black people on Guernsey; I only truly realised that when I moved to Spain and suddenly had quite a few black friends. Sometimes you don't realise how isolated a place is until you leave it. But, of course, it's something Jordan noticed when he came here. How could he not? 'It wasn't too white for you?' I ask Ben.

'I saw a big opportunity for the company and focused on that. There have been challenges, the kids' school in partic . . . You know, Renée? This is your home. We don't need to get into it, OK?'

'OK,' I say, respectfully, a knot forming in my stomach at the thought of what Ben and his family might have experienced here. 'Everything you've done with Magic Marketing is really impressive, you're so young to have all this. I have no idea how to be an adult and apparently, I am one now.'

'I'm not that young. Thirty-two. Married, two kids. I didn't have any of these things when I was your age. I was somewhere in Thailand thinking people who worked in offices were mentalists.'

I think that was meant to be encouraging. But other than being here with Ben, I wish I was in Thailand thinking people who work in offices are mentalists.

'You've achieved a lot. I can't imagine being responsible for that many things. I'd love a cat. But not yet. How old are your kids?'

'Pandora is five, and Sophia is three. They're great. Absolute nutters, but great.'

'So, what does your wife do? Is she a whizz-kid as well?' I ask, intrigued by the woman who found herself this gorgeous man.

'Actually, she's not working at the moment. She's . . . she's not well.'

'Oh no, I'm so sorry. Is it serious?' I ask.

'Yeah, it's serious. But we'll get through it.'

'I'm so sorry,' I say, sensing that it's bad, not wanting to pry.

'Oh, she's not dying or anything. Just, well, it's complicated.'

'You don't have to tell me, I'm sorry I asked, I hope you don't think I was rude.'

'It was a perfectly reasonable question, you're fine to ask. What about you?' he asks.

'Oh, I'm twenty-two, single, just moved back here after a few years away and wondering what the hell my future looks like. I want to write.'

'Oh cool, what kind of stuff?'

'Anything, really. Food, life. I'd like to do fiction one day, but I probably need to live a bit more life before I have the balls to do that.'

'You'll be a huge success, I'm sure of it. You've clearly got lots of character,' he says, just as the lights flicker on and the lift jolts as it starts to move up. 'Wow, I'd kind of forgotten about life beyond this lift for a minute there.' Ben's face is revealed to me again. His skin has a sheen to it, I'm sure mine does too. We've sat in a tiny hot room, and breathed each other in. I can smell him when he moves. I can also smell fish. Our legs or feet were touching nearly the whole time when we were sitting down. He fed me with his hands.

'What was it, thirty-seven minutes?' I say, realising that's ages and that I never got bored.

'Yup, thanks for making it fly by,' Ben says, smiling at me. I smile back as the doors open. We walk back into the office, and I take my seat behind reception.

'Do you mind calling in some sandwiches. I don't want to be responsible for giving half the company food poisoning,' Ben says.

'Of course,' I say, almost adding 'love you' to the end. He goes back to his desk.

Soon after, Flo tiptoes into reception.

'Flo, you'll never believe what happened,' I say. 'I was getting into the lift and . . .' She walks right past me and peers into the office. 'He's back,' she says, out of puff. 'Phil. Has he said anything about me?'

'No,' I tell her. I haven't seen him. The phone rings. 'Flo, I need to answer this, go back to your desk. Order some stuff for the kitchen, coffee and shit, you like doing that. Hello, Magic Marketing.'

'Hello, can I speak to Ben?' the voice says. A rush of something runs through me as I punch in #4.

'Hi Renée,' he says, gently.

'Hey Ben,' I reply, 'call for you.' I listen to a couple of his breaths before putting it through.

Is it possible to fall in love with someone in thirty-seven minutes?

Flo

I could have done without the lift being out of order. There was a power cut, and all the office machinery needed to be rebooted. Our photocopier is complicated. I'm the only person who seems to be able to un-mangle it, but I'm pressing all the buttons and nothing is happening.

'Flo, Flo,' I hear, but I stay focused. One more shove and . . .

'Flo, what are you doing?' I turn to see Georgina standing behind me. She looks confused. 'Why are you punching it? That won't work,' she says.

'I wasn't,' I say. Was I?

'Sorry, you were just being a little violent. Let me see . . .' She stands next to me and lifts the lid, then presses a few buttons. When the machine starts working, she steps back.

'Are you OK?' she asks, looking concerned.

'Yes.'

'You seem a bit on edge.' She leans in. 'Time of the month?' I nod. Even though I haven't got my period. 'I get a bit like that too. Especially on my heavy days. Nothing feels right, and I swear I gain an extra ten pounds every time.' I nod again, even though I don't have the same problem, I just want her to leave me alone.

'I have a trick though, something I worked out years ago that has become my go-to for making me love myself just a little bit more. Wanna hear it?' Another nod from me. 'I buy all my clothes two sizes up. That way every morning, when I get dressed, I have a little "Go me!" moment. It's the little things, huh? Whatever gets you through. I'm here, Flo, if you need to talk.' She walks away, yanking up her trousers as she goes.

I like Georgina, I really do. She is proof that strangeness and kindness can go hand in hand.

'Flo?' says someone else behind me.

'WHAT?' I find myself snapping back. I turn around. It's Phil. Oh God. The rat starts scratching again. Nibble nibble, trying to claw its way out of me.

'All right?' he asks, putting a hand out like I'm a dog that needs calming down. 'Did I make you jump?'

'Yes.'

Why am I monosyllabic today?

'Sorry. Just wanted to say I hope you were all right after drinks on Friday night. My head was banging all the next day.'

I stand motionless. I can't think of anything to say. 'Are you sure you're all right?' he asks. 'You look a bit pale.'

I nod. 'I'm fine.' Why is he smiling? Is he laughing at me? I can't tell if he's being nice or making fun of me.

'I had fun,' he says. 'I won't lie, I don't usually drink that much. I'm more a few casual pints at the pub than a "grind up and down the stripper's pole in Follies" kinda guy. Matt can get wild, he's not the type of person I'd usually hang out with outside of work. But well, I think we all got a bit carried away, didn't we? It was certainly a late one. I hope you slept OK?' His words are just vague sounds, I can't focus on them at all.

'I woke up on the floor,' I say, blankly.

'Yeah, sorry about the wine, I felt awful about that. I tripped when I was helping you to bed. I was going to change your sheets but that felt a bit personal.'

I can't handle this. 'Did we have sex?' I ask him. I just need to know.

'I'm sorry, what?' he says, looking around. 'What did you shout that for?'

'I didn't shout.'

'Yes, you did.'

'Well, did we?'

'How drunk *were* you?'

I just stare at him. He carried me to bed for goodness' sake, he knows how drunk I was. I look at him as if to suggest he took advantage of me, even though I have no idea if he did or not, so I know it's a bit cruel.

'No, we didn't have *sex*,' he says, walking away, looking annoyed. Or upset. Or disappointed. What did he mean? Why did he emphasise *sex*? Does that mean we did something else?

I feel worse than I did before. I go into the kitchen. There is half a bottle of wine in the fridge, left over from a client meeting that Ben had a few nights ago. I look around to make sure no one's watching. I drink some straight from the bottle and go back to my desk.

Why won't the rat just die?

Renée

All I can think about is Ben. What would it be like to be married to someone like him? A sexy man. A boss. A smooth-skinned, shiny-eyed, ripped hunk. Kind, funny, thoughtful. He's everything in one six-foot-three perfect package. I want to marry him and spend the rest of my life writhing around on top of him in a big comfy bed.

But why am I thinking about marriage and babies? Crushes are so weird. When I don't have a crush on anyone, I don't even think about things like marriage and babies. I consider myself to be so independent, the idea of a relationship stresses me out. It would get in the way of my life, my plans. I can't write anything if I'm also juggling a relationship with someone when I get home from work; where would I find the time to do everything I need to do for myself? I struggle with motivation as it is, a boyfriend would straight-up destroy my chances of success. But then as soon as a guy like Ben comes along, my life turns into a romcom. My brain won't shake off the annoying truths of what I want out of life but try my hardest to deny. I want to be loved by everyone, including a good man and, most annoyingly, my dad.

I'll never admit that out loud though, I just won't. The Renée I want the world to see does not need anyone to make her feel whole. Daddy issues really crush my style. This obsession with my boss will pass. He's married, I can't have him. I will let this brush over me so I can get back to living life my way, on my own terms, without the shackles of a crippling crush.

But I think I love him.

I can't stop imagining living with him. Waking up in the morning, wrapped up in a cuddle that we didn't break all night. He'd kiss me, and go downstairs to make tea. I'd throw on one of his shirts and join him in the kitchen. We'd have sex against the sink. We'd walk to work holding hands. I'd smile at my old school friends as they hurry to their boring office jobs and say, 'He's my husband.' Then we'd arrive at work, he'd go to his desk, I'd sit at mine, and we would meet for lunch and hold hands on our way to that little sushi restaurant. They'd screech 'The Jacksons!' across the restaurant when our food was ready. And I would jump up to get it because that would be me, Mrs Jackson. Then, after work, we'd go home to our beautiful home on the west coast and we'd eat dinner while we drink wine, then cuddle up and watch a movie before going to bed, making love, falling asleep, ready to start the whole glorious cycle all over again.

I'm careful not to slam the front door when I get back home; I don't want another run-in with Mrs Mangel. But, just my luck, she's coming out of her flat as I enter the hallway. She's wearing a brilliantly neat Sixties-style coat over her outfit and carrying a large bag which looks like it's full of clothes.

'Hope you're well,' I say to her as she passes. She sort of smiles and rushes off. She's either incredibly busy or incredibly rude, I'm not sure which.

As I walk into the flat, I hear the radio playing in the kitchen.

'Flo?' She doesn't answer.

I get to the kitchen door, but stop before I go in. I don't quite know what I'm seeing. There are lettuce leaves laid out on sheets of kitchen paper on almost every surface in the kitchen. Lettuce leaves? On the table, the work surfaces, the draining board, even on one of the chairs. Flo is wearing an apron and holding a bunch of kitchen towels. She appears to be wiping each lettuce leaf, one by one.

'Flo, what are you doing?' I ask, nervously.

'Oh hi, I'm just washing this lettuce,' she replies, as if this is how lettuce gets washed by normal people. I notice a large glass of red next to the sink and presume it's not her first. It's unusual to see her drinking alone.

'You know you can just put the whole thing under the tap, then leave it on the draining board, don't you?'

She doesn't look up.

'I like my lettuce to be very clean,' she says. 'I can't stand it when there are little bits of dirt in salads.'

'OK,' I say, picking up four leaves from the chair, putting them on the table and sitting down. 'Flo, are you all right?'

'Absolutely fine, why?'

'I just didn't realise you loved lettuce this much. I saw you and Phil talking today . . .' She doesn't seem to hear me, or maybe she just doesn't want to.

'It's Dad's birthday tomorrow. He'd have been forty-seven.'

Ah, I see what's happening.

'Flo?'

'Yes?'

'What do you need?'

'Can you blot the lettuce leaves on the table, please. If we don't get all the water off, they'll go soggy.'

I pour myself a glass of wine and start to dry the lettuce leaves with a piece of kitchen paper. Because that is what friends do.

9

Flo

Your birthday is still your birthday after you've died. It's still the day you came into this world. It's still a day that should be celebrated by those you leave behind. Or so I think, anyway. The anniversary of someone's death is grim. It's like reliving the day itself. But their birthday, that's a day when you can celebrate that they were ever here at all.

Every year I do something special on Dad's birthday. Last year I got the train from Nottingham to London. I visited Big Ben at 2.03 p.m., the time he was born. He'd never been to London, and always said he'd wanted to go. I took a picture of myself with the clock way up in the sky behind me. I got the picture printed and brought it to

Guernsey last summer, where I pushed the photo into a glass bottle and sent it out to sea to be with his ashes. I went back to the beach every day to see if the bottle came back. It didn't, which I took as a sign he'd found it and was keeping it with him wherever it was he'd gone.

Mum still lives in the house she lived in with Dad before they split up. Whether she likes it or not, many of my happiest memories of him are in that house. From BBQs in the garden and the paddling pool he always set up for me, to Christmases by the tree. My favourite picture of me and Dad was taken at the dining table. In it we're both laughing because he'd hidden a fake spider in my scrambled eggs and, when I found it, it made me jump so badly. It's such a joyful picture. My brother Julian took it, apparently. Mum was pregnant with Abi at the time and sitting next to me. She's laughing too. It's a rare piece of evidence that we were once a happy family. It's because of that photo that I find myself getting the bus over to my mum's house on my lunch break, wondering if enough time has passed for us to at least acknowledge that there was love once.

I text Mum on the way: *Maybe we could do something nice for Dad's birthday today? Something just us? I'm on my way over now x*

'Mum?' I say, pushing open the front door slowly. 'Abi?' Even though this has been my home for most of my life, I feel uncomfortable using my key. 'Mum, are you home?' The lights are on, and Island FM is blaring from the kitchen, but no sign of her or my sister. It's the school holidays so maybe Abi's at a friend's house today. I head up the stairs and when I get to the landing, I hear that the TV is on in Mum's room.

'Mum?' I say, knocking gently on her door. I push it open ever so slightly. 'Mum, I've come round to get . . .'

There's a man sitting up in the bed with the covers pulled up to his waist and no top on. He's pointing the remote at the TV like this is his bedroom and his house. He's on Dad's side of the bed. We stare at each other, the sound of the shower seemingly getting louder and louder as the room closes in on me. I can hear my mother singing in the bathroom. The horrible ear-splitting sound of her joyfulness makes me want to throw up. 'It's my dad's birthday,' I say, wanting to pounce and punch this stranger. He pulls the covers up a little higher, then awkwardly says, 'Well, Happy Birthday to him.'

He doesn't even know.

I pull the door shut and run down the stairs, out the front door, and as far down the street as I can manage before my lungs can't take it any more. I stand bent double, hacking as I try to cough up the rat. How could she do that, today of all days? Why couldn't she have called me first thing, or sent me a text? Just something to mark the day, some indicator that my pain matters to her. But nothing. Instead she only thought of herself, like she always has and always will.

I don't even remember the walk, I'm just suddenly here: outside the house where Dad died. He'd separated from

Mum a while before. It was a horrible little house. Rundown and depressing. And now it's painted white and has a bright pink door. There are rose bushes and window boxes and the lawn is freshly cut. Someone has worked hard on this sad house and made it a happy one. I wonder if everything that is sad can be made happy. I hope so.

The last time I ever saw Dad was inside this house. I said goodbye one morning and off I went to school, never imagining the horrible news I'd receive just hours later. This house is precious to me, it makes no sense at all that it isn't mine. Do the new owners even know what happened to my dad on their front lawn?

I stare at the garden, a tiny patch of grass that is having the most made of it. I walk over and slump to my knees on the spot where he was apparently found. The air is loud from the sound of bees humming, the sun is shining. The smell of roses wafts over me and the emotion I've kept bottled for so long starts to well up. 'Happy Birthday, Dad,' I say to the beautiful summer's day. 'The sun came out for you.'

'Can I help you?' a voice says behind me. I turn to see a pretty woman with a baby on her hip. 'Are you OK?'

I don't know what comes over me, but I can't pretend to be OK for this stranger. 'My dad died,' I tell her, staying on my knees and putting my hands on the ground to feel it. 'He died right here, did you know?'

She looks over each shoulder, as if what I said frightened her in some way. But then rather than telling me to leave, she kneels down, she puts her baby on the grass and he smiles. He thinks we are playing.

'I did hear that the previous tenant had passed away,' she says, gently. 'So he was your father?'

'Yes. And it's his birthday today. I'm not mental, I promise,' I tell her, realising how this may look.

'I don't think you're mental. What's your name?'

'Flo.'

'Hi Flo, I'm Annabel. This is Isaac. Say hello to Flo, Isaac.' Isaac looks at me and waits for me to do something silly. I put my thumb on the end of my nose, wiggle my fingers and stick my tongue out. He giggles.

'I'm sorry I'm here, it's not fair. I just . . . I needed to feel close to him and this is where he . . . but it's not fair on you, I'm sorry.' I get up and brush grass off from my clothes. 'I'm sorry, I hope you're really happy in this house. I'm sorry I came.' I walk away.

'Flo, why don't you come inside? I'll make you a cup of tea. You can tell me about your dad? Come in.' I wonder if I should, but I'm not sure I'm made of strong enough stuff to walk into that house, memories of Dad still lingering in the air.

'I can't, but thank you,' I say as I walk away, a feeling of despondency leaving my body. The emotion is there, writhing away, but it feels lighter for the moment. It's amazing how kindness from one person can dissolve the cruelty of another. A smile forms across my face as I walk back down the road. Dad sent Annabel to cheer me up, I'm sure of it. 'Thanks Dad,' I say, looking at the sky. 'Happy Birthday to you.'

10

Renée

Flo is passive-aggressively reorganising the newspapers in reception because I forgot to do it this morning. 'Can you put those in the recycling, please,' she says, flopping yesterday's news onto my desk. Ben enters reception and I feel inclined to say something impressive.

'Funny, isn't it? All that effort to create these papers and then after one day we throw them out, like what happened yesterday doesn't matter any more.' I stare wistfully at the *Guardian* front page. 'Did it even happen if you didn't read about it?'

Flo looks at me and mouths 'What the fuck are you talking about?' Ben says nothing for a while, which makes me think I should probably listen to Flo.

'How profound,' he says eventually. 'I like it. Does it even happen if no one knows about it? What a question.'

'Right?' I say, making a 'Fuck you back' face at Flo, who rolls her eyes. 'I want to be a writer, but I think books, not journalism. Words that will last forever, not just get tossed away.'

'Well, you clearly have a way with words,' Ben says, looking at me with admiration. Flo stares at us, as if she can't believe he is responding to my nonsense. I smile at Ben, he smiles back. We hang there for a moment, admiring each other. Neither of us looks at Flo.

'Do you know what, Renée – and please say no if you don't want to. I need some copy written for a new campaign for the Island Cheese account. Would you be interested in giving it a go?' he says, looking at me enthusiastically, which makes me feel amazing.

'WHAT?' Flo shouts, terrifying us both. She never raises her voice in the office. 'Sorry, I mean, pardon?'

'Well,' he says, smiling. 'Renée mentioned she would like to write, and usually I'd get a copywriter in. But I wondered if maybe you'd like to try?'

I stand up, I must look like I've just won an Oscar. 'Really? Me?' I say in a breathy voice.

Flo, meanwhile, is just staring at Ben with her mouth open.

'I mean, it's no book deal,' he says. 'But if you think you can make cheese sound interesting, then I'm happy for you to try?'

'I'd love to. I mean, I love cheese. Cheesus Christ, I love cheese.'

Ben laughs. 'Great,' he says, collecting himself. 'Island Cheese are looking to tap into the teenage market. Promoting it as a healthy snack as opposed to all the junk food teens are eating these days. I can email you a full brief for the campaign now I know you're open to it.'

'Oh, I'm open. I'm wide open.' I sit down, regretting being wide open.

'Please CC me so I can make sure I'm across it,' Flo says sharply, acting like she's the boss and we're the kids who need to be kept in line. I know she must be wondering what the hell's going on.

'OK, Flo, sure.' Ben nods at her and goes back to his desk.

'Weren't you going somewhere?' I say to Flo, nodding at the bag on her shoulder. She tries to catch my eye, but I can't quite look at her. 'Flo, stop staring at me. I have to work.'

'I thought you found the idea of marketing cheese funny?' she says, sarcastically.

'I get it now. Sorry I laughed before. Are you done? I've got a lot to do.' I pick up a few blank pages of paper and shuffle them like a secretary. I lay them down and write 'ISLAND CHEESE COPY' at the top and underline it three times. 'Flo, what?'

'Nothing,' she says, spinning on her heel, clearly disgruntled. 'Cheese it up, cheese face.'

~~Cheese, it will have you on your knees. Cheese please. Cheese means . . . Eat cheese, please~~

Wow, it's really hard to make cheese sound cool. I have

about fifty Post-it notes stuck to the inside of my desk with scribbles on them. I can't believe Ben asked me to do this. It's so stressful having this much responsibility. Is this how adults who have important jobs feel every day? There was something so nice about just being a receptionist. Since mastering the phones, everything else has been a breeze. Now, it's so much pressure. At least Ben comes to chat to me more now, which always lets some of the steam off. I'm sure he fancies me, or I could be imagining that. But yesterday, he even ate his lunch in reception while he read the paper. He kept sparking conversation with me about various news stories. I'm not that great on politics, so I did a lot of nodding, but at one point he read an article about a cat that barks like a dog. We both did impressions of what that might sound like, which was a pretty unguarded thing for a boss to do with his receptionist. We just get on really well, it's not my fault. And now he's asked me to write a slogan for him, he must fancy me. Or maybe he just believes in me. It's hard to tell the difference sometimes.

I have a theory about his wife. I think she has bipolar disorder. He said it was complicated, that she isn't dying, and that they will get through it. My dad had a bipolar friend in Spain, his wife left him last year because he was so hard to live with. So I imagine it must be really, really hard for Ben. And he probably isn't very happy. It's not like he has the perfect marriage. Is it cheating when you're not in a happy relationship? Not that he is cheating. Other than in my head. All day long. It's really hard to focus on the cheese.

'Renée, any idea where Flo is?' says Chloe, making me

jump as she approaches my desk. I'm sure she's putting on weight, it suits her. She looks overdressed in a sheer floral blouse with enormous puffed sleeves and a neat navy pencil skirt. She has on a selection of statement bracelets and some silver hoop earrings. It's everything I want to look like, but can't afford. Also, she has a little booger. This makes me smile. I wonder what kind of women she sleeps with. I can't imagine her having sex, but weirdly in my head she looks way better with a woman than a man. I don't know why I imagine everyone having sex the way that I do. Always been the same.

'Yes, she's just popped out,' I say, realising I have no idea where Flo has gone. 'Can I help?'

'She was processing an account for me. It's a small file, yellow. Have you seen it, or do you have any idea where it is? I need it for a call in five minutes?'

'Oh, let me have a look on her desk.' I get up and hurry to Flo's desk. I'm aware Ben can see me from his office, so I hold my tummy in and stick my bum out a bit. Chloe is standing on the other side with her arms crossed. She's trying to be nice, but she's obviously pissed off that Flo hasn't given it back to her and feeling very impatient. Her left foot is doing a gentle tap on the floor. I sift through all the files on Flo's desk but don't see it. I open her bottom drawer, nothing. The middle drawer, nothing. Feeling the heat from Chloe's impatience, I hope the file is in the top drawer. I open it, then slam it shut immediately.

'It's not here,' I say to Chloe. 'I've looked everywhere. She must have taken it with her.'

Chloe huffs like a bitchy schoolgirl and stomps back to her desk. I stand still, my heart beating too fast. Slowly, and gently, I pull open the drawer one more time. I hadn't imagined it. There are five empty miniature bottles of Gordon's gin at Flo's desk. What the hell?

'I'm back,' says Flo half an hour later. She walks out of the lift carrying seven packets of copier paper. She has her rucksack on her back and is struggling to see where she's going.

'Flo, why didn't you tell me we'd run out of paper, I'd have come down to help you?' I say, taking three of the packs and following her to her desk. 'Chloe was looking for a file just now. A yellow one?'

'Shit!' she says, putting the rest of the paper on the reception desk and rummaging in her rucksack. She pulls out a yellow file and looks nervously at Chloe's desk. Chloe is on the phone. Flo rushes over, tripping a little but catching herself. She puts the file in front of her. Chloe hardly even looks up.

'So, there's a team meeting at two thirty. Shall I set up the meeting room?' I ask Flo when she comes back.

'I'll do it,' she says, walking towards the photocopier. I watch as she puts some new paper in. 'What, Renée? Why are you watching me?'

I look around the office; everyone is concentrating on their work and not taking any notice of us. Apart from Matt, who is looking at me like a bull that's about to charge. Surely, he'll get the message soon? It's like being stuck in a room with a dog that won't stop humping your leg, he's on a relentless pursuit of sex.

I pull Flo into the kitchen. 'Look Flo, when you were out, I . . .' Matt comes in and starts making a cup of coffee. I'm standing in front of the sink, and he puts both hands on my hips to move me out of the way. 'Excuse me, honey.' It makes me recoil, but I don't say anything, I need to remain focused. If I don't respond, he'll just go away. Eventually, after adding milk, then sugar, then deciding he needs a different mug, he leaves the kitchen. All the while Flo is gathering various crockery items and putting them on a tray.

'Flo, when you were out I . . .'

'Can you fill the jug up with milk, please,' she says, oblivious to my concerns.

I do as she asks and try again. 'So, when I was looking for Chloe's file I found . . .'

'It's so lovely outside,' she says, smiling. 'Town is so pretty in the sunshine.'

'You took ages, I thought you were just going to the Press Shop to get paper?' I just got a whiff of her breath, did I smell booze? 'Flo, we need to talk. I was at your desk and I found—'

'Renée, come on, the meeting starts soon and we—'

I stand in her way, pulling my face into an expression that says I have a problem and we need to talk. 'Flo, you're acting really weird. I know things have been really shit with your dad's birthday and everything, but what the fuck is going on?' I block the exit so she can't get out.

'Move out of my way,' she says, forcibly. I don't know what is happening, but I know I can't move until she has acknowledged my question.

'Flo, what is going on with you?' I say, firmly. 'This isn't like you.'

'Get OUT of my way,' she says, her face turning red. She is holding a loaded tray of china cups and a jug of milk.

'No, not until you tell me why you have empty bottles of gin in your drawer. Are you drinking gin at work?' I whisper.

I see a lump in her throat as she tries to swallow it down. 'I'll count to three and if you haven't moved I'll—'

'Flo, you don't need to—'

'One . . .'

'Flo, I know you are embarrassed about what happened with Phil but—'

'Two.'

'Listen, everyone gets drunk and—'

'Three.'

She raises the tray in the air and lets go of it. Eight cups and saucers crash to the ground, smashing everywhere. We are both covered in milk. It all happens in slow motion, then speeds up again when she pushes me to the side and storms out of the kitchen. I immediately get down on my hands and knees and start clearing up the broken china. I feel tears forming in my eyes. What is going on with my friend?

'Have you been washing your hands in olive oil again?'

says Ben, getting the dustpan and brush from under the sink. He kneels down and starts to put shards of china into the pan.

'Ha ha!' I say sarcastically, wiping my eyes.

'Oh, are you OK? Sorry, I was just joking.'

'I'm fine. Just being oversensitive about something.'

'We have an old set of crockery somewhere; you can just use that. Please don't worry about breaking these, it happens. We won't die of thirst in the meeting.'

He's so nice. So calm. Just what I needed after that. I tip the broken china into the bin and go over to the sink to wash my hands. Ben is standing around a foot and a half behind me. He has a cup in his hand and is obviously waiting for me to get out of the way so he can wash his hands, or fill the kettle, or something. The energy in this tiny kitchen shifted in an instant when he walked in. The tension was so penetrating with Flo, I felt like the tendons holding my eyes in my head were going to snap, and that they were going to shoot out and slam against a wall. When she gets like that, she's impossible. Like a different person. I thought moving in together would be better than this. I thought I'd be the wild one. But something is up with Flo, something dark and I don't know what. It's only been weeks, but it feels like so much has happened, and so little of it has been particularly good. I thought this summer would be the launchpad for the rest of our lives. No September offering us a plan, no schedule to follow. Just a free dive into adulthood with one last hurrah to send us on our way.

I take much longer to wash my hands than I need to. Ben waits patiently behind me. I can feel his eyes on me, I can hear his breath. I can hear the general chitchat of the office, everyone in their own little state of panic about whatever it is they have to do. I need to take control of myself, steer my life in the direction that suits me, make things happen. I can either wait for adulthood to take a hold of me, or I can grab it by the horns. I turn around.

'Ben?' I say, looking at him in a way he understands immediately. We step towards each other. We look into each other's eyes with the undeniable pull of sexual attraction. Where it came from, I don't know. But it's here, and it's forcing us together.

'Ben,' I say, wanting to kiss him. He's so close I feel his breath on my lips. He stares at my mouth, then into my eyes. His body is so close to mine, it seems impossible that we won't kiss. He offers me one more look, showing me that this is not just in my head, and then disappears back into the office.

11

Flo

How do you tell someone you're sorry for being insane? I can't look at Renée. I know I was weird. I know smashing the cups was crazy. I don't know why I did it. I don't know why I do a lot of things I do. I know I have to apologise, I'm just trying to work out what to say and how to say it. Things are getting on top of me, that's all. Being back on the island, Renée being here at work, everything with Mum, with Dad. I gently shut my eyes and inhale long and slow through my nose. With my lips pursed, I blow it out for the count of 10, 9, 8 . . .

'Flo?' My eyes pop open as I remember where I am. It's Phil, he's wearing his usual buttoned-up floral shirt. His crotch is a metre away, level with my face. I wonder if I've seen what is inside his trousers. The rat springs to life and tries to make its way out of my mouth. A big, strange gulp greets Phil.

'Are you all right?' he says, quietly.

'Absolutely fine,' I tell him. My face is burning around my chin as a red blush starts to spread.

'Flo, listen,' he says, leaning in. I move the top half of my body towards him too, so that facing down doesn't seem so strange. Anything to hide my crimson face. I hold myself very still, I don't even breathe. 'Would you like to have dinner with me one night next week?' he says, quietly. I find myself immediately standing up.

'What?' I shout. He jumps. Georgina and Matt look over. When they realise there isn't an emergency and look away, Phil carries on.

'Would you . . .'

'Yes, I heard. Where?' I say, like he just told me one of the toilets is out of paper.

He's obviously surprised by my assertion. I think we both are.

'Um, I can book somewhere,' he says. 'Is there anything you don't like?'

'I eat it all,' I say, my face still burning, but a smile now forming. I feel such relief that I wonder if a plume of smoke just popped out of my head. He doesn't hate me. Why did it take him so long to ask me out? What was he waiting for? I've been in hell wondering if he thought I was a total slut or not. But this is good. We can go for dinner, we can have wine, have a nice time and put an end to this trauma.

'Great. How about next Thursday?'

'That works,' I say, confidently.

'Great.'

He walks back to his desk, and I deflate behind mine. The relief is like a shot of something strong. The scratching in my belly stops. There is nothing like a dose of confidence to shut that rat up. I collect myself and walk over to Renée in reception.

'I'm really sorry about what happened today,' I say. She looks up. 'I've just been really stressed with family stuff. And Mum wants me to go to dinner with her and Abi. You know how Mum makes me anxious. I'm sorry I took it out on you.'

'It's OK,' she says. 'I get it, I promise.'

'Let's do something nice this weekend. Movies and food? I'll take you somewhere fun, too. OK?' I say, relieved she didn't have a go at me. She was well within her rights to.

'That would be lovely,' she says, her smile now unnecessarily huge for this conversation.

'Great,' I say, walking away.

'Love you,' she says, beaming.

'Love you too,' I say back, not sure how or why I got away with acting the way I did. But I suppose that's what friendship is all about.

Back at my desk, I see Renée walk towards the kitchen. A noticeable spring in her step. A few moments later, she skips through with a glass of water. 'Hi Georgina,' she says, as they cross paths. 'Lovely day!' Georgina stops and watches Renée as she bounds back to her desk, emitting levels of happiness that feel overwhelming in a small office.

Being asked to write some copy about cheese has really pepped her up.

Renée

'Aunty Jo?' I say to her back, as she slides new supers into the hives for the bees to build their honeycombs. It's a beautiful, sunny Saturday, and I'm in need of Aunty Jo time after such an eventful week at work. She's wearing her beekeeping suit so looks somewhere between a chef and a spaceman, and likely can't hear me over the sound of the buzzing. 'Do you think it's possible to be happy and sad all at the same time?'

'What did you say?'

'I SAID IS IT POSSIBLE TO BE HAPPY AND SAD ALL AT THE SAME TIME?'

Sensing I need to talk, she slides in the last one and steps away from the hives. 'Come sit, Renée.'

We take a seat on the bench that she had James drag across the garden so she could sit and watch the bees. 'I find them so relaxing,' she tells me. Something I will never understand, I still think they're going to sting me to death. 'What was the question? Oh yes, happy and sad. Of course you can. Why?'

I want to tell Aunty Jo about Ben, but ultimately, I'm

attracted to another woman's husband so I'm keeping it to myself for now, for fear of anyone bursting my bubble. 'Take – I dunno – marriage, for example. Can you be happy and unhappy at the same time whilst being married to someone?'

'Well, where there is joy there is always heartache, I believe that. Pain is the price we pay for love. No relationship can only be consistently one thing and I think ambivalence can creep in without you realising. Look at me and James, we love each other, even if things aren't what they should be at the moment. I can't imagine I'm much fun to be with right now, but I just have to hope he sticks around and waits until this hormonal fuckery is over. I feel about as sexual as this bench.'

I wonder if Ben's wife is going through the menopause. It would be unbelievably harsh of him to describe her as 'ill', though.

'Think of it this way, when I think about your mum I can feel happy remembering her, then sad for the fact that she's not here any more. I can feel love for my partner, but sadness towards my body that's changing. I can feel happy I have all of these gorgeous animals, and gutted that I never had any human kids of my own.'

'And what about love? Can you be in love with somebody, and have feelings for someone else?'

'Renée, is there something you want to tell me?' she says, knowing me too well for a conversation like this.

'No, I'm just wondering.'

'Yes, I think you can love someone and have feelings for

someone else. It's why women like me are so afraid of it. I think being human is a daily battle against temptation. Left to our own devices, we'd all be enormous and be having sex with everyone. So we give ourselves boundaries, like love and health. But people slip, we all do. It takes a lot of work to keep up with what's good for you. Relationships take constant work. Being slim, Jesus, I've been on a diet for twenty years.' She drifts off, staring at the bees, lost in deep thought. 'You know what?' she says, getting up. 'I should cook James and me chops tonight. That's his favourite. Chops would be really good.'

I watch her walk back to the house and sit for a moment looking at the bees, wondering if I can find them as relaxing as she does. After two tense minutes, I discover I can't. All I can think about is Ben. I can't understand how I'm supposed to get through an entire weekend without seeing him. Luckily, bus parties are quite distracting. It's Carla's hen do later. I'm not sure I can look at a giant inflatable penis without thinking about Ben, but I'm going to have to try.

12

Renée

'I hate fancy dress,' Flo says, slumping around the charity shop in a strop. 'Why can't we just wear what we want?'

'Oh come on, it's fun. And you can wear what you want. Just pick a character from a film who wears normal clothes. Oh my God, look.' I pull a blue fluffy cardigan off the rail. 'This is almost identical to the one Baby wore in *Dirty Dancing*. And look.' I pull out a cute white sundress. 'That could pass as Fifties. We just need to get you a watermelon and you're done.'

'Can you go as Johnny?'

I'm not listening, I've spotted a rail that looks particularly inviting. Shining fabrics and puffy skirts, bejewelled cuffs and intricate bodices. I'm particularly drawn to a wedding dress. The neckline is wide, it doesn't have sleeves. It has a satin bodice and a huge taffeta skirt with a beautiful lace overlay.

'I want to wear this,' I say, holding it up to Flo.

'You can't, it's someone else's hen do. Also, the theme is movie characters, so it makes no sense. Can I just wear my trainers? Baby wore trainers, right?'

'Oh my God, *The Runaway Bride*. I'll just wear this and trainers. It's genius. Yes, Flo!' I hold it up against myself, it's so good I could scream. 'And look at this, and this.' I pull a few more dresses off the rail. Brilliant gowns, all with neat bodices and huge puffy skirts. It's like I found exactly who I want to be in this second-hand shop. 'This is it; this is the look I've been dreaming of. I refuse to let Guernsey make me boring any more – this is who I am now. And look, they're only ten quid each. Ball gowns and trainers, why the hell not!'

Like a kid in a candy shop, I drag three gowns and the wedding dress to the till. Forty quid later, I am the proud owner of an extraordinary wardrobe. Flo is looking at me like I've lost my mind.

'People are afraid to express themselves here, Flo. I don't want to feel like that. I want to live big on this little island. These dresses deserve another spin around the block. Now, let's go find you a watermelon.'

We drink a bottle of white wine while we get ready, and listen to the Spice Girls for old times' sake. I keep the music at level six, so as not to disturb Mrs Mangel downstairs.

'You look amazing,' I say to Flo, who is standing in front of me dressed as Baby. She's curled her hair and everything. 'Go on, say it.'

'I carried a watermelon.' We both crease up laughing.

'Here, let me help,' she says, pinning my hair into an 'up do'. The dress fits perfectly; if it wasn't for the trainers, I'd feel like it was my actual wedding day. I get why brides feel so special on their big day now; something about this white dress is making me feel like I want to fall in love. The image of Ben waiting for me at the end of an aisle comes into my mind. I brush it away quickly. 'Shall we?' I say to Flo, as we grab our bags.

'Shit, shit, no,' Flo loud-whispers as she gets to the top of the stairs. There is a *thump thump thump* as her watermelon bounces down the stairs and smashes against the front door. 'Nooooo, now I'm just a girl with a perm and a cardigan!' I find this so funny that I have to cross my legs to stop myself peeing.

'Just sit in a corner all night, people will get the idea.'

Mrs Mangel opens her door around the watermelon explosion. We brace ourselves. 'I'm so sorry,' I say, 'we'll clear it up.' She just stares at me, like she's never seen me before in her life. 'We're going to a party and Flo trip—'

'That's my wedding dress,' she says, slowly. 'You're wearing my wedding dress.'

'What? This? I just got it from the charity shop.'

'I took it there this week, along with some other old gowns. Well, would you look at that. You look lovely, may I ask where you're going?'

Flo is creeping up behind me, clearly also baffled by the friendly tone of conversation.

'We're going to a bus party,' I say tentatively. 'It's a hen do, fancy dress. The theme is movie characters. I'm the . . .'

She looks at my feet. 'The Runaway Bride?' she asks.

'Yes,' I say, a bit worried this is hugely offensive. 'It's such a gorgeous dress. I'm sorry if it looks like I'm disrespecting it. I just really wanted to wear it and, well, there isn't a husband so . . .'

'Disrespecting? Not at all, I'm honoured, and you look beautiful. And you, Flo, are you going somewhere else?'

'No,' Flo says, clearly disappointed by her outfit. 'I'm Baby from *Dirty Dancing*. I was carrying a watermelon, but I dropped it.'

'Oh, that's very good too. You know, I saw watermelons for sale at the corner shop at the top of Mill Street. They've cut them into quarters, maybe easier for you to carry? You two get going, I'll clean this up.'

'Really, are you sure? The bus is due to leave in ten minutes, so we do kind of need to go,' I say, feeling cheeky, but also not wanting to be a literal running bride.

'Of course,' she says, her face creasing into a gentle smile. 'How wonderful for the dress to have another night out. I had wondered if maybe a bride would find it, but no one wants second-hand these days. This is much better. Who'd have thought that my dress would end up on a pub crawl.

This has made my day. You two have fun,' she says, going inside to presumably get a mop.

Flo and I leave. 'Wow, that's so creepy. Her wedding dress is now going on a bus party. What are the chances?' she says.

'I know, so weird. Maybe tonight's the night I meet my husband.' Flo laughs a little too hard, like the idea of me with a husband is completely ridiculous. I join in as though I agree, whilst trying to push the image of me and Ben at the altar out of my head.

The bus party is wild. There are about twenty-five women, including both Carla and Gem's mums, all of Carla's aunties, her boss and various colleagues and future sisters-in-law. Luckily, there aren't any old faces from Tudor Falls. Flo and I only recognise Carla's younger sister, whose name we can't for the life of us remember.

'Betty?' Flo guesses, already hammered on vodka Diet Cokes and Slippery Nipples, our chosen tipples for the night.

'No one under fifty is called Betty,' I say, and we giggle to ourselves at the back of the bus, feeling very separate from the main clique. It's like Carla and Gem are ten years older than us. Carla is dressed up as Princess Leia with a sash saying, 'Bride to be'. She's had her hair and make-up done by her cousin who's also going to do it for her on the big day. Personally, I think the foundation is a touch too orange but her eyes look really good. There's nothing funny in her interpretation of Princess Leia; she would have chosen it so she could look beautiful and not silly despite it being fancy dress. Gem is Holly Golightly. Again, most likely a very deliberate choice to show off her unbelievably perfect figure in a tight black dress. They look good, just boring. But that was always how they were, never outside the box. They were good at everything at school, and both were wild enough to have sex but only with long-term boyfriends and never one-night stands. They told their parents everything and seemed to have a childhood completely devoid of shame and regret. Too sensible to do anything that would damage their self-esteem. Too clever to party so hard their success would suffer.

Carla's friends and family are busying around her, seeing to her every need. The cousin occasionally adjusts her hair. Her mother keeps making her down glasses of water. Others tell her how pretty she looks over and over again. What a lucky man Will is. How she'll probably be pregnant this time next year and how they'll have the cutest babies ever. I don't know why feelings of jealousy keep creeping over me when her life isn't the life I'd want for myself at all, but it's a sobering thought to realise you wouldn't be able to fill a bus full of people who'd treat you that way. For me, it would be more like a taxi, carrying me, Aunty Jo and Flo. And neither of them would think to do anything about my hair.

'They're so . . . obvious,' I say, slumped on the back seat as the bus heads off from the Yacht to the Thomas de la Rue. 'Like, they went to school, they got jobs, they're getting married, they'll have babies. It's nice and everything, but it's all a bit dull, isn't it? And their costumes, like, who cares, that's been done a thousand times.' Flo does a huge burp.

'Shit, sorry,' she says, not really listening. Bus parties were always the wildest form of entertainment on Guernsey. Anything up to forty people, usually in fancy dress, being driven around the island by some poor man who has to endure hours of awful drunk people while he takes them from pub to pub all around the perimeter of the island, ending up back in town where everyone gets dropped off and rages on to whatever nightclub lets them in. This one, due to the number of mums and aunties on board, is one of the most subdued I've been on. Flo and I are like the naughty girls at the back. Carla, however, has now taken off the white dress she was wearing as Princess Leia and is swanning about in a white lace lingerie set with a white tutu over the top. Her mother seems to think it's wonderful that her daughter is running around pubs in her pants. I guess that's how it is when you know your daughter is in love and at no risk of copping off with a random. Personally I don't know why you'd bother wearing that if you're not trying to get laid, but as I've already established, Carla and I are very different kinds of people.

'I might need to drink doubles to get through this,' I say, as we arrive at the Houmet Tavern, a seafront spot in Vale at the top of the island. It's about the halfway point. 'Come on, Flo. Let's steal toilet paper from the loos and stream it out of the bus window to spice this party up a bit.'

We run inside. Flo goes to the bar and I head to the toilets. I come out of the Ladies' holding a giant loo roll, wearing a wedding dress and, by some wild twist of fate, walk directly into Ben. We literally crash into each other in a tiny corridor of a random pub. If ever there was a sign that the universe was looking out for me, this might be it. Although I really wish I wasn't carrying toilet paper.

'Renée?'

'Ben? What – why are you at the Houmet?'

'I'm looking for my . . . wait, why are you at the Houmet?'

'I'm on a bus party. It's a hen do. I don't usually wear wedding dresses, it's fancy dress. I'm the . . .' He looks at my feet.

'The Runaway Bride?' I nod.

'Genius,' he says, laughing. 'It suits you.'

'Are you OK, you look worried?'

'I . . . I'm OK.' He looks like he should go. But he's also looking at me like he could eat me alive. I'm wearing a wedding dress with Ben, I don't even feel stupid. He looks into my eyes, I look into his. Am I in a movie? The kitchen door is to our left, the kitchen is closed but . . . I press the door, it opens slightly. I take his hand and guide him in. He resists at first, but I don't let him go. I have enough alcohol in my system to give me the confidence to get what I want. We stand against the door, our hearts pumping so fast with the fear of someone coming in. We stare at each other. Take a step closer. Forehead to forehead, holding each other's hands. We don't even kiss, our lips brush gently, our breath merges into one hot stream of air that passes back and forth between us. The sound from the pub is so loud, women's high-pitched voices screaming and shouting and laughing as the music is turned up to make their quick visit as fun for them as possible. The beat of the tune makes the door vibrate. I want him more than I've wanted anything in my life. I almost forget what I am wearing.

'I don't know how or why, but I'm crazy about you,' he says, his eyes soft but his body hard as it holds me in my place.

'Same,' I say, gently.

'I can't get you out of my head,' he says, like he's admitting to a terrible secret. Which I suppose this is. 'At work, I have to stop myself hovering around your desk. I just want to look at you all day.'

'Same,' I repeat. Wanting him to feel the water bomb that's just gone off in my knickers.

'I don't know where this came from, I didn't go looking for it.'

'I know.' I feel how hard he is against my leg. Could we do it against this door, will we? But then we hear a voice.

'Ben? BEN? I've found her.' Someone just outside the door calling for him.

'Fuck, Renée, I'm sorry.'

'No, I say. Please. Stay, just a second longer, let's sit, talk.'

'I have to go, I'm sorry. I don't know how this happened, it's you, I . . .'

'It's me?' He's blaming me? He sees my shoulders drop.

'No, I mean, I can't stay away from you. It's my fault, I . . . I'm sorry, I have to go.'

'Ben? She's here, I found her,' the man says again on the other side of the door, less than two feet from my soaking vagina.

'I'm sorry, Renée. I'll see you Monday. You look so unbelievably gorgeous in that dress.' And then he is gone. I am left alone in the kitchen. A jilted bride, I have never felt more pathetic.

I leave the toilet roll in the kitchen and go back to the bus. Flo comes out before anyone else; she's holding two Slippery Nipples. 'There you are. Where did you go?' She steps onto the bus, but I'm done with that now.

'Fuck this Flo, let's get out of here. I need some adventure in my life.'

'Okkkaaaay, but where are we going to go? We're in Vale, we're miles away from anything.'

'We'll find something. Let's down these and go, at least we're in our trainers.' We shot the drinks and I pull her by the hand. I run, I don't know where, I just run. I need to get as far away from the Houmet as I can.

'Where are we going? What about Carla?' Flo says, keeping up purely because I am dragging her. The fresh sea air blowing through our hair. The warm summer night like flapping silk against our cheeks. I feel the island energy running through me. I want to be everything the women on that bus were not. Different, creative, unobvious. I want to be everything a woman whose husband cheats on her is not. Exciting, independent, free-spirited. What spiritual force put me in the same room as Ben tonight? What is this island trying to tell me?

HONEYBEE

'Just run. I don't know where. Just run, Flo.'

We find ourselves in a little marina that neither of us ever knew was here. It feels otherworldly to discover a new part of the island, magical even. The wedding dress glows in the moonlight; I feel like a crystal that is charging.

'Why has no one ever mentioned all these boats,' Flo says, making me laugh. She's silly drunk, the best kind.

'Secret boats, how exciting,' I say, throwing my leg over a gate and jumping onto a jetty. Flo follows me with more trepidation. Sober Flo would be telling me off, drunk Flo joins in. I climb onto the back of a boat. 'Come on, I'll pull you up.' We sit, dangling our feet off the back.

'I'd love a boat,' Flo says. 'I'd sit on it all the time.'

'Same.'

'Do you think they're all trying to find us at the pub?'

'Nope, I bet they haven't even noticed we're missing. They're not our people, Flo. It's good to realise that, I think.'

'It was quite weird of us to run off though, what made you do that?'

I could tell Flo, in this moment, about Ben. She'd get cross, I'd tell her it was a mistake, she'd calm down and all would be well. I could have someone to talk to about this, because it's hard, and that would be nice. But I also know the second I tell anyone about Ben, it's the second someone tells me it's wrong. Tonight was terrible, wrong. But it was also wonderful. Delicious. I wanted more. I'm horny as hell, and just not ready to have anyone tell me I can't have it. There is a loud bang underneath us, and then a hatch flies open.

'What the hell are you doing on my boat?' says a man with a beard, wearing his pants. Flo and I jump into action quicker than we've ever moved in our lives. 'I'm sorry!' I call back to the man as we jump over the gate, 'I thought it was mine.'

We make it quite far down the road before we stop. Laughter and weakness stabbing our lungs.

'I've never laughed so much in my life,' Flo says, bent double, panting. 'You thought it was yours?'

'I know, I don't know where that came from! Anyway, he hasn't followed us and I don't hear sirens, so I think we're good.' It's so dark, just the moonlight bouncing off the road. We're a really long way from town.

'What do we do now? We can't walk. We could call a taxi?' she says. 'But it will take ages. I need a wee so bad.'

'I'll call Aunty Jo, give me your phone, I haven't got any credit.'

Flo wanders off to find a place to pee. There's no one about, but she still can't bring herself to do it out in the open. I look at her phone and see a text message from someone called Katrina. I don't mean to open it, but I don't know how to make a call without pressing the button.

Flo when are you coming back to get your shit? My new housemate moves in here a week on Tuesday. If you haven't taken it all by then I'll chuck it all out.

Katrina . . . She must have been Flo's housemate in London? I scroll back.

You can't just disappear Flo. That isn't how grown-ups deal with stuff.

I'm not telling you again, Flo. If you're not gone by tomorrow, I'll call your Mum.

I scroll back more.

You did it AGAIN last night Flo. WTF is wrong with you. I can't live like this any more; you have to leave.

I've tried Flo, I've really tried. Last night was horrible. AGAIN.

If you won't answer me how can I help you?

Flo, who did you bring back here last night, the living room is disgusting?

Flo, can we talk. Are you OK? I feel like things are getting really out of control, can we have a house meeting? I can't go on like this. You need help. I think you're an alcoholic Flo.

The texts go on and on, and Flo hasn't replied to any of them. My heart starts racing – this is awful. What has Flo done?

'Did you call her?' she says, appearing from the bushes like a mad woman. 'Sorry, I was looking at the stars.'

I quickly mark the text as unread and tap in Aunty Jo's number and call her. She says she'll be here in fifteen minutes. Flo and I sit on a little wall, looking out to sea. It's calm and peaceful, she seems happy to sit quietly. I move a little closer to her, and put my arm across her shoulder. 'I love you, Flo,' I tell her.

'I love you too,' she says.

We listen to the distant sound of waves lapping, the night-time noises of the island. It soothes me, but I can't get those text messages out of my head. And one word stands out above all the others. Flo: an *alcoholic*?

13

Renée

I'm trying to surreptitiously eat a croissant at my desk. It's really flaky and messy, but I'm starving and need pastry. You can't stop halfway through a croissant, it's impossible. It's like only eating half a packet of crisps, or ordering salad instead of fries with a burger, you just can't do it.

I got my period this morning. It came, as it always does, as a massive warm blob with no warning. I'm not one of those girls who knows my cycle; it takes me by surprise every month. I bled through my new blue trousers, so I had to go to Miss Selfridge and buy a new pair before I came to work. They were only £22, but that's a lot to me right now. Everything is so expensive. Every time I buy anything, I think of it in terms of how long I had to sit at this reception desk to earn it. A sandwich is twenty minutes, a bus ride is three minutes, my rent is four days. I've never really thought about money, but adulthood forces you to be obsessed with it. It's all so new, and I'm not sure I like it. Matt walks up to reception.

'Hey hon, looking good today. Nice weekend?'

'I've got my period,' I say, which gets rid of him pretty quick.

I feel bloated and gross. Having a job when you're having a period is awful. Women really should get the week off so they can menstruate in peace. I push the last chunk of croissant into my mouth, just as Ben walks past on his way to the toilet. This is the worst thing about sitting on reception, everyone has to walk past me to use the toilet. It's weird knowing when everyone goes and how long they take. Georgina had been in there for a long time this morning when Chloe went in. I wanted to warn her. 'Don't go in, she's taking ages and you know what that means.' But she went in and took ages herself, both adding to the fruity smells that occasionally drift my way as the door swings open. Ben doesn't say anything, which means he's probably off for a poo. He's been in meetings since before I got in this morning, so we've hardly even made eye contact. I have no idea what to say after Saturday night, it still feels like a dream.

'Renée,' says Chloe as she approaches my desk. 'How are you?'

'Good thanks.' She's going to tell me off for eating at my desk, and it's going to make me blush and maybe even cry.

'Sure? You look a bit . . .'

I look down and see I'm covered in croissant. I look a mess. My hair is shit and my skin is bad. It's like my period is trying to announce itself to the world.

'Just menstrual,' I tell her. She seems to like the woman-to-woman connection.

'Oh, I know. It can be hell. I have painkillers on my desk if you want some.' I don't know why she's being so nice to me. I mean, it's not even that nice, it's just nicer than usual so feels weird. 'Well anyway, just wanted check in. You can always come to me if there's an issue – us girls need to stick together, right?'

'Right,' I say, confused. I try to look normal as she walks off to the toilet, just as I see Ben come out. I didn't have time to go to the kitchen, which is what I usually do when he's been in the toilet for ages. He doesn't seem to mind that I know he just took a seven-minute-long dump and leans over the reception desk.

'Renée, we should talk,' he says. Why now, I think? Why now when I'm covered in pastry and feel too big for my clothes?

'Oh Ben, seriously. It's OK, we don't have to talk about it,' I say, lying. It's all I want to talk about.

'No. We do,' he says firmly but quietly. 'Fucking hell, this is such a cliché, but I want you to know that isn't what I do.'

I momentarily forget about the mess in my pants and the grease on my face. Am I being dumped? I want to cry. But that could just be my period talking. I don't want him to know that I care, because I'm used to playing games with guys and maybe that feels safer than 'talking'.

'It's OK. Things happen, right?' I say, unsure if I have pastry stuck to my lip or not. 'I think human beings have become so civilised that we sometimes forget that, at the end of the day, we're just animals. At the mercy of temptation. You know?'

'I suppose so,' he says, possibly taken aback by my extremely articulate analogy. 'But I also wanted to tell you that I really enjoyed seeing you at the weekend. I hope you're all right and that I haven't put you in a horrible position here at work.'

For fuck's sake, is he for real? He's worried about me? 'I'm fine, thank you,' I say, gratefully. How is he this perfect? Despite the bit about him going into a pub kitchen with his receptionist and gazing into her eyes adoringly while she was wearing a wedding dress. Oh God, it's just too awful.

'OK, now back to your cheese. We only need a line, something snappy that makes you crave cheddar. It shouldn't be too hard, should it?'

'I wouldn't know how hard it is, Ben. Not yet, anyway.' What did I say that for? I sound like a horny mum from an Eighties movie who's trying to get off with the milkman.

Ben opens and closes his mouth like a fish, just as Flo appears out of nowhere. We both jump. 'Ben, hi, I need to take next Monday off quite suddenly. I'm sorry.'

'Oh, all right,' he says, taken aback. Usually requests for holidays go through Georgina. 'I'm sure that's fine, is everything OK?'

'Yup all good, I have to go to London to . . . I just have to go to London. I have a place there and need to move the last of my things out. It might take me longer than the weekend.'

I'm staring at Flo because she hasn't mentioned this to me, even though I already know about it because I read her text messages. She's telling me in front of Ben so that I can't ask her questions and find out what's actually going on. I see right through it.

'I'm sure Renée will be able to cover for you, right Renée?' Ben is looking right at me. I want to make him happy. I so want to be in the office with him without Flo watching my every move. But more than that, I need to know what is up with Flo. I have to think on my feet.

'Actually, Ben. Sorry, but I'm going too. Flo needs help moving out and I'd feel awful leaving her to it all by herself. So yeah, we will both be off, sorry.'

Flo looks at me, horrified.

'Oh, OK, well I'm sure everyone will manage.' He takes a beat. 'I'm actually due to be in London too, we'll all be there.'

Flo and I both look at Ben quizzically. 'That's not in the diary,' Flo says.

'No, I know. I haven't added it yet, we literally just organised it this morning. I need to be in the office on Monday, and it's my brother's birthday over the weekend, so I'm going to have dinner with him first. Renée, if you're up for it, you could spend Monday in the London office? We have a big Island Cheese meeting and it would be helpful, I think, if you were there. Seeing as you're doing the copy.'

'Oh my God, really? I can work in London? I-I mean, I'd love to.'

'Great, and seeing as it's work, be sure to hand in your flight receipts. We can reimburse you for those.'

What is happening? Flo seems to have detached from her body. She's dumbstruck. Ben is cool as a cucumber offering me this, and I feel like I just got handed my future on a silver platter. Both Flo and Ben head back to their desks and I sit staring at my computer, like it's going to answer the burning question of: *what the actual fuck just happened?*

Within minutes, an email from Flo pops up. 'Explain yourself, please.' And then almost immediately one from Ben. 'I'm glad you can come, Renée, will be fun.'

Oh my God Oh my God OH MY GOD.

I reply to Flo: 'London babes, the dream ;)'

I open a Word doc. It's time to be as proactive in my writing career as I am in my love life. I turn Ben on physically, but I want him to think I'm smart too. I can do this; I can come up with the best cheese slogan of all time. But before I do that, there's one more thing on my mind that I need to get straight. I peer into the main office at Flo, my heart picking up. I open the internet browser.

Can you be an alcoholic at twenty-two?

Flo

After work, I stand outside a beauty salon for twenty minutes just staring at the menu in the window.

Brazilian – £20

Hollywood – £30

I don't know what any of it means. Also, how does it work? Do I have to take my knickers off? How many people are in the room? I chicken out in the end and head to Sainsbury's; I'll do it myself with Immac. I've used that on my legs before, it worked pretty well. Getting things like bikini waxes on Guernsey feels risky. If I walk into a pub and the person who waxed me is sitting there with her friends, how can I trust she won't tell them about my flaps?

On the shelf next to the hair removal cream, I also see hair removal strips. I can wax myself? I buy it all and head home.

'I've done sausages for dinner!' shouts Renée up the stairs as I go into the bathroom.

'Yummy,' I shout back. 'Just going to have a shower.'

I take the wax strips out of the box. It says to warm them in my hands before applying so I take off my knickers and do that. I look at my vagina in the mirror. I've never done a thing to it. If I pull the hair, it stretches to about an inch and a half, and the triangle spreads to the top of my thighs. The women in porn have nothing, or a single strip. I don't like either of those, but I do want to tidy it up.

I pull apart the two strips and press one into each of the creases at the top of my thighs. 1, 2 . . . I can't. Oh God, I can't pull it off. I have to, I have no choice. OK. 1, 2 . . . NOOOO . . . I just can't do it. OK, I'll just give myself a minute. I'll trim first. I sit on the toilet with a pair of nail scissors in one hand. I pinch a clump of hair between my fingers and pull it straight. I snip through the hair and it comes off in my fingers. Wow, it's so satisfying. I chop another clump, and then another. I reach underneath and stretch out another clump. I snip, and—

'AHGAHGAHGAHGAHGAG.' Oh shit, I've cut my lip. I keep screaming, the pain is horrific.

'Flo, what happened?' says Renée, banging on the door.

'I cut myself,' I say, wedging an entire roll of toilet paper between my thighs.

'Where?' asks Renée, concerned. 'Do you need help? Open the door.'

What have I done?

'I've broken my fanny.'

'Flo, open the door,' Renée demands. I really don't want to, but I'm scared. Blood is pouring out of me, the wax strips still need to come off. I shuffle towards the door and pull it open.

'What the hell are you doing?' she says, looking at my vagina. A sodden red loo roll underneath it, a wax strip on either side.

'I wanted to tidy it up,' I say, swapping the loo roll for a new one. The second roll at least indicates that the blood flow is slowing down.

'You have to pull those off to get the hair out, you know?' she says, stating the obvious.

'I can't. I'll soak them off.'

'You can't. The wax is like glue, you have to pull them. I'll do it.'

'No you won't,' I say, stepping back. She comes at me until I'm cornered between the shower and the sink.

'Flo, they need to come off, and quickly. Come here.'

I don't know how I get myself into these messes. I shut my eyes.

'OK, bloody do it,' I say, bracing myself. I feel her fingers take hold of each strip at the same time. As I squeeze my thighs together to hold the loo roll in place, Renée says, 'One, two, three . . .' and yanks off the wax strips.

'Oh my God oh my God!' I repeat, until the burning stops.

'There you go,' Renée says, standing back and taking a look. 'It looks nice. A bit raw, but nice.'

I waddle to the middle of the bathroom, managing not to drop the loo roll. I look in the mirror. It does look nice, she's right. It's much better.

'Can I help with anything else? Need me to shave your armpits?'

'Go away.'

'OK, but you should put honey on the sides to calm them down. Aunty Jo says local honey is the world's original antiseptic. Spread a bit of that bee juice on ya puss puss and you'll be ready for whatever it is you're planning to do with it after this wax?'

'I've got a date with Phil.'

'Oh my days, Florence is getting laid. Wow, I never saw you as the "preparations" type. I thought you were too pessimistic for that,' she says.

'Yeah, well, we've obviously already done *something*, so I guess something else could happen after our date, couldn't it?'

'And what happened to not having relationships with colleagues outside of work?'

'Oh Renée, will you just shut up and go and get me Aunty Jo's honey!'

14

Renée

The next day, I take my lunch at 12 p.m. I do this so the phones are covered while the others are out. But it also makes me very happy because I'm starving by 12. I don't know how anyone makes it through to 1 p.m. without passing out. Georgina manages with constant snacking. Chloe drinks green tea all morning. She sometimes brings lunch back and eats in reception while she reads the papers. It's usually soup and a few slices of bread, or measly crackers. I brought lunch with me for two days last week but both times I had eaten it all by 10.30. I'm not allowed to eat at my desk, so I literally ducked down underneath it to take mouthfuls of sandwich, which I swallowed with barely any chewing. Today, I went to the market and got a chic little tray of sushi. I've developed a real taste for it, I just wish it didn't come at such a cost.

Later in the afternoon, I watch Georgina as she lays out what looks like a picnic for five people at her desk. She's seen I'm here and emails to offer me some food. *Happy to share, pull up a chair!* She's by far the nicest person in the office, a real woman's woman. I'm not sure she's ever walked past me without saying hi, and even Chloe softens around her. She has this lovely energy about her that's so caring. I felt quite sorry for Georgina when I first met her, making all sorts of horrible judgements because of the way she looked. I assumed she would hate me because I'm pretty and she's not, but she's so kind to me. It makes me hate myself to know that I thought that. Terrified that someone can hear my thoughts, I try to think about something else.

The phone rings, it's an internal call from Ben's number.

'Go ahead caller, you're on the air,' I say, trying to be funny so he fancies me even more.

'Renée, I thought we could talk.' Oh God, he's going to fire me. 'Are you OK?'

'Yes, I'm OK,' I say, lying. I'm not OK. 'Are you OK?'

'I am, but I shouldn't be. I meant what I said on Saturday night, I'm crazy about you. I hope you know that I'm not taking this lightly. I realise the position I've put you in, but I . . .' I'm so scared he's going to tell me that this – whatever *this* is – is over. I just can't hear the words. 'It's so hard, but I . . .'

I have to turn this around; he can't dump me on the phone. He can't. I'll do what I do best: I'll make it sexy.

'Oh, I see. It's . . . hard, is it?'

He laughs a little, as if he wasn't going to say something awful after all. And then I hear his breath deepen on the other end of the phone; maybe he's going with it? 'Yeah, it's . . . it's really hard. Can you help?' I've still got him, he's not dumping me.

'I can certainly try. Let me kneel down under your desk. I'll get really close, so my lips tap on the tip. I'll have my tongue lick it gently, maybe that will work?'

'It's not working, it's just getting harder and harder.'

I honestly don't think I have ever felt this horny in my life. My fanny is galloping. I press gently down on my clitoris, knowing someone could walk in any minute but wanting to give this everything I've got for both of us. I slide down my chair, so my hand and crotch are hidden.

'Let me take it deep into my mouth. Suck it nice and hard. And then I'll slip my knickers off and straddle you at your desk. I'll let my wet . . .'

'I got you a Crunchie.'

'. . . dishes! Wet dishes are terrible.' Oh my God, it's Matt, pulling me back to reality like I'm a dead animal being dragged out of a bush. 'I saw you eating one once, so I know you like them,' he says, proudly. I scrabble back to upright and try to ignore him. Hopefully he'll go away.

'I'm sorry,' I say to Ben. 'Now, I'd love to help you get this one over the line.' I put my hand over the receiver to look like I'm being professional. 'Was there something else, MATT?' I say, to make it clear to Ben what's happening.

'I can wait,' Matt says, settling in, not getting any hints.

Thinking a Crunchie is the access code to my knickers. I exhale and move my hand from the receiver. 'I'm sorry, sir, it must be very frustrating. Leave this with me and I will get back to you as soon as I can.' I hang up and take the Crunchie. To be fair, the only thing better than the orgasm I was about to have is chocolate. Matt lingers for a while; my vag shrivels back inside itself.

'Thanks,' I say. 'Too kind.'

'Anything for my honey. I like your shirt – let me know if you ever want to hop off with me after work.' He's referring to the frog print. How he managed to turn it into an innuendo is actually really impressive. He heads back to his desk, proud of his advancement, no idea of the devastation he just inflicted upon my libido. Ben hurries past me to the toilets. When he comes out again, a sheen on his skin, a wide smile that looks painted on, I see Flo standing at reception. She has brought me a Blue Boost. I eat that too. If I can't get to climax, I might as well overdose on Cadbury's.

Aunty Jo has cooked us baked salmon fillets with vegetables and potatoes for tea. She's not herself again tonight. James and I have sat opposite her and listened while she's talked us through the eating schedules of every single one of her animals. All of which James and I already know, because we help her with it.

'And of course, the goats never act like they've had enough. They've cleared the lawn and I've run out of hay, again. I'll go straight down with the van in the morning to get some more from the garden centre because I'm on the morning shift tomorrow. Would anyone like to come?'

James and I both shake our heads silently.

'No, of course not. So boring, sorry. God, I'm sure I used to talk about other things. How is work, Renée. All well?'

'Yes, I've been asked to come up with a slogan for cheese. Isn't that cool?'

'That is cool,' James says, relieved for something else to talk about. 'What's the brief?'

'Apparently teenagers are snacking on rubbish, so it's my job to make them choose cheese over Wotsits.'

'"Choose Cheese". There you go, you can have that for free.' James chuckles to himself, Aunty Jo pretends to find it hilarious and does a maniacal laugh as she clears the plate that she hasn't finished. James and I watch her and make eyes at each other. She's being very odd.

'Should I leave you two?' I whisper to James.

'No, no, I've actually got some papers to mark, so I'd better crack on.' Without clearing his plate, he says thank you to Aunty Jo then makes his way upstairs to the spare room that he uses as an office. Aunty Jo puts both hands on the sink and bursts out crying.

'Oh no, what happened?' I ask, rushing over to her. 'What's wrong, are you and James OK?'

'Oh Renée, I don't know what's the matter with me, I'm an absolute blob of emotion. Poor James.'

'No, Aunty Jo, not poor James, poor you. What's going on? Come on, let's go sit by the bees and talk.'

I lead her down the garden with my arm linked through hers like she's an old lady that needs help crossing the road. I sometimes have visuals of Aunty Jo being very old or very unwell and me taking care of her. Sometimes, when my mind drifts, I think of all the awful things that could happen to her. A car crash, cancer, heartache, and I am her hero. I sweep her up and make her better. Getting her everything she needs to be comfortable. I have a terrible mix of feelings after my mind has taken me deep into one of those fantasies. I know that ultimately my brain does this because I want to return the favour. I want to look after her, like she has looked after me. But then I worry that by imagining awful things happening to her, they might actually happen. So right here, in this moment where she is sad, in a relatively undramatic situation, I am happy to be her support.

'What is it?' I ask, as we sit down on the bench. The bees are mostly in their hive for the night, just the odd one making the most of the last rays of sunshine. Not wasting a single second of their day.

'James and I have always been so close, but we didn't have children together. Because of me. We tried for a while but eventually I had tests and we discovered I had more chance of giving birth to a baby goat than a human baby. We grieved together but it was only me who felt the guilt. He promised he was OK with it, he always said that being a teacher meant there were enough kids in his life.'

'And what, he's changed his mind?'

'No, I don't think so. Well, I don't know. But I'm realising something – that maybe by never having children we missed out on an intimacy that other couples have. I don't know how to explain it, but surely if you've experienced birth together, then you break through boundaries of conversation that you never imagined. The man has to become more aware of the woman, because she is going through something so physical. But what if all there ever was between you was emotional support? And now, with this menopause nonsense, and it all being so physical, what if he can't understand it? I tried to open up a bit last night. And I'm sorry, Renée, this is a lot of information from your aunty, but I am so dry. Sex is painful, I just can't do it. I tried to explain this to him last night and he didn't know what to do. I thought we were close, but he panicked or something. Acted like what I was talking about was totally unbearable and he got in such a state he went and slept in the spare room. I just lay there feeling like a disregarded bucket of sand.'

'Well, that wasn't cool. He shouldn't have made you feel that way,' I say, holding back so many questions about her vagina. Do they really dry up? I can't imagine that. Mine is like a swamp, ready for Ben at any given time.

'No, I know he shouldn't but it's hardly a surprise, is it? This thing that happens to us women is a mystery to us, let alone men. I mean, before I spoke to you about it, did you even know what the menopause was?'

'Not really. I mean, I'd seen the word in magazines but I wouldn't bother reading about it.'

Aunty Jo bursts out crying. Loud, ridiculous tears.

'Exactly, "wouldn't be bothered". Who would be bothered with this? It's not sexy, it's not pretty. It's not any of the things women are supposed to be, so why would anyone bother with a woman like me?'

I put my arm around her. 'I'm sorry, I didn't mean it like that. It just seems like something so few people deal with so . . .'

'Renée, ALL woman deal with it, we just don't talk about it. So when it comes, it's like jumping off a damn cliff. And everyone around you gives you a wide berth because it's so awkward, and you act all weird and get all hot and bothered. James hasn't said it, but I know he's just hoping it passes soon and that I'll go back to normal. I don't even know what normal is for me any more. I don't know what the future me will be like.'

'Well have you explained it all to him? I mean, if the problem is that no one talks about it, why don't you talk about it? And not just the dry sex stuff? It's all very well saying men don't understand us, but if we're not telling them what's going on, then how the hell are they supposed to know?'

Aunty Jo raises her eyebrows and stares at the beehive.

'Well would you look at that!' she says, her tears drying up like her vagina, a smile forming on her beautiful face. 'My little Renée is a true grown-up.' She laughs, less maniacal this time. More like she's had a realisation. 'You're right, of course you're right. If men don't understand us, why don't we tell them? It's as simple as that. He's a good man, he can take it.'

HONEYBEE

She puts her hand on mine, and we watch as the activity around the hive completely dies down.

Flo

The London trip is coming up and I'm scanning through my emails, worrying that Katrina is planning something. She once emailed me saying that there needed to be 'an intervention'. An intervention? I had no idea what she was talking about. What if I get to London and she's there, at the flat? Planning whatever the hell she meant. But also, why would she do that; she hates me and most likely never wants to see me again. No, it will be OK. Being in London will be nice for a few days. I can get all my things and close that chapter once and for all. And even though I'm mad she's wheedled her way on to the trip, it will be fun to show Renée the city, it's so crazy that she's never been. I must stop worrying. Katrina will be gone, we will have fun, and all will be well. Please God.

Phil emailed earlier to ask if I like Asian food. I said yes. Does that mean we're going for Chinese? There are so many different kinds of Asians, which did he mean? I'm wearing a black silk shirt with little ladybirds all over it. I'm nervous, but I'm trying to be relaxed because he wouldn't have invited me if he didn't like me, right? I've never been on a date before, it feels so American. Like the kind of thing people do in movies, not in real life. I'm a ball of anxiety when it comes to the opposite sex. Up until now anything I've done with boys has come at the end of a boozy night. The idea of sober sex terrifies me, the idea of dinner just as scary. What if food falls out of my mouth while I'm talking? What if something gets stuck in my teeth and I don't know it's there? I've been writing down ideas for conversations all day:

* Guernsey. Did he always want to stay here, or did he want to move to the mainland?

* Work. We could talk about work, and the company, and if we like our jobs. Which I do. So that should be quite positive. But I don't want it to turn into a gossip session about everyone, that wouldn't feel right.

* TV. We could talk about the latest series of *Big Brother* and how that Liverpudlian guy Craig has now got his own DIY show.

I'm doing what I can to be confident in this situation. More like Renée. Blasé about the boys. She's casual about what happened with Matt; so cool and in control around him, even though he's like a dog that keeps trying to hump her leg. I know she doesn't like him, but still it's how I wish I was with guys, at least a little bit cool. So today, that is who I am trying to be. Carefree and excited for a date with someone I think I might fancy. My vagina is healed. It's good to go, should the opportunity arise to unleash it.

I jump as an email comes in from Phil. *I'll meet you out front at 6.05? Most people will have left by 6 so we can be a little less conspicuous. Not that we're doing anything we shouldn't, of course. A nice early dinner while the sun is still out ;)*

Perfect! I reply. I type three kisses and then delete. As soon as I've sent it, I wish I'd added the kisses. I look over at Phil, he looks at his computer, then at me. He smiles. I smile back. More of a flutter in my belly than a scratch. It feels nice. Nothing to destroy.

'Hows ya vag?' Renée says, coming over to my desk and speaking way too loudly, just as Georgina is walking past.

'Oooooh, girl talk. My fave. What's the problem?' Georgina says, rushing over. I could punch Renée, why can't she learn how to whisper? Or maybe just stay at her desk and send an email. Actually, no, I don't want that question on email either. When will she learn how to be professional?

'Flo had a little slip-up with her scissors preparing for a date.'

If looks could kill, I'd be arrested for murder.

'Ah, been there,' Georgina says, stunning us both. 'Yup, years of the razor blade to make it look pretty. Now I just whip the whole lot off. Bald as a coot down there, have been for years.' She leans in. 'Helps with sensitivity too.' She raises her eyebrows over and over again. As she gets closer to me, I notice that her 'tache is still firmly in place. How fascinating to know she goes to the effort of a full bikini wax but leaves the hairs on her face to thrive. I can now see that Chloe is listening too. She comes over. There is now a huddle of women around my desk whispering about their pubic hair.

'Landing strip for me,' Chloe says, flooring Renée, whose

jaw has hit the floor. 'I have a great girl in St Martin who does it for me if you need a recommendation. She's a honey, we have such a laugh when she does it. Sometimes I even book the last appointment of the day so we can go for a cocktail after. Wax and Cocktails, that would be a good name for a salon, wouldn't it?' Georgina finds this hilarious, and she and Chloe share this moment in the most bizarre representation of the female bond I think I have ever seen.

'Anyway, good luck on the date,' Georgina says, heading off to the loos.

'Oooh, I might go too, before my call,' says Chloe, following her. Renée and I watch them both walk away. I look over to Phil, he didn't seem to hear any of that, thank God. Renée is still standing there, unable to find her words. 'Was there anything else?' I say loudly and professionally. She turns around like a zombie, and heads back to her desk.

'Hi Flo,' says Phil, as I walk outside at the end of the day. The way he says my name is so nice. I always thought he was quite shy, but I think it's a sign of being quite self-assured, when you use someone's name to address them. People don't do that enough. I'm going to do it more.

'Hi Phil,' I reply, confidently.

He tells me he's booked a table at the fancy Chinese on the front. I've had takeaway from there loads of times, but never eaten in the restaurant. This feels very grown-up. We walk, making polite chitchat about various shops, cafés and bars we like. I feel like people are looking at me and wondering if Phil is my boyfriend, but of course they are not. Why do I do that? I'm such a private person and consider myself fundamentally shy, yet I have enough arrogance, or anxiety, or whatever it is, to suspect everyone around me is thinking negative thoughts about me. Why do I presume they care? I just do. It's exhausting, I want it to stop. I try to shake those thoughts out of my head, and concentrate on being reasonable company for Phil. He asked me out. He wants me here.

'I love this place,' he says when we arrive at the restaurant. He's looking around and smiling, like this room is full of fabulous memories. 'My mum and I come here a lot.'

'Oh, that's nice,' I say. Wondering if it is cute or weird that he brought me to the place he likes to go with his mum. I decide it's cute, for the sake of my nerves. 'Whereabouts are you from on the island?'

'I was born in St Sampson. My dad owned a fleet of lorries and his yard was up near L'Ancresse. It's weird, but we rarely came to town when I was growing up. It always felt like so far away when actually it's a six-minute drive.'

He laughs. I laugh. We laugh together.

'Shall we get a drink?' I say, needing one urgently. We order a bottle of white wine and when it comes, I drink the first glass quickly to acclimatise. He fills my glass up again, which I think is very nice of him. I try to drink the next glass a little more gracefully. This isn't a night out, it's a date, there is a difference.

'I drink when I'm nervous,' I tell him, a little looser.

Suddenly feeling like I need to explain why I drink so much when I'm with him.

'I think we all do,' he says. 'Alcohol has a terrible way of making us feel better in the moment. The amount of times I've said, "I will regret this tomorrow" but keep going anyway.'

'Me too, me too. I sometimes think I won't drink tonight and then . . . three bottles later!' I laugh. He sort of laughs. 'Three bottles is a lot,' he says, and I nod because it is.

'My dad drank a lot. He died, actually, at forty-two. He didn't take care of himself. A lot of drinking, a lot of smoking, and the most aerobic thing I ever saw him do was chase one of my sister's boyfriends down the road.' He laughs, but I don't find it funny.

'My dad died too,' I say. 'I'm so sorry about yours. Mine didn't look after himself either.'

'I know about your dad, Flo, you told me all about it that night at your flat. Do you not remember?'

'Oh, of course,' I say, flippantly. 'Silly me.' I could die of shame. I told him about Dad when I was drunk? Oh God, poor Phil, poor Dad. Oh, this is horrible.

'You were very open with me. It was lovely.' OK, it was lovely, maybe things are all right. 'Look at us, though, they'd be proud, don't you think? The best we can do is not follow in their footsteps. Do you exercise?'

'I run to the fridge,' I say, sounding like Renée and finding myself hilarious. Phil laughs too. I changed the mood all by myself, Renée would be proud. This is going well. He raises his glass.

'To our dads.'

'To our dads.'

'And to us.'

'And to us.' I feel some tears gather at the back of my eyes but manage to keep them in.

'I wish our dads hadn't died but I am grateful for this connection, it doesn't happen very often,' Phil says. And we both sit in silence for a few seconds. I feel a responsibility to move the conversation on.

'So, what do you think of the new notebooks I ordered?' I say. He looks up quickly, as if I must be joking to say something so unthinkably lame. He pauses and realises I wasn't. I imagine the look on my face is something between shame and needing to go to the toilet. '"Notebooks"? Wow,' I laugh, 'that's my very own "I carried a watermelon".'

He laughs. I am so relieved. '*Dirty Dancing,*' he says, 'I love that movie. My sister used to watch it all the time. I pretended not to, but secretly loved it. Maybe later we can try and do the lift down on the High Street?' I laugh far too loudly. I even snort. It's the kind of laugh that silences us both again. Like we need to let the air settle after I disrupted it. We look at the menu. He asks me if there's anything I don't like, and when I say no, he just orders for us. Probably what he and his mum eat when they come here. It's OK, I tell myself. That doesn't have to be unsexy.

'I'm sorry if you felt embarrassed after the other night, Flo,' he says, taking me by surprise. 'I realise you were very drunk, and I felt like we should probably talk about it.'

I pick up a prawn cracker and direct it towards my

mouth. The waiter sets down some chicken satay on skewers. I am so relieved that I can continue to put things into my mouth so there is no pressure for me to speak. I have wanted to know what happened that night every second of every day for a week, but now he is sitting opposite me, I don't think I can handle the conversation. I push far too much of the skewer into my mouth and stab myself in the back of the throat. I violently cough, wondering if I have permanently punctured my larynx. I down another full glass of wine to try to clear it away. Phil calls the waitress over to get me some water, instead I reach for his wine and drink that too.

'Wow, sorry about that,' I say, eventually getting my voice back. He's been trying not to look at me for about five minutes, I should have just gone to the toilet. 'Those skewers are long. What were we saying? Oh yes, Guernsey. It's very pretty, no, small. NO, sorry, it's bigger than what you thought, or something. What was it?' I casually pick up the bottle and refill our glasses, his first, to be polite.

'No, Flo, I . . . What I was saying was—'

'Phil, it's fine. We don't have to talk about it. I'm cool, you're cool. Let's just be cool, cool?' I offer him two thumbs up to highlight my point. Who the hell do I think I am, the Fonz?

'I think there may have been some confusion. You don't remember what happened, well I want to assure you I don't take adv—'

'Don't remember? Of course I remember!' I say, sternly. Why, I'm not sure. He knows I don't remember because I asked him if we had sex. And I want to know, and this was my chance to find out, so why the fuck am I ruining it?

'Oh, OK. It's just that I thought you said you . . . but if you remember then that's great. OK, phew,' he says, looking enormously relieved. 'Everything is fine then.'

'Totally fine,' I confirm, kicking myself. I could have had all the answers and now I will never know. I still have no idea if we kissed or did anything sexual. I signal to the waitress for another bottle of wine. 'Sorry, I presume you want more white?' I say, raising my eyebrows.

'Sure,' he says. I detect hesitation but order it anyway. 'It's a school day tomorrow though, so this will be the last one for me.'

So sensible. It's quite hot. I imagine him in thirty years being the driver when we go to friends' houses for dinner parties. He will watch me socialise and think 'look at my wonderful wife, always the life and soul of the party'. And then he will drive me home and tell me I am cute when I am drunk. I shake my face and stop thinking about the future Mr and Mrs Phil.

The rest of dinner goes well, I think. I did spill a glass of water across the table, but the waitress came over pretty quickly to mop it up. It made me laugh. Phil stood up, his chair made a loud scraping noise. Everyone turned to look. Phil didn't really laugh, but none of the water landed on him so it was OK. At the end we got fortune cookies. Phil's said he was likely to make some money soon. Mine said, 'All the answers you need are right there in front of you.' Such bollocks.

We split the bill. I made a song and dance about insisting, even though he didn't offer to pay.

'Shall we go to a bar?' I ask, as we leave the restaurant. It's still light, a beautiful summer's evening. It feels like we're emerging from underground. I hold onto Phil's arm.

'We can, but I'm done drinking now. I have a pitch tomorrow.'

'Oh come on, it's only eight p.m. The sun hasn't even set yet. I'll have you all tucked up in bed by nine, let's go for one more.'

He smiles cheekily and agrees. 'OK, one more. Because you asked so nicely.'

We arrive at Albion Tavern. Having got our drinks at the bar, we make our way into a smaller room, heading for a table in the far corner. But unbeknownst to me there's a huge step that divides the room and I fall off it and collapse like a building that's been detonated. 'Flo, bloody hell!' Phil says, bending down to me. My drink has gone everywhere. Someone starts rubbing me down with blue paper towels. I pretend to be totally fine and laugh maniacally, saying things like 'Phew! That could have been terrible.' And, 'I think I owe you all a drink.' I stand up with the help of Phil, and hobble over to the empty table. The barman comes over with a glass of water and asks if I'm all right.

'Totally fine,' I tell him. 'I just lost my footing.' Phil looks to the barman and assures him we won't be ordering any more drinks.

'Flo, drink some more water?'

'Why?'

'You're not being very . . . you again.'

'Very "me again"? What does that mean?'

'Flo, please, drink the water.'

'Oh, all right.' I pick up the pint of water and down it in huge glugs. Phil tries to stop me. 'No Flo, not like that, you'll hurt yourself.' I slam the glass down, attracting more attention from the barman. And then a sharp pain shoots across my chest, like I'm being stabbed. I grab the sides of the table and screech as tears pour from my eyes.

The barman rushes over, he looks mad. Phil says something about it being gas, that I drank my water too quickly. That he will get me out as soon as I have caught my breath. The pain gets so bad, I drop to all fours and arch my back, then lower it in an attempt to get the air out. Eventually, I silence the rest of the bar with a huge, satisfying belch.

'I'm sorry,' I say outside, the air hitting my face. 'That was embarrassing, and I am embarrassed.'

We walk down the high street. I loop my arm around Phil's and lean on him to disguise any unsteadiness.

'It's OK,' he says, squeezing my shoulders. 'I did warn you not to drink that quickly, but at least you're all right. You seem to have sobered up a bit too, I think? That good old Guernsey air.'

'Sure,' I say, because I think that's what I should say. 'Will you walk back with me?'

'Of course.'

We get to the door of the flat. 'Shall I see you up?' he

says, chivalrous as ever. I try to act sober as we walk up the stairs.

'Renée isn't home, the flat is all ours,' I say, knowing what I want to do and hoping he wants the same. 'Nightcap?'

'Sure, but just one.'

While Phil waits in the living room, I make some drinks in the kitchen. I make two very strong vodka sodas and down them both. I'm nervous again all of a sudden. Phil is here, he came back, are we going to have sex? I make two more drinks, normal strength this time.

'Would you like to come upstairs with me?' I say boldly, handing Phil one of the drinks. *I can do this, I can do this.*

I hear a voice, like I'm underwater and someone is shouting from above. The voice speaks again.

'Flo, seriously. I told you if you did that again, I'd leave.' I see someone standing over me. A man. A big blur that slowly comes into focus. It's Phil, he's doing up his trousers. Where am I? Did I zone out from the booze?

'What?' I ask. Was I asleep?

'You heard me. We were kissing and it was so nice, and then . . . I . . . I told you three times I didn't want to do that, but you kept pushing it. I mean it, Flo, I'm going to go home.'

I can't have been asleep. What was I doing? I realise my trousers are on the floor, my ladybird shirt is open. What just happened?

'What did I do?' I ask, coming round.

HONEYBEE

'What game are you playing, Flo?'

'Game? What game?' I ask, reaching for my trousers and pulling them back on. I do up my shirt, as I try to remember something, anything. These blackouts happen, I wake up in a different world. 'Phil, I'm really sorry.'

He rubs his hands over his face. 'Look, it's fine. I just, how many times did I have to tell you I don't like that? I'm going home, I'll see you at work. Dinner was nice. The rest of the night . . . I dunno Flo, I think you . . . it's not my place to say. Get some sleep, I'll see you at work.' He leaves.

'DON'T SLAM THE FRONT DOOR!' I shout after him. He doesn't, because he is nice. I lie back on my bed, my head thumping for so many reasons. What the hell did I do? No matter how much I try to remember, I can only recall getting home, downing the two drinks in the kitchen. It's 10.30, an entire hour just gone.

The door of the flat flies open, Renée is home. She pounds up the stairs and nudges open my bedroom door.

'Just saw Phil on the way out, he seemed stressed. Was tonight OK?'

'Fine. Yup. He just has a presentation tomorrow. Tea?'

I go into the kitchen, put on the kettle and get two mugs ready. As I stand there waiting for the kettle to boil, the rat comes to life in my belly again. It pulls and scratches at my insides, trying to get up my throat. Its red eyes burning holes, its sharp teeth trying to bite. No breath will calm it down this time. I open the cupboard to the left of the sink. There is a half-empty bottle of vodka. The rat flinches at the sight of it. As the kettle gets louder, I reach for a glass. I pour as much of the vodka as will fit and drink it all in one go.

I'm not going to let that rat wake up again. I'm going to kill it.

15

Renée

It's the weekend and the weather is gorgeous. A perfect summer's day. I put on some cut-off denim shorts and a red vest. It's boring, but I turn the shorts up extra-high so I feel light on my feet, pretty and happy. I have a mission to complete today but, first, I decide to do something very grown-up and buy a Sunday paper and pop into Dix Neuf for a coffee and a croissant.

As I walk in, I see Mrs Mangel sitting at a table in the corner. Damn it, what a buzzkill. I take a seat at the only table left, just behind her. She sees me, we smile awkwardly at each other. Things are a little less tense since she saw me in her wedding dress, but we're a long way from joining each other for breakfast. She looks snazzy again. A green shirt with a large brooch and a pink scarf wrapped around her head. As always, she has her make-up on, rosy cheeks with bright lips. She's always alone, I wonder why she bothers to get so dressed up.

The place is busy but calm. A very different sight to the weekdays where there is loud chatter and a constant stream of people coming in and out. I find myself glancing over at the old lady, fascinated by her. She's reading a copy of the *Telegraph* very intensely. I am so terrible at reading papers, I skim the politics and read all the silly little articles about people who get stuck in trees or marry their cousins. She has hers laid out on the table, above her plate. I do the same with mine, maybe I can learn a thing or two from her. Let's just brush over the fact that the paper I got is the *News of The World*. I'm acting like a grown-up, and it feels very nice.

I read the menu and think I'll treat myself to scrambled eggs on toast and a cup of tea. When it comes, I squirt ketchup onto my eggs, and swoop the bread up and around, then stare back at my newspaper and pretend to read it. This is a new Renée on Guernsey, where I don't just lie in bed all Sunday morning or ride a bike around aimlessly until someone else cooks me food. I like this version of me, it's civilised. All that's missing is someone to do it with.

And then a sound fills the air. A sound so loud, so full, so vulgar that it can only be one thing.

It's a fart.

A massive, enormous fart.

'What the f . . .' says a man at the table beside me,

turning his head sharply to Mrs Mangel, along with everyone else in the café. No one is mistaken, that fart resounded right out of her bottom, and her bright red face is all the confirmation anyone needs. No one knows what to do, it's such a shock. The force of it. The volume. How did a little old lady create that deafening sound? A few people shake their heads, as if disgusted. Two young teenagers giggle as their mother kicks them under the table. Mrs Mangel looks terrified, and like she might cry. She's gathering her things. She's trying to get money out of her wallet, but her hands are trembling. I can't remember if music was playing, but now it's silent. I feel bad for her, she must be so embarrassed. I want to help her, but how?

I have an idea.

I laugh.

I laugh as hard as I can. I bang the table with my fist and allow tears to pour down my face. And as I laugh, I get up and walk over to her table. I take a seat, and I look deep into her petrified eyes as I laugh even harder. I call upon her happiness with mine, and eventually it comes. Her eyes brighten, her mouth reaches up at the corners and a full, throaty cackle pours out of her mouth. It takes just seconds for almost everyone else in the café to join in, and before long we are all, somehow, sharing a moment of total joy.

We find humour in a fart. Like a bunch of kids when someone lets rip in a classroom. A fart so loud, that people would talk about it for years. A fart like all farts should be, so funny that a group of strangers abandon all their social graces, just to laugh. Is there anything more liberating?

'Don't worry love, it happens to us all,' says a man who had originally barked in disgust.

'I'd have paid money to have something make me laugh like this today. Made my bloody day,' says a lady from another table.

'Your breakfast is on me,' says the guy behind the counter. 'Yours too love,' he says to me, still chuckling to himself. Mrs Mangel is giggling too, she looks completely different. 'You're welcome,' she says to people on her way out. Which they find even funnier. Her face is now its original colour. We walk a little down the street together, still chuckling.

'I've lived around here for my whole life,' she says as we get outside. 'What a way to finally make a name for myself, eh?'

'Your bum will be the talk of the town, toots,' I say, jokingly. She laughs again. She's so relaxed, like a different person.

'Thank you, Renée. That was a brave reaction. I've not laughed like that in so many years, I had forgotten how it feels.'

'I couldn't bear to see you sitting there looking so embarrassed. There was a time in all our lives when farts were the funniest thing imaginable. When did we decide to make them the worst?'

'Grown-ups, we ruin everything, don't we?'

'We do,' I say, enjoying being called a grown-up by someone I presumed saw me as a kid. 'Can I walk you home?'

'No, thank you. It's beautiful. I'm going to enjoy the sunshine for an hour or two. I don't work on Sundays.'

'You work?'

'Yes Renée, of course I work. I am a dressmaker and do alterations. Have you not heard the loud buzz of my sewing machine?'

'No, never.'

'You're surprised, aren't you? That I am my age and that I still work.'

'I . . .'

'It's OK, it's unusual. You must think I am a terrible bore complaining about the noise of the door, but when it bangs, I jump, and I do wonky stitching.'

'I understand, I'm sorry.'

'Hopefully you'll be long retired by the time you're my age. I'd much rather be out on the town like you girls.'

'So *why* do you still work?'

'Ha, Renée, what a funny question. I work to pay the bills, of course. My husband is in a care home, it's expensive. He's been there eight years, I'll have to work until he . . . well . . . You know, I have to keep the money coming in.'

How could I have got this person so wrong. I guess it goes to show that if all you ever do is tell people off, they're going to think the worst of you.

'I'm sorry about your husband,' I say. 'What's the matter with him?'

'Alzheimer's. He hasn't known my name for over four years. But I still visit every day, because you have to, don't you?'

'My gran had that too. She was mad as a box of frogs.'

'Yes, he says some very funny things. I can laugh about it, sometimes. My name is Lillian, by the way.'

'Hi Lillian,' I say. 'Enjoy your day.'

'You too. And thanks again, that was very brave what you did in there. To support someone rather than laugh at them. Unusual. You're a lovely woman, Renée.' I buckle at being called a woman. It feels silly and weird and like she's got me all wrong. 'I hope you have someone special in your life, Renée. A lovely man to give you everything you deserve.'

'I'm working on it, Lillian. It's complicated, but I think it's going to be OK.'

'All the best love stories are complicated, Renée. Just don't lose yourself in the quest for love. There is nothing more attractive to a man than a woman who knows her worth. Have a lovely day.'

I watch her walk away. An entirely different person to who I thought she was.

The terrible thing about being in love with your boss is that you have access to personal information on the work computer and therefore know exactly where he lives and have calculated that it would take exactly twenty-three minutes to cycle there if I borrow Aunty Jo's bike. The house is on the coast road in Castel, just down from Vazon Bay. A lovely place to be cycling, should someone see me and ask me what I'm doing there. 'Just enjoying the island,' is all I have to say. 'Ben, really? He lives nearby. How HILARIOUS.'

HONEYBEE

I have it all planned. Which is how I find myself just down the road, staring at a cute house. A detached two-storey with a garden that wraps around the whole thing. There are a couple of kids' scooters in the front porch. Down the side of the house is a surfboard, which turns me on. Just the thought of Ben on a surfboard makes me want to rip my knickers off. The house looks new. It's not wildly interesting as a building, but I guess if you're from London and have two kids, this simple, functional house, a stone's throw from a golf course and a beach, is probably the lap of total luxury. As a born-and-bred islander, though, this wouldn't be my taste at all. I see Ben and me in a large Guernsey farmhouse made of traditional granite, with six windows along the top and four on the bottom with a colourful front door. Ivy would crawl up the house, roses on the lawn. I'd wave him off to work every morning, maybe a toddler by my feet, a baby in my arms. I'd sit in the kitchen all day, close to the Aga for warmth, and I'd write books while the children sleep.

Why is it that in my fantasies I'm so wildly different from who I am in real life? I don't know if that's who I wish I was, who I really am, or that I'm horribly delusional. Either way, it's where my imagination takes me and I'm happy to go along with it.

I park my bike up and sit up on the seawall. I have a perfect view of the house, but I'm far enough away that Ben won't see me if he's home. Home. I've never truly felt at home. Growing up, I was always in 'Pop's house.' He never made life easy. For Pop, love and anger went hand in hand.

He loved so hard that it made him cross, like an aggressive tiger protecting his young. He only knew one way, to defend. At the time it was hard, but I see it now, that everything he did came from a place of love. Loving everyone but himself. When I moved in with Aunty Jo, I felt welcome and safe, but disjointed and sad. Only because I would imagine the other kids my age and know that they'd likely had the same bedroom their whole lives, eaten breakfast at the same table, come home to the same amount of people in their family. But by the time I was eighteen, I'd lost a dad, a mum, and I'd moved house three times. I think now, if I was to be really honest with myself, I am programmed for change, but I crave stability. A family that stays still, a home that feels like my own.

    I duck behind the wall as a car drives past me and turns into the drive. Ben steps out from the driver's seat; he's in casual clothes. Tracksuit bottoms and a surf T-shirt. Gorgeous, as ever. He helps two little girls out of the car. One hurries to the porch, where the door is opened by someone I can't see. Ben carries the other child in, holding her up in the air and making her laugh as he goes. The front door closes, and the family is inside. Those little girls are safe and secure. Two parents who love them, a home that is theirs. It's the dream. And yet, Ben can't keep his hands off me. Maybe there is unhappiness in every home. Doubt in every spouse. The threat of disconnection just one power cut away.

    What am I doing?

    I jump down from the wall and get back on my bike. As I cycle back to Aunty Jo's, I take in the world around me.

HONEYBEE

Bees buzzing in the hedgerows, boxes of produce for sale from people's gardens. The air feels silky, the sky bright blue. As I glide along the roads, the various smells waft over me, from honeysuckle to the salty sea. The roads are calm, the cars drive slowly. The island breathes gently beneath us, holding us all up. I think I'm falling in love with Ben, and maybe I'm falling more and more in love with Guernsey too.

16

Flo

Work has been awful. I don't look at Phil and he doesn't look at me. It's Renée's fault. If she hadn't forced me to overstep my own personal boundaries and go for office drinks on that first Friday, none of this would have happened. People who work in offices cannot drink alcohol together because they WILL end up fucking. It's a fact and I knew it and I have proved my theory right and now I am entangled in a horrible, dark and twisted mess. I'm haunted by what I did to Phil to make him so cross. How bad was it to make him angry enough to leave? The only thing I can think of is trying to stick my finger up his bum. I have never wanted to do that to anyone, but I do think about it. At university I had quite a slutty friend called Karen.

She was obsessed with sex. She once said her boyfriend liked 'a finger up the bum when he cums' and now I think maybe her words came back to me that night when I was drunk. That I tried to be someone I'm not with Phil and tried to insert my finger into his anus against his will. Oh God, just the thought of it makes me want to cry.

I open my drawer quickly and peer inside, just checking the Gordon's gin minis are there. Alcohol is the only thing that offers me respite from the breakdown that I know will consume me if I allow it to. I know people have noticed. I know I haven't kept this a secret. I know what I'm doing isn't right, but even people knowing isn't worse than me not drinking. Everyone on this island drinks – who's to say it's just me with the problem? Binge drinking is part of the culture, and yet when I do it, people get all weird with me. I can't cope right now without it. It won't be forever. What's so wrong with a coping mechanism that gets me through a tough time?

I have dinner with my mother tonight. I have to go because my sister Abi will be there and I've barely managed to catch up with her since I got back to Guernsey. Mum texted me yesterday to remind me and I just replied with the word 'yes'. I'll put on my big girl pants and try not to look her in the eye.

Mum and I can be cordial if we try. But it isn't real. When I left for uni she changed a bit. She acknowledged she should have done better, but she soon lost momentum for making any effort once I was out of sight. We kept in touch, largely by text. Maybe a phone call once a month, but she generally put me on loudspeaker when she had a friend over, and we'd both give our best performances to make them think we are a normal family.

The more I think about how she was when I was a kid – the way she rejected me, didn't help me when Dad died, allowed a headmistress to tell me he had been found dead outside his house rather than tell me herself – the more I want to attack her. I don't mean physically, I mean with words. I want to tell her she failed. That she is a disgrace of a mother. That I don't believe I will ever truly be comfortable in myself, because of her dismissal of my feelings. I want to tell her what a shit mum she is. But the problem is, she isn't a shit mum. She's a brilliant mum to Abi. Who, to the best of my knowledge, had a perfectly happy childhood with a mum who loved her very much. Mum dumped Dad soon after Abi was born, so without him around, she actually got to enjoy motherhood and Abi was none the wiser.

It's just how it is. I have to accept it and take advantage of her guilt-fuelled olive branches, like the one she is reaching out with tonight. Dinner in a fancy restaurant for the three of us. A 'Girls' Night' as she so agonisingly put it. The problem is, no matter how much you deny it, the relationship you have with your mother will be the backbone to your entire existence. Unluckily for me, that means my backbone is broken. It says a lot about the state of my life.

Renée

My head, body and soul are fully submerged in this crush. I think about nothing but Ben. I dream about Ben. I think about touching him when I'm in the shower. I pretend to be on my phone when I'm walking to work so I can have imaginary conversations with Ben. I have imagined our wedding. I have imagined our children. I had never imagined I would be this person.

Something is building, I can feel it. Every time he walks by me, every time we pretend that we need to be in the kitchen at the same time, every time one of us deliberately walks too close so we can touch, every time he comes to ask me to do something when he could email me, it draws us closer and closer. Everything he does, everything, makes me want to go back in time, find the person who invented lifts, and thank them endlessly for creating the tiny box that forced this amazing man into my life.

Amazing, apart from his wife.

I try not to think about her. He told me it was complicated. He isn't happily married. It's not my fault. He's not a bad person. If it hadn't been for the lift getting stuck, this would never have happened. I truly, to the bottom of my heart, believe that. This is cosmic. It was given to us. It isn't something we can control.

My thoughts are wild, and I have to hide them all. I wonder what horrendous, cruel and inappropriate things I would hear if I stepped into anyone else's head in this office. I bet Chloe is planning her next workout. I bet Georgina craves filthy sex as much as she craves doughnuts. I bet Matt wanks about me in the toilets. I bet . . .

'Flo?' I say, standing up as she walks into reception. She looks a bit wild, like she's just run up and down a mountain five times. I switch the phones to 'out-of-office' and drag her into the toilet, locking the door. 'Flo, your hair is down, what is going on?'

'I just wear it down sometimes, I'm fine.'

'No, you don't. You never wear your hair down because you think it makes your nose look big.'

'Does my nose look big?'

'No, Flo, it never does. But you're clearly consumed with something else to be so chilled about wearing it down, so what is going on?'

She sighs and drags her hands down her face. 'It's driving me mad, Renée. What did I do? What did I do to him?'

'Oh God, not this again. You have to let this go. I'm sure the date was fine, lovely even. Come on, get to your desk, focus on work, then have a nice dinner with your mum and Abi tonight. Try not to think about Phil.'

'I'm not going tonight. I just want to go to bed and have a breakdown on my own.'

'Oh no way, you're absolutely going.'

'Why? My mum will just find another way to disappoint me and I'll feel even worse. Can't we just stay in and watch *Dirty Dancing* or something?'

'Look, why don't you go home now, I'll tell everyone you're ill. Go to bed, get some rest, have your breakdown or whatever it is you have to do, then go to dinner. I'm not denying your mum is an arsehole, but Abi will be gutted if you don't go. Do it for her?'

'I have to empty the dishwasher in the kitchen.'

'I will do that.'

'Will you get new milk? Semi-skimmed, must be local.'

'Flo go, OK, I'll handle it all.'

I steer her outside and watch her walk away in the direction of the flat. It's lunchtime, that's plenty of time for her to chill out before dinner. Ben must have seen me leave with her because when I turn to come back in, he is standing by the lift.

I look at him. He looks at me.

Oh God.

'Any idea how to make one of these things break down?' he says.

There are no more words. He presses the button and steps inside. I follow, feeling faint.

We kiss immediately. We have resisted each other and tried to hold back so many times. We have behaved. We have been gentle. We have been safe. But now it's real, it's raw. Holding back is impossible now. This thing, whatever it is, has to happen.

'Ben, Flo will be out tonight. From six. If you're free, maybe you can come over?' I say, pulling my mouth away while he kisses my neck and squeezes my body with his hands.

'Yes,' he says without hesitation as the doors ping open. Reality forcing us apart. 'I'll get your address from the system. See you at 6.30. Can't wait.'

He goes back to his desk. I dissolve into a puddle on the floor.

I thought maybe the ball gown was a bit much for a night in, so I've gone with denim shorts and a T-shirt. I want to look cute but not like I'd tried too hard. I want Ben to see what I'm like at home. Wife material. Relaxed, casual, sexual. Flo is out for dinner. For a moment I thought she wouldn't go, but she did. She knows she can't avoid her mum forever. I think she'll end up having a nice time and maybe things between them will get easier. I heard Lillian go out at 6.15, which is perfect because I wouldn't know what to say if she opened her door when Ben arrives, or how to introduce him.

At 6.30 exactly, the doorbell rings. I freeze for a second. How do I answer the door? I feel like Hollywood has been preparing me for this moment all my life, but I've forgotten everything. I will open the door slowly and smile casually. I won't say anything. But that's weird, there is no need to be weird. We will walk up the stairs holding hands, I'll lead. I will open the door, we will go inside the flat, we will shut the door then he will push me against it, and we will stay there until we have had our first glorious fuck. After that, we will laugh, and I will show him into the kitchen where I will make us some drinks. And we will drink them. And then we will fuck again on the kitchen table. Halfway through I'll lead him upstairs. And then, in my room, we will fuck and fuck until we can fuck no more.

What actually happens is that I slip on the stairs and bump down four of them on my bottom, it hurts. I open the door and I'm clearly sore. 'If you heard that, I didn't fall, I danced. I danced down those stairs and I looked amazing,' I say, rubbing my buttock.

'I heard nothing,' he says, lying.

Ben is nervous, I can tell. He knows why he is here but doesn't want to presume anything. He might be cheating on his wife, but he is also a gentleman. This whole thing has been a good lesson in realising two things can be true at once. While screwing one person over, you can be making someone else very happy. Surely it would be worse to make no one happy? At least he is putting something good into the world. That being his penis in my vagina, any minute now, hopefully. He is holding a bottle of red. So classy. We walk up the stairs without saying much. My heart is beating hard, I feel silly and like I don't know what to do. A feeling that this is sordid creeps over me. An affair, what am I doing? Nothing about this can end well. Where did he tell his wife he'd be tonight? But he is here, this is a decision we made together, good or bad.

We walk into the living room. I look at the couch, wondering if I should throw myself onto it and demand he joins me. Damn it, I should be wearing a nightie, not shorts. But I don't seem to want to do that. Maybe I'm a little worried he won't do what I say. Hollywood makes these moments look so much easier than they are in real life.

'This place is cute,' he says, looking around. 'I didn't realise you were such a hippie?'

'Oh, I'm not. It's Flo's brother's place, he's travelled loads. I've never been to any of the places, apart from Spain. Drink?'

'Sure.'

I go into the kitchen, and he follows me in. We must be thinking the same thing. When do we kiss? When do we do what we came here to do? I struggle with the cork. 'Here,' he says, 'let me.' He pops it out effortlessly, it's so sexy. I open the bottle of red wine and pour it into two proper wine glasses. Usually, Flo and I drink out of tumblers because we are so clumsy and knock them over all the time. I pass him one, we say cheers and take a sip. This is very sophisticated. This isn't how I imagined it. More than ever, I'm certain that Ben hasn't done anything like this before. I know what men who want to get laid are like, they come on strong physically. Ben has a whole life at stake. Is he thinking about his wife? His kids? Is he wondering how he got here? A random power cut offered him an opportunity and he took it. He didn't go looking for this. He never hit on me at work, or anything inappropriate, we just had a bizarre bonding experience that landed us in the position of liking each other. It's real attraction. Who are we to turn down such an aggressive call of nature? But still, what to do next . . . I really have no idea.

'I could make meatballs?' I say, bending down to get a frying pan out of the cupboard. I freeze when I get to my knees. 'I can't believe I just offered to cook us meatballs,' I say, looking at him apologetically, but also laughing. 'I'm so nervous.'

Ben exhales a huge breath. I can almost hear his anxiety leave him. He sits down on a chair and relaxes. 'Meatballs, the ultimate ice-breaker,' he says. 'I'm nervous too.'

'Maybe we should just . . .'

'Kiss?'

He stands up, presses me against the sink and kisses me. He holds my face. He stops to kiss my cheeks, my neck. He looks into my eyes. He kisses me more. 'I've been wanting this so much, wanting you.'

'Me too,' I say, as his lips leave mine. 'It's all I've wanted for so long.'

I don't feel shy to tell him how I feel. I don't want to play games. I just want him to know that I cannot and will not resist him. I take his hand, and I lead him upstairs.

Flo

'Flo!' says Abi excitedly, running towards me with her arms wide. I'm so happy to see her. She will always be, no matter how grown-up she looks, my baby sister. The one person I can always pull myself together for. The one person I will always stay strong for. I feel my power come back a little as I hug her. My feet find their place on the ground, as if real love, without question, does exist in my life.

'You look amazing,' I tell her. She's a little shorter than me, five foot four, but in that pre-teen phase where she's still growing into her limbs. She has perfectly plump and pretty cheeks that look squashed by her constant smile. Her hair is dark and curly, she's wearing blue jeans and a red jumper. She looks well put together and happy. Her backbone is not broken.

Mum hovers behind her, doing a weird smile that has given her three extra chins. She is looking at us like mothers should, but I know she just wants to get her hug with me out of the way so she can sit down and order some wine.

'Flo,' she says, holding out her arms. 'Mum,' I reply, moving myself towards her. Our bodies touch as we embrace. It's gentle but makes the sound of a thousand cymbals crashing together. I can't believe I'm the only one who heard it.

'So, Abi has exciting news, don't you darling?' Mum says, as we all sit down. A waiter asks me what I would like, and I order a glass of champagne. Mum tries not to react, and I refuse to look fazed. She's brought me to a posh place to make herself feel better about our relationship. The bill is not my concern.

'You do?' I ask Abi.

'Yup. I got the main part in the school play. It's about a creature that wakes up in a strange forest and has to get home. I'm the creature,' she says, bursting with self-pride. I am so relieved that she's too young to enter into the world of lewd sex acts that she can't even remember. I hope she bypasses this stage entirely, and goes straight from being adorable to being an adult without these terrible complications.

'Congratulations,' I say, raising the glass of champagne

that is now in front of me. I clink my glass with her Diet Coke and sense Mum is trying not to say something. The words fighting like a tiny monkey trapped in her mouth, making her cheeks ripple. Eventually she just can't hold it in.

'Abi's going to do so well. I joked to her form teacher that she has all the hallmarks of an Oxbridge student and she said "absolutely, she does". I cried right there on the spot.' Here we go. 'She's head and shoulders above her class, aren't you love? It's very exciting to think about what you'll achieve in the future.' Abi smiles sweetly and accepts the compliment. She doesn't see half of the things Mum throws at me because she's never had them thrown at her. I finish my glass of champagne, call the waiter over and order a whole bottle. Mum flinches again. *Is she really doing this?* I can hear her think.

Yes, I am. I really am.

'So Mum, how's your job going?' I ask facetiously. Mum hasn't worked since she married a guy called Andrew then divorced him and rinsed him for half his cash. She coughs awkwardly and chooses not to answer me.

'Order whatever you like. It's so rare I have both of my girls together, I thought we deserved a treat,' she says, staring at the champagne like someone has just put a live chicken on the table.

'Thanks Mum,' Abi says sweetly. Mum pauses, as if waiting for me to add my praise.

'Yeah, thanks Andrew,' I say, which causes her to put her glass down a little too hard. She blows out her nose like a bull and scrapes her top teeth across her bottom lip. It's like watching a kettle boil, but no steam is escaping. It gives me a jolt of pleasure. The rat springs into action. I'm drunk now, and the one person in the world I enjoy upsetting is my mother. She got me at the end of the wrong week.

'Can I take your order?' our waiter says, slicing through our hatred.

'I'll get a ham sandwich,' I say to him. I haven't even looked at the menu. It's just what I want.

'I'm sorry, we don't do sandwiches.'

'Don't or can't? Because if you can't, it's very easy, I could come and show the chef the basics?'

'Flo, darling, have a look at the menu and stop being silly,' Mum says in her stupid fake posh voice. It riles me up even more.

'We *don't* do them,' the waiter says. 'We don't have ham and we don't have sandwich bread. Is there anything else you would like?'

'Right, well, I can fix that,' I say, picking up my bag and storming out of the restaurant. I walk with pace out of the hotel, up the street and to the supermarket which is pleasingly very close by, because I might have aborted this idea if it wasn't. I purchase some bread and some ham and storm back into the restaurant and sit back down. I don't know why I am doing this. I know it's mental. But I appear to be committed.

'There! I say, sitting down and handing the bag to the waiter. All you need for a lovely ham sandwich. I'll have it with chips, please. I assume you have those?'

'We do,' he says, taking the bag into the kitchen, hating me with every inch of his soul. Abi and Mum look like they haven't taken a breath since I left.

'Did you order?' I ask to break the ice. They both nod. I drink some more champagne. I really don't like champagne, it tastes like farts.

'So, Flo, any boyfriends I need to know about?' Mum says, like we're a group of girls who have met for drinks and nibbles and to talk about boys. I buckle at how uncomfortable it makes me feel. I'm not really in the mood to sugar the pill. I want her to realise the mess she made of me.

'No boyfriends, no. But I think I shagged a guy from work last week. Not sure though. You? Any more lovers we should know about?' This time Mum slams her glass down so hard that the stem breaks. The waiter rushes over to clear it up and asks if we would like another bottle. I say 'yes', mum yells 'no!' The waiter appears to be on my side despite the issue with the sandwich.

'Flo!' says Abi, clearly embarrassed. This probably isn't what my little sister needs to hear, but I can't seem to stop the word-vomit. 'What do you mean you *think* you slept with someone?' she says, wondering if I was joking, hoping I was.

'I can't remember if we did or not. It's fine, though, women have one-night stands all the time. There is no reason why I should carry any shame about it. It was as much my experience as it was his. It happens, it's fine, right Mum?' I spurt, as if Renée were feeding me lines through a secret headset.

Mum stands up and brushes her clothes with her hands, as if my words have soiled them in some way.

'Oh Mum sit down, it's just sex.'

'Or no sex?' says Abi.

'Yup, or no sex,' I say, confidently. As if I don't regret saying this at all. I fill my glass up again.

'Flo, can you stop talking about sex in front of Abi!' Mum says sharply. 'And why are you acting like this? Is it because—'

'Because my mother messed me up so badly I can't bear intimacy and don't trust that anyone will ever really love me?'

'OK Flo, come on now,' says Mum, looking at me nervously. I realise I've stood up, so I sit back down. I'm not so drunk that I don't notice she looks scared of me. That wasn't what I was aiming for. I sip some water.

'You can hardly talk about relationships, can you?' I say, trying to sound level-headed.

'I am seeing someone, actually,' she says, proudly. 'And let's not forget I was married to Andrew for four years.'

'And before that?' I ask, hoping the ensuing silence will cause Abi to question Mum's perfection.

'What about *before that*?' says Abi.

'Oh Abi, there is so much you don't know.'

'What do you mean?' she asks, looking so fragile.

'Oh, just that Mum didn't bother telling me herself that Dad had died and then pretty much left me to grieve on my own while she found herself *another* boyfriend.'

'Flo, what are you doing?' Mum says, looking around

nervously. The waiter comes over to ask if we want another drink. Mum says no, I order a gin and tonic.

'I'd visit him,' I say. 'He'd got himself into such a mess. He'd lost his job, his marriage, his self-respect. And you never once went over to see if you could help him. The father of your children, probably someone worth looking out for. And then his heart blew up inside him and you let my headmistress tell me rather than tell me yourself.'

'I couldn't stop her telling you.'

'Any normal mother would have made sure that couldn't happen. Wouldn't they?' I say, the rat crawling up my throat. This time it's really angry, not just at me, but at her.

'I am not a normal mother,' she says, proudly. As if I should be grateful for the fucked-up experience she gave me, rather than one that involved love and understanding.

'Guys, please. Can't we just have a nice time?' says Abi, getting younger and younger by the second. I start to feel bad. But I'm in it now, I'm getting to Mum. It's as addictive as the gin itself.

'Flo, you're obviously carrying a lot of hurt connecting to your dad. And that is understandable, but this isn't the time to take it out on me.'

'Why, because it's embarrassing for you?'

'No, because Abi is here and doesn't need to . . .'

'Doesn't need to know that she is your favourite? And that you do weird things like organise fancy dinners to make yourself feel better about being such a bitch to me?'

'Flo, don't speak to Mum like that,' says Abi, as a vision

of the rat in my stomach flashes in my head. It's got my mother's face.

'OK Flo, enough. He was not my responsibility. I organised tonight so that the three of us could spend some quality time with each other. But you obviously hate me too much to allow that to happen so I think the best thing is that you leave.'

Classic passive-aggressive Mum.

'Oh sure, shut it down. Push it away. Act like it isn't happening, that's what you do, is it? Well maybe *you* should leave? Maybe Abi and I can have a nice dinner together. Right Abs?'

Abi looks at me and shakes her head. 'No Flo,' she says, firmly. She and Mum both stare at me, waiting for my next reaction. I want to sit down and cry and tell them I am sorry. I want to lie to Abi and tell her Mum didn't really abandon Dad. That she was sweet and tender towards me. That I said it all because I'm drunk. That I didn't mean it. But those words don't come. Instead, I pick up my glass, finish my drink, say, 'This family is a fucking joke', and storm out of the restaurant taking my ham sandwich with me. I walk purposefully for about five minutes, long enough for Mum to catch up with me if she tried. She doesn't. I turn around to make sure, but the pavement behind me is empty.

Renée

'You're so comfortable,' I say, pushing myself into Ben. I can't get close enough. He runs his fingers down my spine. My left boob is lying across his chest. He strokes it.

'You have such a gorgeous body, Renée. Everything, every bit of it is perfect.'

He rolls onto his side so he's facing me and reaches down to my bottom, my soft thigh. These moments with men can be hard. When the sex is done and the lights are on, and you're just naked with someone you don't know well. I've wanted to leave these embraces so many times. Worried my bum is too big, my stretch marks are too shiny, my belly too floppy. But with Ben, I know it's what he wants. I can tell. He loves grabbing onto me, he wants every single inch of me. I don't need to be anything else with him. He strokes my face.

'I love this,' he says. I tell him I love it too. 'So, does Flo know?' he asks, catching me off-guard. I wasn't expecting him to care, really. It's not like she's my wife.

'No way,' I say, sitting up. 'I wouldn't do that to you, I promise.'

'It's OK. I wondered if you'd told her. What will be will be. I know that nothing's off limits in the realms of true female friendship.' He smiles at me, as if he would have just accepted it. He's cheating on his wife but he's not trying to pretend this is right, or make me lie, or talk about this like it's the dirtiest secret. 'What will be will be.' He's right, it will.

'Flo has no idea, and I want to keep it that way. She's not in a great place right now, and . . .'

What am I saying? This is Flo's boss. I can't talk to him about her. I stop.

'Oh, why?' he says, sounding concerned for her. Or maybe for his business. I can't believe I said that.

'Oh nothing, really. She's fine.'

'I have to say, I noticed she was being a bit off this week. She seemed distracted. I was going to ask her about it but, well, Flo doesn't give the impression she wants to be asked questions. She's quite private, isn't she?'

'Yes.'

'What's the matter?' he asks, now concerned for me. 'You look worried, is Flo in some sort of trouble?'

'I don't know', I say, giving into the warmth of his body. And the warmth of his heart. 'She's been drinking, I think . . .' Ben sits up quickly.

'Drinking? How much?' He looks really concerned.

'A lot. And all the time. I shouldn't have said anything, it's her business, not mine. Shit Ben, please, forget I said anything.'

He gets out of bed. He seems far more upset about this than he should be.

'It's OK, Ben. She can still do her job. I shouldn't have said anything.'

'OK, OK, but we need to keep our eye on it. Where's your bathroom?'

I tell him and fall back onto my bed. I smell my sheets, they smell of sexy Ben.

I then I hear the toilet flush and the front door slam at the same time. No no no, surely not. Please no. Please say I imagined that slam. I stand up and pull the duvet off the bed, it's been squashed down the side of the mattress. I wrap it around me and hide underneath it. I don't want to face this, I don't want this to happen, but if that door slamming was Flo coming home . . . oh shit! I hear her pounding up the stairs. She bangs on the bathroom door.

'Renée?' she says, 'Are you in there? Let me in.'

I stay quiet. Maybe she'll get bored and go looking for me somewhere else.

'Renée, open the door.' She's slurring and getting annoyed. 'Renée, please. What are you doing in there? I need to talk to you, I need to talk to someone. I just had an awful argument with Mum and I think I tried to put something in Phil's bum-hole. I need you, come on, please open the door.'

I wrap the duvet around me and open my bedroom door slowly.

'You're in there?' she says. 'Well then, who is in the bathroom?'

Ben opens the bathroom door slowly. He is holding our pink hand towel in front of his dick. 'Hi Flo,' he says. 'We should probably have a chat?' She backs away.

'Oh my god. When did this start?' she asks, looking like every last modicum of happiness has been squeezed out of her. 'You shagged Matt *and* Ben from the office. Wow, Renée, a personal best.'

'Flo,' I say, horrified. Ben looks at me in a way I didn't even think he was capable of.

'You shagged Matt?' he asks, softly.

'No, I didn't shag Matt. OKAY? We didn't shag. Can we not use the word "shag" anyway, it's horrible.' Ben is still looking at me. Does he think I'm a slut now? It turns out there is shame in one-night stands when the guy you think you're in love with finds out about them. 'It was in the first week of being at Magic, I didn't know you and I . . . fucking hell I don't have to explain myself. I didn't shag him. You're fucking married, Ben.' He buckles at that. I feel horrible. But also, get lost with the one-way shame.

'Flo, I was going to tell you,' I say, lying. I should have told her when it started. After the power cut, when Ben and I started flirting, I should have told her.

'You were?' she asks. Not believing me. Ben steps back into the bathroom and reaches for a bigger towel to cover himself with. He's so gorgeous; even when things are this dramatic, his body is so distracting.

Flo looks devastated.

'Flo, what happened with your mum?' I ask, softly, realising something bad must have gone down because it's only 8.30. Tears start to pour down her face. They must have had a fight, it's usually why she turns like this.

'What is happening?' she says, gently, obviously referring to the greater picture of her life as if it's all just come crashing down in front of her. Three people on a tiny landing is too many people. None of us knows what to say next. You can't be prepared for a moment like this, you just have to wing it. Flo flips: the sides of her mouth drop, her eyes soften and then close. The depths of her innocence suddenly so vivid. Her sorrow becomes unbearable to share a space with. She turns around and runs down the stairs. A few seconds later, a slam.

'If you need to go, it's OK,' Ben says, suggesting I follow her. But I don't. I stay.

'Ben, about Matt, I . . .'

'Renée, I'm in no position to tell you who you can and can't sleep with outside of this relationship,' he says, being reasonable. But I don't believe him. He looked winded when Flo said it. Just because he knows he has no right to be hurt by it, doesn't mean he isn't.

'All right, but I didn't have sex with him. It's important to me that you know that.'

'Now I know. Let's move on?' he says, nicely pushing past me to get his clothes. 'Shouldn't you go after Flo?'

'I can't leave you with this in the air. I can't. Flo is impossible right now; she doesn't want me to follow her. She'll walk around and blow off steam for a bit, then come home. I'll talk to her tomorrow, on the way to London. It will be better, please don't go.'

'If she has a problem with alcohol, she won't realise it herself. You'll need to help her Renée, she'll need you.'

'I know, and I will. But just for now. While I have you here, please come to bed and fuck my brains out. You're driving me wild just wearing that towel.' I pull him towards me, and we fall back onto the bed.

Part Three

Queen Bee

It's December 1999. A letter arrives on Flo's doormat. It's from Renée in Spain.

Flo, you haven't answered any texts or calls. So I'm trying an old-school letter because up until very recently you really liked sending me those. My address is still the same, I AM STILL THE SAME.

I know you think you hate me, but you don't. I was a dick when I came to stay, I'm sorry, but you can't ignore me forever. I can't keep saying sorry. Here it is one last time: SORRY. Now can we move on?

I've been thinking a lot about the things I said and why I said them. I came to Nottingham hoping that we would have a really nice time together. But there was no 'together'. All you talked about was how busy you were. Really busy with your course, really busy with your job, really busy with literally everything except wanting to be really busy with me. I guess I got jealous. It took me months to save for the flights and get some money together so we could have fun. I was desperate for fun. I wanted to go out, drink stupid amounts, snog boys I didn't know. Do silly things with you. But we couldn't because you were . . . yup, TOO BUSY.

See it from my point of view Flo? Or are you too busy for that too? I was upset. I'd missed you and then you didn't seem to care that I was there.

I see it clearer now I'm back here. We're not the same Renée and Flo that we used to be. Our lives were so entwined in Guernsey. We did everything together, we couldn't escape each other. We were part of the same world, and now we're not. You have your world, I have mine. You're at uni and want to have a career, and I still work in a bar in Spain and dream of being a writer. We are on totally different paths. We are our own women. Aunty Jo said the day you realise you are your own woman is the day you become an adult. She's right, that's what we're doing. We've changed. I can't expect you to behave how I want you to any more, and the same goes the other way around. But do you know what I think? No matter how much we fly off in different directions, there is no Renée without Flo, and there is no Flo without Renée. We need each other to survive. (Stop rolling your eyes Flo, I can see you doing it.) You know it's true.

The fundamental route to our survival as women is our friendship. So answer your fucking phone when I call you and stop being so busy that you'll throw away the best friend you could ever have. THAT'S ME BY THE WAY.

HONEYBEE

I love you. You're my number one.
Friends Forever?
Renée.
P.S. SORRY (OK that really IS the last time).

SEPTEMBER 2001

17

Renée

Aunty Jo has just dropped us off at the airport. Flo and I are off to London on our own, alone in the city to do whatever we want. As we walk into departures, I get two egg sandwiches from the fridges. At the counter I also grab us crisps and ask for two muffins, one blueberry, one chocolate. Aunty Jo gave me £100 for the trip, I feel loaded.

'Party time,' I say to Flo's miserable face. She's been talking to me in monosyllabic grunts all morning.

'You didn't get any wine?' she says, looking at the egg sandwich like it's the worst thing she could possibly imagine. I had thought about getting some miniature bottles, that's what we'd usually do, but it feels wrong giving alcohol to Flo at the moment.

'You need to eat, you're very pale,' I tell her. 'Are you feeling sick?' She shakes her head. I unwrap the sandwiches and put one in front of her. I tear open both packets of crisps and put them in the middle so we can share. I fill my sandwich up with some salt and vinegar than make orgasmic noises as I take my first bite. 'Ahhh nothing better,' I say, masticating. Flo just stares at hers.

'Look Flo, I was going to tell you about Ben. I was. You were going to be pissed off whether I told you at the start or now, so I just wanted to enjoy it for a bit before I got a bollocking.'

'Of course you're going to get a bollocking, Renée. He's our boss. I knew something like this would happen when you got the job. I *knew*, and you acted like I was the crazy one. I saw my boss wearing just a towel and now I have to work in an office with him. How could you bring him to our flat?'

'Where was I supposed to go? I can't exactly go to his house, can I?'

'Aren't people who have affairs supposed to go to hotels and rent rooms by the hour?'

'Well not us, it's not seedy like that. We really like each other, it's special.'

'Sure.'

She can get lost with this pure angel routine. 'So how come you need to go back this weekend anyway? It's a bit weird that all your stuff has just been in that flat in London, isn't it?'

'Not really,' she says, loading a sandwich with crisps as a distraction. 'I'd paid up until the end of the month and so Katrina was really chilled about it when I moved out. She was gutted when I said I was moving back to Guernsey, she didn't want me to go.'

'Oh, well, I'm sure she will be really happy to see you.'

'She won't be there. She's going to her mum's.'

'Oh, why are you going when she's away?'

'What is this, Renée? Ask Flo as many questions as possible to distract from my affair?'

I stop there. She doesn't know I read Katrina's messages. Something weird happened and I will get to the bottom of it, but Flo is in no mood to talk about it. I can wait, if she lays off me as well.

'Flo, can we just try to have a fun weekend? This is my first proper grown-up trip to London; I'm so excited. I don't want this dark cloud hanging over us. I'll end it with Ben, OK? I know I have to and I will, but let's not think about it this weekend, yes? Can we just have fun?'

'OK, we can move on, for now.' She takes a bite of her sandwich and chews it for ages before eventually swallowing like it's a brick. 'I've got knots in my tummy for some reason, like something awful is going to happen.'

'Something awful? Like what? We've got three days in the big smoke. We can pack up your stuff, party, walk around, see the sights, and I'll go blow everyone's minds with my creative genius in the London office on Monday. It's going to be great. I love saying that: "The London Office". "Hey Flo, I'll be in the *London office* if you need me."' I'm making myself laugh. Trying to cheer her up whilst hammering through the snacks.

The flight is so quick. Forty minutes from little Guernsey to Gatwick. I've only ever passed through Gatwick before, on my way to Spain. I've never actually left the airport and followed signs to London itself. Flo hardly said a word on the flight. I had no idea she was a nervous flyer. Her hands were trembling. 'I don't know why,' she kept saying. 'I just feel really anxious. Something weird is in the air, I can feel it.'

'The only weird thing in the air right now is you,' I said, trying to calm her down. She smiled, but then locked her stare out of the window, as if the clouds were going to explode and she didn't want to miss it.

'It's probably just moving all your stuff out,' I said, reassuring her. 'Moving is always hard. But we can pack what you want to keep and donate the rest, it will be fine, I promise,' I say, knowing there's more to the story than she's telling me. I'm hoping this trip opens her up a little, but I have to play it well for that to happen. Flo is like a wild animal: if she feels unsafe, she'll defend herself. Approach her in the right way, and she'll cuddle up and surrender.

'We'll get the train to Victoria then jump on a bus to get to Dalston. It's a bit of a mission but the cheapest way,' Flo says, leading me down an escalator towards the Gatwick Express. We only brought hand luggage so that we can load up with all her things on the way back. It's a good job, I'm not sure how we would manage with cases. There's so much walking and we're not even out of the airport yet.

Flo seems happier now she is out of the sky, more

confident. I, on the other hand, feel suddenly aware of how lost I could get. 'Flo, slow down,' I say. She turns and laughs. 'It's OK, Renée. I won't abandon you. But you're in London now, you have to keep up.'

The Gatwick Express is quick and exciting. I love trains, a novelty when you come from somewhere like Guernsey. Victoria Station is like something out of a film. It's huge with so many people. 'If we ever get lost,' Flo says, 'meet me under the clock. OK?'

'Can I just call you?'

'Yeah, but isn't it romantic that people had to say that and if they didn't show up, they'd never meet?'

'I suppose.'

We line up at a machine to get what Flo has referred to as a 'travel card'. Apparently, it will last us the whole time we're here and we can use it on buses and trains. It costs £27. Why is everything so expensive? 'Can we not walk?' I ask her, finding all this quite stressful. There is something very disconcerting about being surrounded by so many strangers. No one makes eye contact; they all seem to know exactly where to go. They're all so . . . busy.

'No, Renée, we can't just walk. But as long as you don't lose this, you won't have to spend any more money on transport. It's a pretty good deal when you look at it that way.' She takes my money and feeds it into the machine. A ticket pops out. 'Put it in your pocket, the one with the zip. Do not lose it and you'll be fine.'

I look at the Tube map on the wall. 'Jesus, you'd need an A level in Geography to work this out.'

'You'll get the hang of it. Just remember, millions of people travel to London on holiday every year, and they all work it out, don't they. And don't worry, like I said, we're getting the bus.'

Flo walks off and I follow inches behind her. I cannot let her out of my sight. Outside the sound of traffic is so loud, why aren't people walking around with their hands over their ears? And the smell, it's like being stuck in a garage with a car that's on and leftover pizza boxes. It stinks. There are so many buses, what if we get the wrong one?

'That's the number thirty-eight stop right there,' she says, and we run towards it. Soon, we will be on the bus and out of this mayhem, and it will all look like it does in the movie *Notting Hill*. Pretty, tree-lined streets with cute bookshops and lots of posh people in nice clothes. It will be fine.

I follow her, ducking in and out of people's way. Trying to stay away from the kerb for fear of getting smacked in the head by one of the many bus wing-mirrors. How many people die by being thwacked by a bus mirror every day in London? Thousands, I imagine. I keep hold of my bag and suitcase, certain someone will snatch it off me any minute.

When the bus pulls up, I stand staring at it in disbelief. Flo gets on and turns back, realising my feet have not left the concrete pavement. 'Renée, come on, it will leave without you.'

'But . . . there . . . there's no door?'

'No, you just hop on, and hop off. Come on, quick, they

don't hang about when it's this busy. Renée, come, it's fine, honestly, it's just a bus.' A river of people have ignored my anxiety and piled onto this vehicle. Flo reaches out her hand. 'Take a big step, come on, you have no choice.'

I close my eyes and take the big step. Suddenly I feel the rumble of the engine beneath my feet. Flo pulls me in, where she sits me down on a long bench. She sits on the bench opposite and laughs. 'Wow, Renée. You've been the biggest fish in every room we've ever been in, and look at you now. My little island girl, out and about in London and all afraid.'

She seems to be getting some kind of kick out of this.

'I'm not *afraid*, Flo. I just, there's no fucking door, we could fall off any minute. You know I get weird when other people are driving. This is a lot.'

'You're right, I'm sorry,' Flo says.

I sit back in the seat. The bus stops all the time, it's like we've barely travelled any distance at all. Flo tells me the journey will take fucking FORTY MINUTES. No wonder. The sound of the traffic is so loud. Constant beeps and screeches and a million other noises that merge into one deafening angry growl. Thousands and thousands of people crossing roads, jumping on and off buses. Shouting, barging past each other, sitting so close but not making any eye contact. No one smiles, everyone is looking down. I always thought I'd be a city girl, I've been so excited about getting here. But now I'm here I don't like how small I feel, how insignificant. Already I'm missing the chirpy disposition of small-town people.

Flo doesn't seem bothered by all this. I could never have imagined her being confident enough to cope with this level of aggression, but here we are on a London bus. Me feeling like I'm about to get trampled to death and her casually reading a newspaper she found on the seat. How can she touch that? God knows whose hands have been on it before. It's all just so dirty.

'I thought maybe we could go for dinner tonight, a pub by the flat?' she says.

'Do they sell crisps?' I ask, sarcastically.

'Look, I know you're worried about money, but tonight is on me. I've been earning longer than you and have some saved up. Just don't worry, OK? You're right, what you said at the airport, we have to enjoy ourselves.'

How can I not worry? London isn't anything like I expected it to be. Where are all the stylish posh people skipping around all jolly with bunches of flowers and tote bags? It's not like that. Everyone looks so sad, like they're forced to be here. And the clothes so far are shit. I want to go home.

'Where is this?' I ask Flo, looking out of the window.

'The Essex Road.'

There is an old lady dragging a shopping trolley along, and two young guys in hoodies walking dangerously close to her. Are they going to mug her?

'Where is the flat?' I ask, hoping she says, 'a long way away from here.' I don't like it here at all.

'Dalston, it's not far. Just around the next corner,' Flo tells me, and I hope that whatever is around that corner doesn't reek of poverty and crime like this road does. Did I just think that? That was so snobby. Maybe I am a snob. I've only ever lived in Guernsey and Marbella, that's not normal. Is the Essex Road normal? Is that why no one else wants to call the police every time they look out the window?

'OK, this is us,' says Flo, after another long ten minutes on this stinky bus. She jumps up, but I stay sitting down until it has stopped completely. 'It's about a five-minute walk, then we're there, OK?

'That caff is amazing,' she continues as we pull our cases along, pointing at a shitty-looking builders' café with horrible bright lights and a menu written with a black marker in the window. 'They do the best fry-ups, you'll love it.'

Will I? I think. Will I LOVE it? It looks crap. But sure, the smell of bacon wafting out of it isn't terrible. As we walk along the pavement, Flo points out a bus stop over there, a library over there, the back entrance to the supermarket, the pub where we're going to tonight. But I can't focus on what she's saying; it's already an information overload and my brain feels like it might explode.

'Are you OK?' asks Flo, and I realise I have stopped and am staring all around. 'Renée, what's the matter?'

I shuffle up to her. 'Nothing just, everyone is . . . different.'

'Oh. You'll get used to that. I felt the same when I got here. I quickly realised we have lived very sheltered white, middle-class lives and that multiculturalism is a big part of London life.'

She's so worldly. I feel like I just crawled out of a cave.

'It's not the world we were brought up in. But you get used to it. In fact, it's kinda great. I'll take you to Whitechapel, that's a more Islamic community, amazing kebabs. It feels good to be among other people, like we're actually part of the real world and not in some weird, island bubble. I love it. OK, we're here.' We stop at a large, terraced house. It's pretty and calmer on this street. It's still not like the movie *Notting Hill*, but it's better than the Essex Road.

Flo opens the front door, we go inside and I immediately feel the relief of the journey being over. We go up one flight of stairs, and she opens the door to the flat. It's cute, with wooden floors and mismatched furniture. There is a lovely big wooden dining table and fun pictures on the walls. I can see a kitchen through a sweet arch-shaped doorway. It's warm, and homely, and I collapse onto the sofa feeling like I just climbed an eight-thousand-foot mountain to get here. Flo's nervousness seems to return almost immediately. Like the hectic London hustle distracted her from it, but now, in the silence of this living room, she is face-to-face with herself once again.

'Are you OK?' I ask her.

'I just need a minute.' She leaves the room, disappears up a corridor and shuts a door behind her. Pleased to have a moment alone, I sink into the sofa and relax.

HONEYBEE

Flo

I left in such a hurry that morning. Katrina and I had a big fight the night before. She said she was sick of my behaviour. I had no idea what she was talking about, she just went on and on about how impossible I was being. I ignored her and went to sleep. I slept through my alarm then packed whatever I could squeeze into my case and bolted for the airport. I left a note saying I'd come back to get the rest after the funeral, but I obviously never did. Now she's found a new housemate and needs it all out. She didn't even want to be here when I came back. Living with friends can go so horribly wrong, I still get scared for me and Renée.

I walk around the room, taking in the memories. Katrina was right, there is a smell. I find a very hard pair of pyjama bottoms stuffed under my bed. They have dried to a crisp and smell awful. I put them into a plastic bag and open the window. I light a joss stick and strike a few matches, which helps.

Katrina was my friend at university and things were always OK there. It was when we moved to London that her issues with me started. She said I turned into a different person when I drank and that she didn't want to be around me when that happened. It left me with a horrible feeling of shame that I couldn't shake. She said I did awful things but never told me what they were. I wondered if that was because I didn't really do anything that bad and she'd just changed her mind about living with me because she wanted the flat to herself. The problem was that I felt happier when I drank. It made me feel like I fitted in, it still does. Why could she drink and get hammered and do crazy things, but I couldn't?

My room looks sad. I pull a large suitcase out from under the bed and start to fill it with clothes. I have a vase that mum got me for Christmas once, and a few pictures that I'd hung on my walls. There's some bedding that I keep out for me and Renée to use, we'll have to do head-to-toe. There is a cushion that I like and some make-up and a small mirror. Before I know it, I've packed it all and it all fits neatly into one suitcase. Coming back for this seems ridiculous. It also strikes me how simple I am. I don't have 'stuff'. Renée and I have only lived in our flat for a month or so and her room is already bursting with things. I don't know where she gets it all, but she's always coming home with bits and bobs. 'Stuff to make a house a home,' she says, like she just knows how to create a homely space. Picture frames, trinkets, things she found in charity shops or that Aunty Jo gave her. She gathers and gathers, adding to the stuff that makes her who she is. I don't have stuff. I am basic. Simple. I always liked that. But now, seeing my life packed neatly into a suitcase, I feel fucking boring.

I head back downstairs. I feel a scratching in my belly. In the kitchen there's plenty of alcohol, as usual. Giant bottles of vodka that Katrina and I split the cost of when we first moved in. We thought it was fun to have the cupboards bursting with booze. It made us feel grown-up.

Although the fun of it wore off quickly and she got annoyed with me any time I drank anything. I hold up a bottle of vodka that's half full. There's a black line drawn on it. Katrina did it with a Sharpie one morning, saying the rest was hers and she'd know if I drank any. I bring it to my lips, but something stops me. A voice from somewhere deep inside tells me I don't need the extra booze today. That I can handle this weekend, and I can handle the things that cause the rat to scratch and my lip to sweat. I put the vodka down, and head to the living room.

'Right then,' I say to an exhausted-looking Renée. 'Let's hit the town.'

I'm not sure how we get from the local pub to central London, but suddenly I'm ordering 'two for a tenner' bottles of white wine and a portion of chips at the All Bar One in Leicester Square. This kind of drinking is different to the kind when I drink alone. This is fun. This is allowed.

Renée got a bolt of confidence after a few drinks and said she wanted to see the sights. We got off the bus at Tottenham Court Road and walked through Soho. Renée dragged me into a sex shop then ran out screaming when a gimp walked up to her with a whip and said it was only five quid to watch 'The Show'. Even Renée and her filthy mind found that too much. We've laughed the whole way here. We needed this. I love being back in London, not feeling like the streets are loaded with my dark side. Sure, I have some London tales to tell, but I don't feel like my past is out to get me here. I love how invisible I feel, how no one is looking at me, or worried about what I'm doing. It's not that I want a big life here in the city, it's more that I want my little one to go unnoticed. And of course, my mother isn't here, which makes me want to sing and dance down every street like I'm in a West End show. I like London me. London Renée though, she's not what I was expecting.

'You could go out every night and never go to the same place twice,' she says, looking out of the window. 'I think it would feel stressful, no familiarity. Where do people go to relax?'

'There are lovely parks, and you can walk for miles along the river. If you go out a bit there are more chilled places than Dalston, especially south of the river. You just have to be adventurous to find your places. It takes time.'

'I can't wait for tomorrow. "The London Office". You'll write it all down for me, won't you? How to get there?'

'Of course I will, stop worrying. Let's finish up here and go back into Soho. The drinks are expensive but it's more buzzy.'

Renée's eyes are wide with wonder as we walk down Old Compton Street. It suits her, even if she doesn't quite feel it yet. There is a crowd outside Bar Soho. It looks like a media event of some kind; there are paparazzi, and everyone is dressed really trendily. 'Oh my God, look, a proper showbiz bash,' she says, joining the line to get in. 'This is what I'm talking about.'

'Renée you can't just go in, your name isn't on the door.'
'Oh Flo, shhh.'

Someone comes outside and the paparazzi cameras go bananas. 'Who is it?' I ask, I can't see with all the flashing.

'It's the weather girl from *The Big Breakfast*. Wow, this is so cool.'

Suddenly we are at the front of the line. Names are being checked off a list, the woman with the clipboard turns her head for a split-second and Renée pulls me inside.

'Renée, we can't do this!'

'Why not? Come on, look.' She charges towards a man holding a tray of cocktails. She picks up two and gives me one. 'This is it, Flo, this is the London life I've been dreaming of. Oh my God, look, there's Felicity Mellors.' She drags me over to where Felicity is standing. 'Felicity, hi, I'm Renée Sargent.' She says it so confidently that I'm impressed. Felicity is a columnist for the *Observer* magazine. Renée never seems to read it, but she's said it's 'her dream job' so many times.

'Hello, sorry, have we met before?' Felicity says, sipping her cocktail. She's wearing a very cool black blouse with puffy sleeves and tight black leather trousers. She is stick thin and utterly beautiful. She's so cool that it's impossible not to feel like a giant blob of dorkishness in her company.

'I just wanted to say I love your work, I read your column every week,' Renée spouts. 'I'm actually a writer too.'

'Oh, thanks. I appreciate that.' She turns back to who she was talking to, but Renée is not done.

'I wondered if you had any advice on how to make it as a writer like you? It's all I want to do, all I've ever wanted to do.' Felicity takes a breath, as if this happens all the time.

'That's great, what have you written?'

'Well, nothing yet. But I want to, I've always wanted to. I'm currently writing a slogan for cheese.'

'Cheese? Listen, love, everyone wants to be a writer, but if you haven't written anything you're not a writer, you're a wannabe writer, like everyone else. Writers write, it's not rocket science. Got it?' She turns aggressively now, back to her group, and makes them all laugh by saying, 'Jeez, I need to get that on a T-shirt, the amount of times I've had to say it.'

Renée steps back, humiliated and embarrassed. As she should be, that was brutal. The cheese bit was particularly terrible.

'Are you OK?' I ask her, knowing it's now my job to boost her back up. 'What does she know, anyway? You're the most talented writer I know.'

'Let's get out of here, Flo. This isn't my crowd. I need to be on top form tomorrow. I bet she couldn't come up with a slogan for cheese if I smacked her over the head with a slice of Edam.'

It's not the time to remind Renée that it's been over a week and she still hasn't thought of a slogan for cheese, though I'm sure the energy of 'The London Office' will squeeze it out of her. We finish our cocktails and head for the door. The photographers outside ready themselves, but relax when they realise we're no one special.

HONEYBEE

'Renée Sargent!' she shouts at them all, making me want to run for cover. 'Remember that name!' They raise their cameras again, looking at her intensely, but no, they got nothing. It's not even worth the snap, just in case.

18

Renée

I have an hour to pull myself together. I can't believe this. I had planned to wake up at 6 a.m., have a shower, get ready and walk to the office, feeling bright. But I've hardly slept, I have a hangover and I feel like shit. I was supposed to sleep in Flo's bed but she got all weird about it so I ended up on the couch.

    I blow-dry my hair with a hairbrush so it looks neat and smooth. I put loads of eyeliner on and make my cheeks nice and peachy with a blusher I got free with *Cosmo*. I wear extra deodorant and some of Katrina's perfume that I found in the bathroom. I'm wearing my frog shirt and the green trousers, which I'm getting bored of, but it's still the best outfit I have. I did consider one of the ball gowns, but wondered if it was overkill for day one. Next payday, I'm getting some new clothes. I'm realising more and more how much I want to express myself through what I wear.

Ben texted last night to say he can't wait to see me. I've never looked forward to anything more in my life. It's been hard not to mention him, but it's just not worth it with Flo. She thinks I plan to end things, which I don't. But if she wants to think that for now, fine, whatever keeps the peace. I've promised her I will come home tonight so she knows there will be no London rendezvous at least. God, I'd love a London rendezvous with Ben.

'Bye Flo!' I shout as I hurry out of the door. 'I'll see you tonight for dinner!' As I hurry towards the bus stop, I see the number 38 pulling up. I pick up my pace. It stops but I get another bolt of fear. Pure determination to see Ben launches me from the pavement to the shuddering bus floor. I grab onto a pole as it sets off. 'I did it!' I say to the conductor. 'I did it all by myself!' I get off at Holborn after spending the entire journey asking, 'Is this Holborn?' every time the bus stopped. If I do nothing else today, I will have accomplished that journey.

On the streets people are rushing in all directions, and nearly everyone is holding a coffee. Do people not have time to sit down and drink coffee in London? We don't do that in Guernsey, we go for coffee and sit in cafés. I'm terrified of someone banging into me and spilling the hot contents of their paper cup all over me. Soon afterwards, thank God, I find myself on Russell Street looking at a green door with a little plaque that reads: MAGIC MARKETING. I press a buzzer and the door snaps open.

'Hi, I'm Renée,' I say to a very fashionable receptionist who I immediately feel in competition with. 'From the Guernsey office.'

'Oh, hi, yes, Ben said you were coming. Weird.'

'Weird?' I ask.

'Yeah, weird. You're just the temp receptionist, right? And he's asked you to come for a creative meeting. Weird.'

'Well, I'm not just the receptionist, actually. I'm working on some copy for the cheese campaign. That's why I am here, to work on the copy.'

She silently mimics what I say and picks up her phone.

'Ben, I have Rrrrrrenéeee for you.'

'Why did you say my name like that?'

'Why did you say my name like that?'

What the fuck?

'Renée, you made it,' Ben says, coming into reception. 'Come this way, I'll show you your desk for the day.' I follow him, looking back at the receptionist who is staring at me and snarling. An actual snarl, like a dog.

'What's her problem?' I ask Ben, quietly.

'Oh, don't mind her. That's Lisa. She's been on reception for four years. She's so horrible we can't promote her or fire her because either way she'd make our lives hell. Take no notice. Here, this is the hot desk, and today it's all yours.'

Ben is so good at being 'work Ben'. It's a lesson I need to learn. All I can think about is him bending me over the HOT DESK and doing me from behind.

I sit down. It feels strange being in the open-plan office, I'm usually all alone on reception and that feels a lot more comfortable. The London office is bigger, more people. A quick count reveals about twenty. I have spoken to a few of them on the phone before, taking messages or putting them through to Ben, but mostly I've had very little to do with them. I know Jordan must be here somewhere. He's always rude to me when he calls, always talking like he's in a massive hurry. Like marketing is the most important job on earth and he has no time to waste as he gets messages about new kinds of cheese out into the world. Rude git, I dread hearing him on the other side of the—

'Renée, this is Jordan,' Ben says, as a handsome black man reaches out his hand to me. I had imagined him as short and fat. Angry with himself, more than anything else. But that's not who's in front of me. He's not as tall as Ben, but he's as good-looking and clearly goes to the gym a lot. I reach my hand out and shake his.

'I'm much nicer in person, promise,' he says. Ben smiles.

'I told him to go easy on you. Your first day in London is a big deal, how was your journey in?'

'Oh easy, yeah, just hopped on and off a Routemaster, no problem at all.'

'Look at you, London gal about town!' Ben says. 'Well, you're very welcome here. I told Jordan how you were hoping to move to London soon, so if today goes well, maybe we can look into some future options.' Ben looks chuffed to bits with what he said. But all I can think is: is his plan to pack me off to London to get me out of the way?

'Consider this an interview,' Jordan says, rushing back to his desk. Ben hovers over me; I'm trying to hide the fact I want to burst into tears. Why is he so keen for me to move to London? Doesn't he love me like I love him? I don't like it here. But he can't know that, so I pull myself together.

'Lovely to meet the team,' I say, confidently.

'We set the company up together just after we left uni, thought it would last five minutes but, turns out, we're quite good at it.' He senses that maybe I don't feel 100 per cent comfortable. 'You OK?'

I lean back in my chair, unusually quiet. Ben leans closer to me, probably to offer me a job in Australia. 'Have you got plans tonight? I mean, I'm sure you do. But if you're alone in London then I could take you for a pint?'

'Take me for a pint'. Is that romantic or not? It doesn't matter, he wants to see me. Who cares if it's just a pint? 'No, I have no plans. That sounds great.' Flo will understand, I'm sure. I'll tell her it's work. And I won't be late, we can still have dinner later. I reach for my phone to text her. Shit, I left it at the flat.

'OK great, but first, Island Cheese. We're actually going to have the meeting in a local hotel. It's good to get out of the office sometimes, I said I'd treat them all to brunch.' A brunch meeting? In London? OK, things are looking up, that's the most impossibly glamorous thing I've ever heard.

We walk to the hotel together, all nine of us. I make friends with a lady called Rebecca who says she's worked for Magic for five years. She manages the accounts for some really cute clothes brands. She says if I do end up moving to London and working on them, I might even get free clothes. Ben walks behind me, I love the thought of him watching me. I make sure I walk with a little wiggle and laugh loudly so he can see what a joyful person I am.

The Charlotte Street Hotel is one of the fanciest places I have ever been to. To the left is a restaurant, but we're not going in there. We're shown into a private room with a huge table and a sign in the middle saying 'Magic Marketing'. There is tea and coffee set up for us to help ourselves to and pastries on the table. No one takes any, which drives me mad because I'm starving. Everyone is given a menu and told to order whatever they want. I go first and order the Full English with extra toast, which I see Ben laugh at. As the waiter goes around the table and takes everyone else's orders, they mostly order the granola and yoghurt, or toast with preserves. Ben goes last and orders Eggs Benedict, probably just to make me feel like less of a pig. When all the food comes, I plan to just eat the toast and eggs, but it's the most spectacular plate of food I could ever imagine. I manage the eggs, toast, beans and bacon while everyone else nibbles on their wholegrains. But eating the sausage in front of everyone is a level of gluttony even I can't muster. As the waiter takes it away, I look at the sausage like I'm sorry for rejecting it. I hope it doesn't go to waste and that some lucky KP gets to scoff it while he scrubs pans. That was a job I actually enjoyed, washing up in a kitchen. I got all the scraps.

The meeting starts and most of it is absolute jargon to me. I sit and nod politely. Ben is so sexy at work. He's so clever and funny. He lets everyone speak and looks at them as they do. Even if he doesn't agree with what they're saying, he responds with, 'thanks for that', and then comes up with a brilliant explanation as to why it won't work. Everyone respects him, and I can't be the only woman who fancies him. I drift off, imagining him coming home from work after being brilliant all day long. He'd sit at the kitchen table and say it was a good day, but that he's tired. I'd massage his neck. He'd put his hand on mine and pull me round to sit on the table in front of him. I'd have had the forethought not to bother with knickers. And then he'd bury his face into my . . .

'Renée? Renée?' Ben says, trying to pull me back into the room from wherever it is I went. Everyone is looking at me.

'She's regretting not eating that sausage,' one of the men says, and they all laugh. If only they knew what sausage I was thinking about.

'Sorry, yes?' I say, embarrassed. 'What was that?'

'The slogan,' Ben says, 'I know you've been working on it. Did you have anything to pitch to us today?'

To 'pitch' to them? I was supposed to 'pitch' to them? I mean, of course I was, why am I so stupid? Did I think I was just coming to this meeting to listen when I had specifically been asked to come up with a slogan? A writer who doesn't write, a slogan creator with no slogans. I am a fraud on all levels. I'm getting sweaty and red; everyone is staring at me. It's either really hot in here or I'm about to have a heart attack right here on this table. I was supposed to prepare something. What an idiot. I see a flyer on the table showing the different cheeses for the campaign. I pick it up, as if I am about to say something profound.

'Whenever you're ready,' Jordan says, that nastier side to him creeping through. Ben shoots him a look, then offers me some supportive eyes. I don't want to let him down, I can't. I look at the flyer, and then it comes to me.

'Sorry,' I say, 'I just wanted to get the words straight in my head. Yes, I've obviously written hundreds of ideas down, but there is one that I keep coming back to. Teenagers, all they care about is growing up, right?'

'Right?' says Jordan. Ben nods and smiles, as if to say, 'Come on, Renée, spit it out.'

'Cheese, Something to be Mature About,' I say, letting it sit in the quiet room while it seems to take an age to travel into everyone's ears.

'I love it,' says my friend, Rebecca.

'Me too,' says someone else.

'It's actually really good,' Jordan says, disappointed he didn't get to be disappointed.

'It's brilliant,' Ben says. 'It's perfect.'

My body temperature drops immediately. My heart goes back to normal pace. There is a hum of enthusiasm around the room and then a round of applause. I smashed it. Somehow, despite being horribly unprepared, I absolutely smashed it. It seems I am a natural. In your face, Felicity Mellors!

The rest of the afternoon was amazing. I sat in on a few other meetings and was so chilled and relaxed because my work was really done. I have to be honest though, literally nothing except the writing interests me. I have no doubt that is all I want to do. Marketing is fun, it's energetic and exciting if you give a shit about brands, but I don't think I do. In the meetings, they talk about the consumers a bit like they're idiots. Just numbers. Not real people. And it struck me halfway through one discussion about how 'if you tell someone it will make their hair shiny, their hair will shine' that I, too, am just a consumer. That somewhere a bunch of marketing people are probably sitting around talking about me like I'm an idiot. No, this isn't the career for me. But that buzz I got today, that thrill for writing something, even if it was just a tiny line that people responded to and loved. That's the thrill I'm chasing. I want that over and over again.

At the end of the day, I leave ten minutes before Ben and head for the meeting spot we discussed. I remember I didn't call Flo. I'd meant to ask the moody receptionist for her number, as it would be on the system. I was going to tell her that there was a late meeting and that I wouldn't be home until eight. But now I have no way to reach her. I could call her from Ben's phone, but if I do she'll go apeshit at me. So, she's just going to have to wait. I'll blame it on the bus, or something. I'll make sure I'm back soon.

'Hi,' Ben says, walking towards me and kissing me on the cheek. My heart is beating like I'm about to deliver a speech to a thousand people. It's different here in London. In the office, I'm flirting with a colleague. Out here I feel like the words 'HE IS MARRIED AND I AM A SLUT' are tattooed on my face. He throws a hand into the air and hails a cab.

'Where are we going?' I ask him.

'Let's get away from the office. My hotel has a nice bar.'

'Can't we just get the bus?' I say, thinking London cabs look terrifying.

'No, it's fine,' he says, as one pulls up. I hesitate to get in but other cars start honking almost immediately. Ben doesn't put a seat belt on, I struggle to get mine to work.

'You don't need to wear a belt,' he says, like that's no big deal.

'I want to,' I say. 'I have to.' This is really killing my mood. I want to be relaxed, but this is very triggering for me.

'Where you going then?' asks the driver grumpily.

'Park Plaza, Victoria,' Ben says, confidently. I hold on tight to a handle and take a few deep breaths.

'Are you OK?' Ben asks, concerned. 'It's fine if you've changed your mind, it's OK, this is . . .'

'No, it's not that,' I assure him. 'Ben, I was in an accident a few years ago and . . .'

Before I've even finished he's telling the driver to slow down. He puts his arm around me and I'm not sure I've ever felt safer in my life.

'OK, this is it,' Ben says as we pull up to the hotel a few minutes later. He pays the driver, it was 27 quid, which I try not to have a panic attack about. I stand on the pavement for a minute and take a few long, slow breaths. 'Next time we get the bus,' he says, firmly. And I'm so happy he said 'next time' that I look him in the eye and say, 'Can we go straight to your room?'

I lie draped across the left-hand side of Ben's naked body. Mine feels perfectly peachy against his slim, firm frame. Somehow, he is still comfortable to squash myself against. His body makes my body feel good. I reach for his penis and give it a little shake. 'Hey boss,' I say, and we both laugh.

'I feel like I should smoke,' he says, gently.

'You smoke?' I ask, surprised. He doesn't seem like a smoker.

'Nope, not for about ten years. But sex like that makes me feel like I should smoke.'

Sex like that? That means he loved it. I stroke his chest and kiss his cheek. He turns his face to me, and we kiss properly. So slow, so soft. I could go again right now, but I know he needs a minute. I realise, as I lie here, that I've only ever shagged before. All sorts of boys, all sorts of men. Good sex, bad sex, some fun, some awful, but all for show. All just shags. The quick shags were either passionate or mistakes, both entirely forgettable. The longer ones like a performance, doing all the things you're supposed to do in bed. Uncomfortable positions, just to try them. Filthy words, just to say them. Kinky outfits, just to wear them. All for their pleasure, never mine. I'd rather be naked, just like this. This sex was proper, grown-up sex. The kind of sex that they call love-making. I've not made love before, not like this. I thought I had, but I haven't, I know now. Not this tender, this slow, this hard, this deep. We weren't trying to be filthy just for the sake of it, we were equal, every step of the way. My pleasure, his pleasure. It made me realise how so much of the sex we have as women is about being a vehicle for men to try new things or live out their fantasies. Their own kinks disguised with their soft hands. Our orgasms are for their ego, not our satisfaction. Our experience is only important when we tell them how good they are in bed. Our desires are seen as deviances to turn them on, not pleasures for us to receive. I squirm at the number of men's eyes I have looked into, them being so excited at the prospect of what I might do for them sexually, with zero interest in what I could do emotionally. Their thrill is always the priority, no matter how many times I scream in the throes of it all. I don't know why it has always been engrained in me that I must perform well in bed for the approval of men. It's sickening, now I think about it. Now I know how this can really feel. I have never in my life so wholly believed that my body could be sacred and magical, in the way that I just did with Ben. It was spiritual. Otherworldly. It was the real thing, should the real thing even exist. Which now I know it does.

I run my fingers through his chest hair. It looks so short, but when I pull it, it's long. 'Boing,' I say, making him laugh. I am smitten. Besotted. The luckiest girl alive. I've found my soulmate. I've—

'FUCK, Flo. What time is it?'

'Nine p.m.'

'Fuck! She's going to be so angry.' I jump up and start looking for my knickers. 'I promised her I'd be home for seven. We were going to some Thai place. BYO, whatever that means.'

'Bring Your Own. It means you can take wine. Always the classiest joints.'

I'm frantically looking for my underwear. I get down on all fours and look under the bed. Not there. Under the little sofa. Not there either.

'Well, this is fun,' Ben says, watching me. He reaches for his perfect penis which is now rock hard for the third time tonight. 'Don't mind if I do this while you look for them, do you?'

I try to ignore him, I really, really do. I want nothing more than to go and find Flo and see London town rather than just the inside of a hotel room. But . . . but . . . his cock is better than the sausage I rejected this morning and I simply cannot make the same mistake twice.

I see my knickers, they're hanging off the bedside lampshade like they would be in any romcom. I unhook them and put them somewhere less likely to start a fire. Then I climb back into bed with the most gorgeous man on earth, and eat the sausage.

Flo

Fuck Renée. So much for us being in London together. I don't know why I always hope she'll be different; she would dump me for someone else any time of the week. She's blatantly with Ben. She dumped me for her filthy affair. I sit at home and swear furiously at the TV until 10 p.m. then turn it off. I call Abi, longing to hear my little sister's voice. It rings out. I try another five times and the last time it cuts off early, like she's hung up. I scroll through my messages just to make sure I haven't missed one from Phil. Nothing. No one is thinking of me. No one wants to be with me.

I take my bag and a bottle of gin and I leave the flat with no real idea where I'll go at 10 p.m. I just want to make a point and not be here when she gets home. I'll show her, standing me up. I have a life beyond her disloyalty. The outside air is cold, I should go back and get my coat, but what if she comes home and I'm still here. The plan will be ruined. As far as Renée's concerned, I'm out galivanting with friends and I do not need her. Not one tiny bit.

I walk to the top of Kingsland Road and head towards Shoreditch. It's busy at first. I walk purposefully with no particular destination in mind. Maybe I will go to the Mother Bar. I'll pretend my friend is on her way and get chatting to other people and then I'll say she got held up, and they will be my friends instead. We will go to a club, if there is a club open on a Monday night. And if not, we'll go back to their house and drink all night like friends do. Look at me, Miss Independent.

As I get further down Kingsland Road, I hit the part with fewer restaurants, less life. It suddenly feels very dark. A man walks past me. 'Hey honey,' he says, like a total sleaze. I'm not safe, this isn't safe. I run, faster and faster between small groups, big groups, men on their own. No women on their own, it's too dark and dangerous for that. What woman would be here alone, asking for trouble? I keep running, I take a right onto Old Street, I slow down. It's busy again here, less scary, less dangerous. There is no queue at the Mother Bar, not on a Monday night, but the bar is busy enough. I order a double vodka and Red Bull. Then quickly add another. 'My friend is on her way,' I say to the hipster behind the bar. He doesn't care. I drink them both and order a Slippery Nipple and a Blow Job 'for my friend'. Two girls start dancing. They're drunk too, it's OK to be drunk and out on a Monday night, it's what people do. I dance up to them, they don't like that. Two men are drinking. I ask them their names; one says he hasn't seen his friend in a long time so could I leave them to it? I order another Slippery Nipple. I laugh my head off; the barman doesn't think it's funny.

'OK love, out, now,' says a voice above me.
God?
'Come on, I mean it now.' A dark blur comes into focus, I make out the words 'Pussy ALL DAY' on a wall. 'Seriously, hon, I'll break down that door if I need to.'

OK, not God.

I look up. A man with a beard and glasses is looking down at me. The barman. I see now that I'm in a toilet cubicle, he must be standing on the toilet seat in the one next to me. My door is locked.

'OK, OK,' I say, as if he's being ridiculous. I look on the floor for my bag, I don't see it. I stand up and open the door, the floor is wet, I can feel it in my socks. The barman comes out of his cubicle and stands intimidatingly close to me. 'You woke up just in time, I was going to call the police,' he says, putting both of his arms out, as if herding an animal into a pen.

'OK, OK, I'm going,' I say, as he pushes me gently on my shoulder. 'But I need to find my shoes and my bag.'

As we walk out into the bar, I see it's empty. One woman is washing glasses, she puts a glass of water on the bar for me. I don't take it. I don't want water.

'OK, there's the door,' says the man again.

'My bag, my shoes,' I say, again. And then again.

'Out,' the man says.

'Let her look for her bag, Pete. Come on, it will have her keys in it.'

'Yes!' I shout, punching the air. 'The sistership in action.'

Pete rolls his eyes; the woman helps me look but we can't find my things anywhere.

'I don't see a bag, you'll have to come back tomorrow when the cleaners are here. Will you be OK getting home?' the woman says.

'I don't know,' I say, but her capacity to care seems to have reached its peak.

'Out now, come on,' says Pete, who is being unreasonably forceful now. Out on the street, I look back at him. Why is he being like this? He locks the door behind me. I look down, panicking about my shoes. They're on my feet. My socks are soaking inside them. Where am I? It's cold. My watch says it's 1 a.m.

'Where am I?' I ask a man who walks past. He just laughs at me and carries on. Then I remember. I walk back towards Kingsland Road, my feet making a squelching sound in my shoes. There isn't much I can do about it now, I need to get back to the flat. Thank God the keys are in my pocket. One thing my mum told me to do before I moved out of home: 'Always have your keys in your pocket, not your bag, in case you lose it.' I hate that she was right.

I see a bus coming. I run to the stop, but my foot gives way, or I trip, or my shoe slips, I don't know what. I'm suddenly face down. My left cheek is burning. Someone is helping me up.

'I'm OK!' I bark, slapping at them to get off me. Dragging my foot behind me, I pull myself onto the bus. The driver looks at me and shakes his head. Why would he do that? The judgemental arsehole. I take a seat.

'You have to pay,' he shouts, looking back at me. I ignore him.

'Oi, love, you have to pay.' People behind me start swearing. He won't drive the bus. They are yelling at me to get off, so he can leave. 'I LOST MY BAG,' I shout at everyone, wobbling on my ankle. A man puts me on a seat. I see him go to the driver, I think he pays my fare. He comes back.

I'm falling asleep. My head knocking against the window as the bus starts to move. I'm suddenly so deeply, desperately tired.

It's 7 a.m. I wake up with the driest mouth and need to pee. I look around the room, thank God I'm at Katrina's flat. I rub my eyes, I go to the kitchen. I drink some water, it's incredible. Waves of despair hit me as I remember Katrina said we have to be out by 10 a.m. latest, before the cleaner arrives. I can't go back to bed.

I put my sheets and last night's clothes into a bin bag. I'll dump them on the way out. I tidy the living room. Fragments of memory coming over me. I remember falling, a lady lifting me. Me wanting her to get off. Something about a toilet. Something about wet feet. I lost my bag. I think I remember looking for it somewhere. The Mother Bar, that's right. The woman, she said I must go back to get it. Vague memories of a bus. There was a woman, she stayed with me. I think she got me to the front door.

Where is Renée? She never came home. I see her phone in between the cushions on the sofa. I don't know what to do with her things. What if she's lost and doesn't make it back in time? I wanted her to be jealous when she got home. But she's not here, what if she's hurt? I don't want to care, but I do. I really do. I need to get my phone.

I fill a bin sack with all the things I don't want to take. I do one last sweep of the kitchen, the living room, the bathroom. I have to leave, it's 9.30 a.m. I cannot be here when the cleaner comes, what if Katrina comes too? I cannot see her. But where is Renée? I pack her stuff into her case. I get it all. I take her case and her phone and leave the flat. I put a note on the door. *'Flight at 5.30, I have your case. Be at Victoria Station at 3. The 38 bus goes all the way there. Flo.'*

That feeling washes over me again, a dread I can't name. Is it the hangover? Or something bigger? I think of Renée, looking so small in the big city. Things are weird between us, but it suddenly feels like the most important thing that she's all right.

19

Renée

The deepest sleep in the most comfortable bed. A peaceful room, a pillow like marshmallow. I feel reborn as I open my eyes. Ben is dressed, I can smell the soap he used to wash his body. It's all so perfect.

'Order breakfast,' he says, 'I have to be in the office by nine thirty.'

'Breakfast?' I blink. 'Why, what . . .'

He opens a curtain, it's bright outside.

'Shit, no, did I stay the night?'

'You did indeed, I'm not sure an earthquake would have woken you.'

I jump out of bed. It's 8.30, we have to be out of the flat by 10. I've fucked up, I've really fucked up. God, Flo must be so angry. 'How far am I from Dalston?'

'At this time, forty minutes to an hour.'
'FUCK!' I get my clothes on. 'I have to go.'
'How will you get there?'
'I don't know. Bus? It's the thirty-eight.'
'Renée, get a cab. It's easier.'
'I can't . . . I . . .' Jesus, this is embarrassing. 'I can't afford one, it's a really long way.'

Ben takes £60 out of his wallet. He hesitates, he knows how this looks. But he gives it to me anyway. I could hang my head in shame. To end that perfect night together, in the loveliest hotel room, to feel so equal, and then to end it with him giving me cash. Why do I always feel like such trash no matter how classy my sex is? But I have no choice, I have to get back to Flo.

'Thank you. I'll pay you back.'
'Don't worry about it. Let's call it a bonus for giving us such a good cheese slogan.' He must notice my shoulders drop. 'I mean, it's worth more than sixty pounds obviously. And I'll make sure you're paid properly for it, but call this a loan until you get it. Cool?'

'Cool, thanks Ben. I don't do slogans for blowies, OK?' He pulls me close to him. We kiss, it's perfect, but I have to go. 'I'll see you in Guernsey then.'
'You will.'

I leave. I don't feel good. I wish I did, but I feel like I just screwed someone else's husband. Because that's exactly what I did.

*

HONEYBEE

I hammer on the door and ring the bell all at once. *Please still be here Flo, please be here.* A lady answers the door, the cleaner. 'I'm staying here,' I say, running in. Flo has gone, my bag has gone. My phone is nowhere. I see a Post-it note in the kitchen.

'Victoria Station at 3.' Oh Flo, thank God. Thank you thank you thank you. I'll see her there, she will be mad, but we'll work it out, we always do. As I'm leaving the flat, I see someone's coming up the stairs.

'Flo?' I call, desperately. But it isn't Flo. It's Katrina, I recognise her from the time I visited Flo at uni. Shit, she wasn't supposed to see us, that was the whole idea.

'Who are you?' she asks, defensively. I'm surprised she doesn't recognise me, I stayed in her house for three days. But people who live on the mainland can't possibly retain the faces of all the people they ever meet. There are just too many people here.

'I'm Renée, I'm Flo's friend. We met a few years ago, in Nottingham. I came to help her pack.'

'Is she here?' Katrina says, looking really annoyed.

'No, no she's left. I just popped back to look for my phone.'

'Good. And yes, I remember you. You came and had a massive fight; it was after that that she went fucking mad.' Katrina walks past me. 'Glad to see the place isn't destroyed. Did she get all her stuff out?'

'Yes, it's gone. Katrina, can I ask you what happened? I'm worried about Flo, she's been . . .' I don't know if I should say it. 'She's been . . .'

'Let me guess, getting blind drunk, bringing random people back, and pretending not to remember anything?'

Woah, OK, this Katrina bitch doesn't like Flo, but there's no way she is talking about my best friend like that.

'She's been drinking, yes. But nothing like that,' I say, lying. It must be obvious.

'I knew she wouldn't change. That girl has a problem. Alcohol makes her crazy, like proper crazy. I'd never know which Flo I'd come home to. The sweet one who was shy and awkward but kind and easy to be around, or the wild one who was volatile and did mad things that she'd forget about the next day. It was a rollercoaster, and I just couldn't take it any more, so I told her she had to go. I gave her a month to be nice, but she just went and left half her stuff. I didn't want to see her, so I went to Mum's for a while. I have a new roommate coming tomorrow, she's American. Sounded pretty straight on the phone, way better for a nice flat like this. I bought it, you know, my dad gave me the deposit. Great right?'

I don't like Katrina. She's a stuck-up rich kid who doesn't take care of her friends. I shouldn't care, but I hate there being so much bad energy around Flo. I try to be reasonable. 'Katrina, Flo has a problem with alcohol, we know that, but please don't hate her. She's troubled, but she's one of the kindest, sweetest, most loyal friends imaginable. She's been through so much. She and her mum have a bad relationship, her dad died . . .'

'Flo's dad died? When?'

'When she was fifteen. She never mentioned it?'

'She never mentioned it. Wow, that's fucked-up.'

'Yeah, it is. And so is she. But she's going to be OK. Please don't hate her, you don't need to see her again now. It's done. But just in your heart, don't hate Flo, please.'

'OK Renée, I won't hate Flo, if that makes you feel better. Fine. I hope she's happier in Guernsey, it sounds like a mad place.'

'It's a brilliant place. It's beautiful and calm and safe. And we have each other. She'll be fine. Bye Katrina, I hope your new housemate is really boring and that your daddy gives you everything you ever need so you don't have to live in the real world and have a fucking heart.'

'Excuse me?'

I slam the door really hard on my way out.

The bus, as usual, takes forever. I cry the whole way. Poor Flo, she's been hurting so much. To never mention to her uni friends that her dad died, that's some next-level closeted grief going on. And the drinking, and the guys, oh God. That's it, when we get back to Guernsey, I am making her address it. We're going to throw every drop of alcohol away and get her through this. I'll even do it myself; I'll never drink again if that's what it takes. Where is she now? What if she's on a massive bender and misses the flight? And all because I went off to have sex with a married man. I'm the worst person alive.

I feel immeasurable relief when the conductor finally says, 'Victoria Station, this bus terminates here.' My heart stops racing for the first time in hours. The flight doesn't go for a couple of hours, we have time. London is a real anxiety boost, I can't lie, I've really missed the slow-paced, salty-aired Guernsey vibe that I thought I was so desperate to get away from. But as I approach the station, something in the air doesn't feel right. I don't know if it's my imagination, but the sound of sirens seems to have really picked up. Behind me, a crew of about fifteen policemen charge past, nearly knocking me down. The sound of mobile phones ringing becomes overwhelming. People answer them and look terrified at what they're told. The sirens, they're getting closer. Louder. Three people run out of the station. The chaos doesn't feel normal. Not even by the standards of the London I've experienced so far. This feels wrong. People look scared, what is going on?

I run in circles. People are heading out of the station in their droves. There are men in suits shouting into their phones. A woman bursts out crying and falls to her knees. Someone else gets annoyed. 'Watch yourself,' he shouts. Something isn't right.

'Flo?' I call pathetically as fear inside me rises. 'FLO!'

I see the entrance to the Gatwick Express. The staff are on their walkie-talkies. More and more police gathering by the minute.

'FLO!' I call, desperate now. A crowd is gathering by the trains, the staff are being told something. I can't find Flo.

'When is the next train?' I ask a man in a high-vis vest.

'Trains are cancelled, sounds like the airport is shut down?'

HONEYBEE

The airport is shut down? How will I get back to Guernsey? My island, where I am safe. What is going on? I don't know what to do, where to go. And then I see the clock. She said if we ever lost each other, to meet under the clock. People are zigzagging through the station. Shouting into phones, running, tripping over their bags to get out. Why, why is it like this? I get closer to the clock, and I see her. She is there, waiting for me. Just like she said she would be. She looks scared too. She drags her suitcase in one hand and mine in another. I run to her, and we hug like nothing else matters but the fact we are together. 'Flo, something has happened. Something is wrong.'

'I know,' she says. 'I went into that pub, there's a TV. Two planes have crashed into the Twin Towers in New York. They think it's terrorists.'

I've never felt a fear like this before. The fear of being somewhere so big, so busy. 'Are they coming here? The terrorists?' I ask, feeling like a child. I have never heard of the Twin Towers, I feel so small. So horribly afraid. So stupid.

'Apparently the airports have shut down in case of further attacks,' she says. 'They said it on the BBC.'

'Further attacks? What does that mean?'

'I don't know. I don't know, but we can't go home. We can't go to the airport.' We stand in the middle of the station, motionless, embracing, while utter chaos reigns around us. We don't know where to go, we don't know what to do.

'I have an idea,' I say. 'But you can't be mad at me. OK? Not until we make it home.'

'OK, I won't.'

'Follow me.'

With a case each, we go as quickly as we can out of the station. I see the Park Plaza Hotel. 'In here, quick,' I tell Flo, and she follows because we have nowhere else to go. I see Ben in reception, he's on his phone. 'I'm safe,' he's saying. 'I'll get home to you all as quick as I can. Don't worry, OK? I love you, I'm safe.' He catches my eye as he says, 'I love you.' It's the most painful 'I love you' I have ever heard.

'Renée, Flo, are you OK?' he says, rushing over to us.

'We were going to the airport, but apparently there's been a . . .' I can't finish. I drop my case and bend over. I hyperventilate. 'I can't handle this, it's too much. It's too scary.'

'It's OK,' he says. 'Sit here.'

He goes to reception, speaks to the man behind the desk and hands him his credit card. Flo and I sit silently. She is sticking to her word, she isn't cross. We just need to get home, whatever it takes. Ben comes back with a key. 'Here, go to this room. Stay there. I'll work this out and text you later. OK? Go, go to the room.'

Flo and I do as he says. We go to our room. We get into bed, and we watch in horror as the news unfolds.

HONEYBEE

Flo

I've never seen Renée so scared. She is like a child quivering beside me. I'm scared too. More than scared, I am terrified. Mum calls me: 'Flo, Flo, tell me you are safe. Flo, tell me you're OK, where are you?' I try to calm her down, tell her to breathe. 'Mum, I'm OK. I'm safe. I'm with Renée, our boss got us a room in a hotel. He's booked us onto the boat from Weymouth tomorrow and has a car to take us there at six a.m. We will get home. We're safe.'

'Oh, Flo thank God, thank God. When I saw the second plane hit, I knew it wasn't an accident, how could it be? I was in the hairdresser's, people screamed. One lady said her son works there, in the second tower. She couldn't reach him; his phone wasn't even ringing. All these local finance people that leave to work there. Guernsey, so far away but connected to it all. The world is so small. I thought of you, Flo, and what it would feel like if you'd been there. Why are you in London now, of all the times? Why now?' She sobs down the phone. Bawling, hysterical, nothing I say will calm her. I give up in the end, it's quite nice to hear it.

'I'll see you tomorrow, Mum,' I say softly. 'We're in safe hands with Ben. He will get us home.'

Renée shivers for most of the night. I find an extra blanket in the wardrobe and put it over her. I wake her at five-thirty a.m. and help her get dressed. She needs me right now, I need to take control for her, to help her through this.

It's what she would do for me. Nothing else matters. Her and Ben, we don't need to address it now. We'll talk it through when we get to Guernsey, and we will talk about other things. Both of us. We're lucky to have the time.

The drive to Weymouth takes hours and is largely silent other than Ben taking calls for work and from his wife, who sounds like she's in a terrible state over him not being home. He speaks gently to her, he keeps his voice low, as if he would rather we didn't hear. Right or wrong, it must be crushing for Renée to listen to. Between his calls, he asks the driver to turn up the radio so we can listen to the news. Renée sits silently with her knees up to her chin the whole way. She stares out of the window, terrified. A little girl again. Not able for this.

'They jumped out of the windows,' she says, meekly. 'They had to choose how to die.'

The thought is so petrifying. It's almost impossible to contemplate. I snuggle up to her in the car and she rests her head on my shoulder. 'We're nearly there,' I whisper. 'We're nearly home.'

20

Renée

Almost every time I've returned to Guernsey, I've felt a feeling of crushing disappointment that I haven't achieved more. But this time, as the boat pulls in, I have never in my life been so happy to be anywhere. Flo's mum, her sister Abi and Aunty Jo are waiting for us at the harbour; we spotted them as the boat got closer to the shore. 'Take the rest of the week off, OK? Look after yourselves,' Ben says as we leave the boat in single file. I want to hug him. To feel his skin and his warmth. But I can't, not here. He isn't mine.

Aunty Jo's hug cures me of a million things. She wraps a blanket around my shoulders, like I was in the attacks myself, and leads me to her car. Flo's mum is crying dramatically. 'Thank God you're here, Flo. You made it home.' Out of the corner of my eye I see two small children run towards Ben. His huge body engulfs them. I do my best not to look at the third person I see behind them.

We get to Aunty Jo's and she puts me to bed. It is not lost on me that I wasn't in New York, I wasn't anywhere near the Twin Towers. I knew no one who was, I have lost nothing, I am not hurt, I know I am privileged. But I've never been as scared as I was in London – so out of my depth. I felt like a tiny, vulnerable insect in a sky full of giant birds. I couldn't look after myself, I needed Flo, I needed Ben. I needed anything but to be alone. I was pathetic. I always thought I'd be so London-savvy. I thought the pace of the city would thrill me when, actually, it terrified me. The noise, the smell, the constant roar of engines. The ground trembled with trains below us, there was energy coming at me from every angle and it was just too much. I missed the sea air, the fields, the flowers.

For four days I stay at Aunty Jo's. For the first twenty-four hours I don't even get out of bed. She brings me honey on toast and hot-water bottles for my top and toes. She doesn't push me to get up. 'Shock is the same as any illness, it takes time to recover,' she says. After a day or two, she convinces me to help her clean out the chicken coop. 'It's good to be active,' she says, and we laugh a little, remembering that I'm not ill, and nothing bad had actually happened to me. 'You can't milk this any longer,' she says a day later, being absolutely right as always. She doesn't know about my breaking heart. We take a seat on the bench by the bees.

'How are you?' I ask her. Once again allowing her to take care of me when she's the one who is really going through something. 'Did you talk to James?'

'I've tried. I got as far as "heavier periods", and he made up some bullshit about us having run out of toilet paper. He was in the car and off to the shops quicker than I could say "HRT". Which I'm considering for the future, by the way. I was scared because of your mum's breast cancer, but after having to strip down to my bra in Marks and Spencer's because I got so hot and bothered, I'm starting to wonder if I should.'

'Whatever helps, right?'

'Yeah. You think you're going mad, and no one tells you you're not. Honestly, if women didn't have each other, we'd all be doomed. I found a forum, do you know what a forum is? It's a group of people on the internet who . . .'

'Yes, I know what a forum is.'

'Right, of course, it's all so new to me. Anyway, on this forum, women were writing all the things that they have experienced and so much of it has been the same for me. It was like reading about myself. I got chatting to a few of the women and I couldn't believe that this huge change is afoot and the only place I can really talk to anyone about it is on the internet.'

'When I write my book, I'll make sure there is a character who is going through the menopause so women can read about it.'

'Yes, Renée, brilliant idea! I will be your research subject. Look at you, planning all your material. How exciting.'

'I don't think I'll move to London now,' I tell her. 'I can work here, write in my spare time for fun. Writing doesn't have to be my job.'

'Now Renée, what happened in New York was awful, but it's not the way the world is. You can't have it shatter your dreams.'

'It isn't just that. I hated London. I hated everything about it. I hated feeling invisible. Like, what would I have to do to get noticed in a place like that? I don't think I can be bothered. I can write anywhere, so I'm going to stay here for now. And I feel fine about it, better actually. I mean, writers all over the world would love to live on Guernsey and write by the sea, wouldn't they?'

'Yes, they would. This is your hive, my honeybee, you'll keep coming back. I never thought I would, and look at me now. I love it here so much.'

We hear James's car rolling into the driveway.

'Right, might as well rip this HRT patch off, as it were. I meant that to sound like plaster, did you get it? I said HRT patch instead of . . . Oh God, why am I so nervous? He's my partner, the love of my life. All I have to do is talk really honestly and make him understand what I'm going through. OK, it's happening. Time to make myself heard. Here I go.' She starts walking towards the house.

'No, wait, you should talk to him down here, it's your favourite place. I'll tell him to come down.'

'Yes, yes, that's nice.' She sits back down on the bench.

'Aunty Jo would like to talk to you, she's down by the bees,' I say to James as he unpacks a ridiculous amount of toilet roll onto the kitchen counter.

'Talk to me, why?'

'James, Aunty Jo is going through the menopause. It's very difficult but it's very natural. Go and talk to her, listen and do better. OK?'

'"Do better"?'

'Yes, stop treating her like she's going mad and buy her a couple of fans. Go on. She's waiting for you.'

He nods robotically and heads down the garden. I watch them from the kitchen. Aunty Jo starts talking and gesticulating. She talks for a while, longer than I think she should without him talking. But then she stops, and he hugs her. They hug for ages. And then they move closer together on the bench and she rests her head on his shoulder, and they watch the bees. And suddenly, the world feels back on track.

Fancy chips on the bunker? I text Flo, missing her so much.

Yes! See you at the chippie at 6 x

I love every second of the bike ride across the island. The roads are so quiet, the temperature balmy, history at every turn. 'Hi Renée,' says an old schoolteacher as I stop at a white line outside her house. She's putting out her bins. The familiarity overwhelms me. 'Love to Aunty Jo,' she says when I set off. It's lovely, how could I ever think I didn't want that?

Flo and I throw down the bikes and run to each other,

both arriving at exactly six o'clock. 'I've missed you so much,' we both say, over and over again. 'I mean, it's only been four days.'

'Yeah, but you try eating Mum's cooking every day,' Flo says. 'I've missed our dinners. Ahh, chips.'

With a cone of chips each, we walk along the wall to the bunker. Neither of us suggests getting wine.

'How's it been, at Aunty Jo's?' she asks me.

'Good. She's just the best. How's it with your mum?'

'Good, she's trying. It's been good. And spending more time with Abi has been lovely.'

We dip chips in the little boat of ketchup that we've made between us. And then both say each other's names at exactly the same time. It's funny. 'You go first,' I tell her.

'No, you.'

'OK, I'm going to end it with Ben. I mean, I think it's already ended but I know I have to let him go.'

'And how do you feel about that?' she asks me, doing very well not to tell me off.

'Horrible. I feel like I've met the person I'm supposed to spend the rest of my life with, but I can't have him. And so I have to be really grown-up and put an end to it, when all I want to do is beg him to leave his wife and kids and run away with me to live happily ever after with all our babies. But I can't, and it sucks.'

'Yeah, I'm sorry. He's a really special guy. I know I got mad but obviously I totally get it too.'

'Hey bitch, you hitting on my man?'

'Ha, no. But I'm just saying if I'd got stuck in a lift with

Ben and he hand-fed me sushi, I'd probably have felt the same way.'

'Maybe you would have. I keep wondering if something would have sparked with anyone at some point. Maybe I was more what he needed, than what he wants.'

'No, Renée. He wanted you. Because you're special too, and lucky him for having the chance to have you.'

'Thanks Flo, that was nice. What were you going to say?'

'Oh yeah, that.' She lays her chips down carefully so none spill, and turns to me. 'Renée, I know I have a problem with alcohol. I know I do. And I know I need to stop.'

I can't think of anything to say, so I lay my chips down too and I hug her. 'We'll do it together, OK?'

She pulls away, she wipes tears from her eyes. Those really big tears that come before you even realise you're upset. And then she laughs. 'Fuck off "we" will. Drunk Renée is the best, it's drunk Flo that needs to go.'

'Fair,' I say, smiling and picking up my chips. 'I'm pretty funny when I'm drunk.'

Flo

I'm under no illusions that Mum will keep this up. After all, we've experienced this kind of thing before: there's a drama and she worries about me, and then overcompensates and showers me with love and attention to prove that she does really care. It's how it goes, and honestly, I'm just so grateful that we manage to do this at all so I roll with it. She brings yet another tray of overcooked food to my room, despite me saying I felt perfectly OK to come down and eat it at the table.

'What are you doing?' she says, putting the tray on my bed.

'I'm looking for photos,' I say from the closet. 'I want the one where Dad put the spider in my food.'

'Oh, hang on, I know where that is,' she says. 'Out the way.' She reaches up and rummages around, then pulls a big grey box down and puts it on the floor. 'That's the Dad box. All the pictures of him are in there. I was saving them all in one place for you and Abi.'

'Shoving them well out the way, more like,' I say sarcastically, but with enough humour that she knows I'm not going to kick off. I open the box, it's full of pictures. There must be hundreds, and they're all of Dad. I tip the lot onto the floor and spread them out with my hands. Abi appears at the door.

'What are you doing?' she says, a look of concern on her face. Likely assuming Mum and I are having another argument and that things are about to kick off.

'Just looking at old pictures. Come in,' I say. A smile creeps over her face and she skips over and kneels next to me.

'Is that Dad?' she says, pointing at a picture. I buckle at how little she remembers him. No matter how my relationship improves with Mum, it will always be my job to tell Abi about Dad.

'Yes. This was the day Dad got his new car. He was so proud of it, look at him, that grin is huge.' Mum says nothing, I don't let it bother me. 'And this one, your first birthday, Abs. Oh look, Dad's card that he made you. He's showing it to you, see? It was the first time you said doggie, do you remember? He drew a dog on it.'

'Doggie,' Abi says in a baby voice, making me and Mum laugh.

'Oh my God, I'd forgotten about this. That's the first lobster he caught in his lobster pot. He'd go out on his little boat and collect our dinner. We'd have crabs and prawns.' I keep looking at the pictures, Mum's feet in my periphery. They turn, as if to leave, then turn back.

'He was a good fisherman too,' she says, sitting down on the floor next to me. 'Look, this is the day he caught that giant seabass. It was so big he made it into the *Guernsey Globe*; he was chuffed to bits.'

I smile at Mum. She smiles at me. Abi watches us both, and then goes ahead and proves that she is more grown-up than either of us put together. 'I'm going to go to my room, so you two can be together. Maybe you can show me the photos another time?' Mum and I both nod as Abi disappears. Mum puts her hand on my leg and I stare at it, fighting my reflexes to push it away.

'He was a big part of my life too, Flo. It didn't end the way anyone wanted, but that doesn't mean thinking about the good times isn't very painful for me.'

I have so many 'buts'. I don't know if I really believe her. But, this is Mum showing a hint of sensitivity towards

Dad, and so seeing as it's one of the first times I've seen this happen since he died, I think better than to question it. We sit on the floor looking at pictures, telling stories about Dad, for another hour and a half. It's the nicest time I have ever had with my mother.

'What about I go grab a bottle of wine?' she says, getting up. 'I could sit here all night doing this, a drink would be nice. Oh, my knees.'

'No, Mum, please don't,' I say, knowing that if I drink, this won't end well. 'Mum, I'm going to stop drinking. Actually, more like, I think I *have* to stop drinking.' Deep breath. 'Mum, I think I'm an alcoholic.'

'An alcoholic, at twenty-two; oh, get over yourself, Flo.' I had expected that reaction. She won't be the first to have it.

'Mum, I'm serious. Our dinner with Abi, the whole ham sandwich thing, that's what I do when I drink. It's not OK.'

'We all act like that when we're drunk. You don't just label yourself a damn alcoholic.' This is about her, and the fear that one of her friends will hear about it and judge me, judge *her*.

'Well, Mum, I'm trying to be honest with myself about something and I think I've realised that I have a problem with alcohol. I do crazy stuff. Sexual stuff that I don't want, I've drunk at work. It's bad, and I know it is.' She huffs, quite loudly. 'Look, Mum, all I'm saying is I'm going to give up drinking, for Christ's sake. To make me happier, to make my life better. I'm sorry if that's such a problem for you.' I might as well have had the wine. We ended up here anyway. Some of my tears fall onto a picture of Dad. I wipe them off gently with my sleeve.

'Oh look, there it is,' Mum says, sitting back down. She pushes a few pictures around and reveals the one of the day Dad hid the spider in my food. 'Look, love, here it is.'

It's as good as I remember. I laugh, then push it into my chest and cry. Eventually, Mum's hand reaches out and lands on my knee. 'You know, I have a couple of friends who are in AA, they meet every Thursday in a room at the hospital. I could drive you there if you want?'

'Yes. Yes, please, I think that would be good.'

21

Renée

I've missed Ben. I've missed him so much. To be so close to him in that car, on that boat, and not be able to touch him was torture. We were all dumbstruck. All so numb. I wonder if he's been at work this week or if he's been off like us. I know what I have to do, but until the words are said, until we've told each other it's over, it's not over. But it will be. He loves his wife, I heard him say it.

It's weird being back at my desk. Everything is the same, but different. A new energy is in the office, in the world. Since the attacks, life has been slower. Pubs quieter. Roads less busy. Like everyone just needs a minute. Chloe and Georgina come to reception to see me. They seem different now too, softer. Like we're a team, not like it's them versus me, the temp on reception.

'Are you OK?' Chloe asks. 'We were so worried about you. Honestly, it must have been so frightening to be in London with all that going on, I hear they deployed an extra thousand police officers.'

'Yeah, it was pretty scary. Kept looking up to the sky expecting to see a plane.'

'Makes you realise how lucky we are to be here in lil' ole Guernsey, doesn't it?' Georgina says. 'If you forget about the whole Germans taking over the island for five years thing.' She rests her head on Chloe's shoulder, which Chloe doesn't seem to mind. We all stare and contemplate for a few seconds.

'We're here for you if you need us, OK?' Chloe says. All of her harshness evaporating. A new, softer version poking through. She looks happier. I hear the lift doors open, please let it be Ben. Please, please. It is. Chloe and Georgina go back to their desks. Ben walks straight over to me; he looks exhausted.

'Are you OK?' I ask him, standing up and walking around the reception desk. 'I think the fact that we were in a traumatic situation together means we have the right to hug.' I put my arms around him, and hug him the way a friend would. Something has changed. The usual energy between us, I can't feel it.

'Are you OK?' he asks.

'I'm good. Thanks for the week off. I mean, nothing even happened to us, but it was still awful.'

'The entire world is traumatised. This, on top of our individual traumas. It raised a lot of things for a lot of people. I'm glad you're OK.'

'I am Ben. But can we talk?'

'Yes, we will, I promise. I need to get to my desk now, though. But we will. I'm so glad you're OK.'

I sit back down. Does that mean I have to wait for him to suggest a time, or can I suggest a time? God, affairs are complicated; ending them is even harder. Matt appears at my desk.

'Hello,' he says, hovering over me.

'Hello Matt.' I try not to look at him in a way that would give any sort of encouragement. 'Do you need to make a booking?'

He looks awkward. 'Renée, did I do something to upset you?' he says, softly. Like a real person. With feelings. That are hurt.

'No, of course not,' I say, feeling terrible and acting like I have no idea what he is talking about. That everything is fine. And that I didn't make a very deliberate decision to ignore him and make him feel small and insignificant.

'I know I act like I might, but I don't sleep with many girls,' he says, quietly.

'We didn't sleep with each other, Matt,' I remind him.

'No, I know that. But we did . . . I just wanted to say that I came back to yours that night because I think you seem really smart. And you're gorgeous, and I thought we had a connection. I still do.'

I laugh a little. Is he joking?

'Matt, it was just some drunken fun. I'm sorry you wanted more but I'm not really up for a relationship right now, OK?' I say, lying so hard I could cry. I'd marry Ben in my lunch hour if he asked me.

'OK, well I just wanted to tell you that I liked you,' Matt says. 'Because I thought if you knew I wasn't into messing around, then maybe you'd view me differently. But you don't, so . . .'

'No Matt, I don't. I'm sorry. You're a decent guy, just not . . .'

'Not your guy?'

'No.'

'Well, whoever your guy is, they're very lucky, Renée.'

OK, now I feel bad. 'Thanks Matt, and I'm sorry. I really didn't mean to hurt your feelings.'

Imagine if you could just love whoever was available. Wouldn't that have been the kindest gift Mother Nature could have given us? For love not to be so selective, but to be spread willy-nilly with whichever person is up for it, rather than the one who isn't. Matt isn't that bad. He's a bit of an oaf and needs some training but with time he would be OK. He's got a good job, looks all right and – despite the sexist overlay – there is obviously a heart in there somewhere. And yet, it's just a no. Not even a maybe. I want nothing to do with him. Life would be easier out in the wild, where a mate is something you stumble across when foraging for food. You'd stick your ass in the air, let them do the thing, then bugger off with your babies and move on to the next. The love bit makes everything so difficult. And I love Ben, I do. I love him so much, and I cannot for a second believe that he doesn't love me too.

As the weeks roll on, the monotony of professional, grown-up life sets in, and I can report that if this is adulthood, I want out. Let me try uni again, I'll go this time. Put me back in A levels and tell me school will be the best years of my life, so I don't wish it away. Let me try to crawl back into my mother's womb and see if I can start it all again and do it differently. Because somehow, I've really ballsed this up.

    Life revolves entirely around work. And if I know anything, it's that this job is not for me. I imagine some people, like Carla and Gem, are riveted by the nine to five. For me, it's a rigmarole I want to live without. I can't go to bed late, because getting up is too hard. My alarm wakes me up every weekday morning and most Saturdays too because I always forget to turn it off. Meaning the weekends generally start with Flo being angry at me for waking her up too. We go to work, we come home. One of us cooks. We watch TV, we go to bed, we do it all again. At the weekend we cycle around, getting chips at the beach. We walk the cliffs, go shopping in town. It's just as it was. We left, we came back, we slotted straight back in. I swore that would never be me. I'd be so much more than the same old thing. If we could look into the future and see where we end up, we'd probably be a lot less judgemental of other people along the way. It's so easy to dream big when you're young. To imagine the people you'll meet, the places you'll go. You believe that you will be enough to get you what you want. No one tells you that it probably won't happen.

This island is safe, but it doesn't feel like my island any more. It's for younger people and families. I can't help the feeling that I'm not supposed to be here. I am the demographic that is supposed to be away, striving, thriving, making shapes. More than ever before, I notice heaving groups of seventeen- and eighteen-year-olds everywhere I go, downing shots and shouting over each other. Young, loud and horny. It looks so exhausting to be that free, what do they even do all day? It's their island now, not ours. I never imagined feeling old at twenty-two, but my guess is that no matter what age you are, you'll feel old if you're not where you should be. And yet, a voice inside is telling me that I can't leave. That this is where I am supposed to be. I remain in a constant state of confusion. Who am I? Where should I be? Why is being a grown-up such a goddam slog?

I am trapped inside this cage of an office, possibly dying from a broken heart for eight hours every single day. Ben is like an expensive house I can't afford, a dress that won't fit, a meal that makes me sick. He is everything I want and can't have. He's staying out of my way. Not being rude, not being mean, just keeping it professional. Like the last month never happened. The days have never felt so long. I've tried a couple of times to suggest we talk, but he's always busy, it's never the right time. Doesn't he just want it over with too? Maybe not. Maybe until we say it, there is still a chance.

I don't understand how this has all happened in just over a month. Guernsey truly is the tiny thing where big things happen, in absolutely no time at all.

Flo

It's taken a week of polite smiles and 'oops, don't mind me's' in the kitchen. But finally, Phil comes over to my desk with more purpose than he would if we'd run out of copy paper.

'You seem well, Flo?'

'I am, thank you, Phil.' Said like a woman who didn't do anything inappropriate to his bum-hole. Despite the last fortnight being a huge distraction, I'm still desperate to know what I did to him that night. It remains, even with everything that is going on in the world, the last thing I think about before I go to sleep at night. I just want to know.

'I was worried about you when you were in London, I'm very pleased you got back OK.' He's being very nice. Does that mean he's forgotten whatever it is I did? And if he has forgotten, would I be an idiot to remind him?

'Thanks. Honestly, it was scary, but we weren't in any actual danger. Ben got us home in one piece. We had each other.'

'So look, I was wondering if you'd like to have dinner with me tonight? I thought we could go back to the Chinese restaurant. I think you liked it?'

'I'm sorry, Phil, but tonight I am going to my first Alcoholics Anonymous meeting and I'd better not miss it, because well, I am an alcoholic.' I had not intended to tell a single soul about this. Ever. Let alone anyone at work. Let alone Phil. But I suspect that what just happened is that my paranoid brain was simply desperate for him to understand that I wasn't myself that night. And so, I just outed myself for going to AA. I mean, I literally said the word 'anonymous' out loud. I hate myself, and I'm not even drunk.

'Well, Flo. I'm really proud of you,' he says. 'That takes balls.'

'Did someone say balls?' Matt says, butting in. 'Flo, we're out of bog roll in the Men's.'

Damn him, I was about to ask Phil what I did that night. The confession of alcoholism seemed like a really nice run-up to getting the information I need. But Matt and his big, brutish man ways just stole the show. 'No problem,' I say, the consummate office manager. 'I'll get that sorted right away!'

Later on, we pull up to the hospital and Mum seems more nervous than me. 'What will you say?' she asks, parking up.

'I don't think I have to say anything at my first one. I hope. I don't know, it depends how many people are there.'

'Small island, lots of pubs, I'm sure it will be busier than you think. You'll have to tell me if there is anyone we know in there – Anne would never tell me. She said it would break "the code".'

'Then I won't tell you either, Mum, and don't ask me. OK? Don't make this harder than it is.'

'OK, OK, I won't ask.' I raise my eyebrows at this, she hasn't kept a secret her whole entire life. Even her own affairs were public knowledge.

I put my hands on my knees and take three long, slow breaths. 'OK, I'm going in.'

'Good girl, I'll wait here in case you change your mind. But if you stay the full hour, that's OK. I have my book.'

'Oh, what are you reading?'

'*The Secret Life of Bees* by Sue Monk Kidd. It's wonderful, I'll pass it on to you when I'm done.

'What's it about?'

'Motherhood, I suppose. And the many different forms it comes in.'

I have to hide my shock at the thought of my mother reading a book about motherhood. I thought it would be her least favourite subject and that she would actively avoid any book that had anything to do with it. But she's trying, and right now isn't the time to rock the boat.

'Come on, in you go,' she says, opening the book to a page with its corner folded down. 'Take your time.'

I walk in and take a seat at the back. I'd expected a circle with about ten people, but it's more of an audience set-up, chairs in rows and a lectern at the front. There are around twenty-five people. I keep my head down, terrified I'll meet someone I know. I appreciate that we are all here for the same reason, but still, this is my journey and right now I'm not interested in sharing it with anyone else. I didn't come to make friends. I want to learn how I give up booze, because I know that I can't do it on my own. I hope I don't have to stand up and say I'm an alcoholic, like I saw in a film once. I just want to sit here, go unnoticed, and hear what it's all about.

'Hello,' says a man taking the seat to my left. I half smile and glance quickly at him. I can see his body is big. It's spreading over his chair and touching me. I don't want to be rude. He's here for the same reason as me. But I don't want to talk. 'I've seen you about,' he says. Oh God, I know him, this is horrible. So embarrassing. How could I think this was a good idea on Guernsey? Why didn't I just wait until I got back to London, where that glorious big-city anonymity could swallow me up? 'I've seen you down the Ship and Crown.'

I turn to look at him. Wow, oh wow. It's the guy from the Ship. The one who was there after Sally's funeral, who was there before we left years ago, always alone with a pint.

'Hello,' I say back. 'You're here.'

'Third time. Couldn't go on like that. Time to turn that ship around.'

Wow, I thought the mission ahead of me was long. This guy has been sitting in the same seat, in the same T-shirt, in the same pub, for as long as I can remember.

'Well done,' I say to him, offering my hand. 'Flo.'

'Dave.'

The irony of us being in the same pub so many times over the years and never saying hi, and it only taking one AA meeting to force an introduction. 'I hope it works out for you this time,' I tell him.

'You too.'

We sit up straighter, as someone at the front begins to talk.

'Well, who was there? I mean, how was it?' Mum says, rushing towards me, having been leaning on the back of her car.

'It was sad, mostly. And inspiring, and then sad again. It made me realise I do have a problem, and it made me realise that I'm not alone. But I'm not going back in Guernsey, I'll do it in London. I can't bear the idea of people being there that I know.'

'London? Well, when are you going to London?'

'I'm going to move back, Mum. It's better for me. I'll visit, of course, but I want to go back.' I walk to the car door and get in.

'But Flo,' she says, considering her words as if they could upset me. 'I'll miss you, you know.'

'Yeah, Mum. I know.'

Renée

To take my mind off Ben, I see if Carla and Gem fancy a night out. We meet in the Albion for wine, the Ship for shots. The De La Rue for a couple more. I do my usual hilarious routine of being their court jester, so they laugh and cheer me on, like I'm the hired entertainment at a posh party. Carla goes on and on about the wedding. The seat covers match the tablecloths. She's doing 'sugared almonds' as the favours. Her bridesmaids are wearing sage green. I laugh and coo and tell her it sounds wonderful and fantastic and romantic, when really the whole thing sounds ridiculous and unnecessary. If I married Ben we'd run away and get married on a beach, just our closest friends and family there, our bare feet in the sand. None of this chair-cover nonsense, just pure, undeniable love.

I writhe around the stripper's pole in Follies, my ball gown landing around me like a blancmange when I fall to the floor because I am too drunk to hold on. At 2 a.m. we get chips. They share theirs, I eat all mine with extra mayonnaise. They get a cab together, I start walking with some guy who may or may not be handsome. I guess I'll find out in the morning.

The sun comes up. He isn't handsome. I leave his house at 8.15 a.m. and walk that dreaded walk of shame back to Mill Street. It's raining. The roads are busy with people who have their shit together. Adults going to work. Adults driving their kids to school. I just don't know where I sit in this world at this age; there is nothing for me. The in-between bit. The perineum. The utterly useless time in your life when you wander around in a ball gown at 8 a.m., trying to work out who you are after a one-night stand with a guy whose name you didn't catch but who had an overweight cat called Pamela Anderson that watched you have bad sex.

There was a smell of chemicals in his house. When I asked him what it was, he said he'd spent the day spraying furniture protector on his clothes to make them waterproof, to save him from having to do so much laundry. And there he was, in his own flat, cavorting as an adult.

My boobs ache. My period will come today. I feel particularly heavy. Heartache, hangover and PMT is a nasty and heady mix. I can wear this ball gown as much as I want but it won't make me more interesting. It won't change who I am. Like Pamela saw last night, you peel off this fancy exterior and the girl underneath has lost all her mojo. I think I fell asleep on the poor guy in the end. Not my best rodeo.

'Renée?'

No. Oh God, no. I can't bear to look around.

'Renée?' It's Ben's voice. I'd recognise it if I was fifteen thousand feet below sea level and every creature in the ocean was screaming all at once. I shouldn't be surprised. Guernsey is a tiny island; if you sleep with someone, you will just casually bump into them when leaving another man's house. I have make-up down my face. I haven't brushed my teeth. But what fool storms off in a ball gown pretending not to hear the man they love? I turn around.

He is on a bike. He is pulling a little cart with a rain cover over it. I assume he's just dropped his kids off at school.

'Ben, hi. I'm wearing a ball gown and it's 8.30 in the morning, how are you?'

'I see that. Fun night?'

He feels like my boss, and not the only man I have ever made true love to. 'This is not the walk of shame. I feel no shame. I slept on a friend's couch, I . . .'

'Renée, it's none of my business,' he says. I want to lie down on the pavement and bang my fists on the ground like a toddler who doesn't want to eat carrots. I want to scream that it *is* his business. I am all of this because of him. Everything I am in my whole life right now is because of him. I am his business, and he has no idea. To him I am just something extra. I see that now.

'Can I give you a lift, unless you're planning on coming to work dressed like that? In which case I will go ahead and lock all the doors.' He's being funny with me again. It feels like ages since I saw him smile.

'No, I'll go home. I am queen of the quick change. I'll see you there.' I keep walking. I never imagined wanting to get away from Ben but, right now, I need him to stop seeing me like this. I worry the smell of sex is radiating from me and I just want to be clean. I am a hussy, a slapper. I bet he doesn't see himself that way. No matter what he does on the side, he is still a husband, a father, a boss. I'm just a broke receptionist that he screwed.

'Renée, come on, it's raining. That taffeta won't age well if you get it wet.'

HONEYBEE

I don't know why I agree to squash myself into the small, rainproof cart that Ben is dragging on his bike. I have to sit to the side, my knees up to my face. In my gown. Wet. Hungover. Stinking of sex. When in, he pulls down the rain cover and does up the poppers. He then takes off, struggling a little with the weight of me, but soon we are gliding down the Grange, along the front and then up past the market and to the base of Mill Street. It's quite honestly one of the most humiliating ten minutes of my life. Like I'm being dragged and paraded for all the town to see and shame. I'm surprised no stones are thrown. When he unpops the lid, I find my knees have seized up and I have pins and needles that are so intense, so agonising, he has to lift me out and put me on my doorstep like an empty milk bottle.

'Please never mention this and eradicate all of this from your memory by the time I see you again.'

'In twenty minutes, you mean? When you're at your desk?'

'Sure. Ben . . .' I step closer to him, just to kiss him on the cheek. No one would think that was strange if they saw us, just a person, kissing another person on the cheek, saying thank you. In a ball gown. I hold still for just a second longer, just a second to feel his breath, to feel his cheek next to mine. He holds there too, I feel him wanting me. But something has changed.

'Renée, I have to go, I have a nine a.m. call. I'll see you in the office, go on, you've got seventeen minutes.'

I watch him cycle away, I want to run after him and tell him I love him. But it has to end, I know it does. Even though a part of me, a big part of me, still thinks he's going to choose me over his wife. I go up to the flat and collapse onto the sofa. The clock says it's 8.43 a.m. I roar with tears. With love. How is this what comes from something so fulfilling? Total emptiness.

I hear a noise. A buzz. A wasp, oh God, a wasp. I hate them so much. I hate them I hate them I hate them. It's clearly in here, the buzzing is so loud, and no one is here to save me. I get up, a rolled magazine in my hand, and I head towards the window. I'll smack it. I'll smack the shit out of it. But it isn't a wasp, it's a honeybee. Maybe one of Aunty Jo's, she said they flew for miles. I can't swat it, I need to save it. Just like Aunty Jo did. They don't want to sting you, it's only if they're scared. That's what she said. So, the trick is not to scare it. I hold out the magazine, it climbs on but rolls off. I remember how Aunty Jo did it. She laid down her finger, the bee climbed on, and she let it go out of the door. Easy. I can do that, I can save the bee.

I open the window first. I lean down, the little thing is tired, she must have been trying to get out for hours, the windows have been closed all night. Her little body is heaving. I lay my finger next to her, she walks onto it, as if she knows it's her ticket out of here. I raise my hand up and just as I am about to let her go, the curtain flaps in the wind and brushes against my other arm. I think it's a thousand wasps attacking me, my fist snaps shut, squashing the bee into my hand. She stings with every ounce of her might. I scream so loudly that people on the street below look up. The bee falls to the ground, leaving behind a small sack that pumps venomous poison through my skin. Oh God.

'Renée?' says a voice behind me. 'Renée are you all right?' It's Lillian, she must have heard me scream.

'No. I am not all right. I am a terrible grown-up. I killed her. The poor bee, all I had to do was get her out of the window safely. She trusted me. And now she is dead, because I can't do anything right.'

'Oh come on now, don't blame yourself. Those little bees might be strong but they're also fragile. OK, you're all right,' Lillian says, plucking the sting out with her fingers, then guiding me by the shoulders down the stairs and into her flat. 'Come on, come with me. I'll get you right.'

'This isn't about the bee, is it?' Lillian says, pressing a piece of kitchen towel filled with ice onto my finger. 'The scream I get, the hurt, but the self-loathing. That's about something else.'

'I'm sitting here in a ball gown crying my eyes out at nine a.m., what could possibly give you the idea that something is wrong?'

'Well, what is it?'

'Lillian, thanks for taking care of me, but I have to go. I'm going to be really late for work.'

'Oh, be late. What are they going to do, fire you? I'll wrap up your finger really well, tell them you slammed it in the door and had to go to hospital to get it looked at.

You're staying, and you're talking.' She's right. I relax. What's Ben going to do, fire me? Do I even care if he does?

'Lillian, I am a terrible person. I am having an affair with my married boss. I know that makes him sound awful, but you have to believe me when I tell you he's one of the best people I've ever met. He just . . .'

'Met you?'

'Yeah, he just met me. But I must end it, because he has a wife and kids and it's too messy. And I promised Flo, and if she can give up drinking, I can give up Ben. And oh my God it's all such a massive cliché. How am I someone's "other woman"?'

'OK, well first thing to understand is that he is the married one, not you. So, where you are right to have a conscience about it, it's him who should be ridden with guilt, not you. The second thing to understand is that you need an entirely new wardrobe.'

'Sorry, what? Why?'

'Because love challenges your self-worth, and so doing things for yourself helps to rebuild it. I have been alone for eight years, while my husband lives just nine minutes' drive away but doesn't even remember my name. I've felt like you feel right now most mornings for that entire time. Helpless, lost, alone. But I get up, I choose an outfit, and I get dressed for my day. And it helps. You need to do the same. I've seen that frog shirt; it's cute, Renée, but you can do better than that. I can help.'

I don't know how this has become about clothes. But

HONEYBEE

Lillian has finished wrapping up my finger, very professionally I might add, and she is walking towards another room.

'I'd love to buy loads of clothes, but I'm broke. Being a poxy receptionist pays diddly squat.'

'Well then this is your lucky day!'

She opens the door and inside is an entire bedroom full of clothes. Everything from gowns to trouser suits, cashmere jumpers to printed scarves. 'What shoe size are you?' she asks me.

'Six.'

'Ah, what chance. Go on, go in, pick out what you like, take whatever you want. I have my favourites in my bedroom, I was taking all this to the charity shop bit by bit, but much better if it goes to you.'

'Are you serious? All of this?'

'Yes, absolutely. I'm eighty-two years old, I have no need of it all. Go, enjoy yourself. Pick what you want and take it up, you can come and get the rest later.'

With my big swollen finger, I run my hand along the rails. The most brilliant, stylish clothes, way better than what you can buy on Guernsey. I feel my personality rising back up through me. I'm going to go to work today and hold my head up high. I might be late with a fat thumb, but I'm going to look like a queen.

22

Renée

Despite the hangover and swollen finger, I am sitting at my desk looking brilliant. I have on a pair of pink 'cigarette pants' as Lillian called them, and a shirt with blue waves and puffy sleeves. I'm having a few issues with the buttons across my boobs, they keep popping open. As I'm premenstrual my boobs are massive and really sore, worse than usual. But maybe that's because I'm sad. My period will come any minute, and then the buttons will close.

'Looking snappy,' Chloe says, walking past reception. It feels like the highest praise from her.

The phone rings. 'Hello, Magic Marketing,' I say, politely.

'I need Ben,' a female voice says. She sounds worried. 'I need Ben, please,' she says again.

'Of course, who can I say is calling?' I ask, grateful for her urgency, it means I will hear his voice. I'll say something cute when he answers the phone. Something to make him laugh to remember that feeling.

'It's his wife,' she says. And the world stops turning.

I can't say anything. I just freeze. 'Hello?' she says, sounding irritated. 'I need Ben now, please.'

'Of course, just a second,' I say, breathless.

I press hold. My heart is thrashing around in my chest. What do I do? If I say he isn't here, she'll call his mobile and he'll know I made a decision to hang up on her. If I put her through, I have to say who it is. And it will be so awful. I don't know what to do. I have to do something. I press #4.

'Hey,' he says quietly, as if I called him for a little chat. I give it a second, as that 'hey' rebounds around my body.

'Hey, there's a call for you.'

'Who is it?' I listen to his breathing for a few seconds. I suck his little sounds into my ears and close my eyes and hold on to him in my head, just for a moment.

'Your wife.'

Pause.

'Renée, I . . .'

'It's fine. Honestly. I'm putting her through now. OK?'

'OK.'

I press the transfer button and throw the receiver down like it's covered in bees.

*

HONEYBEE

I get up to organise the newspapers on the coffee table in reception. Flo likes them done in a certain way. A fan shape, starting with the tabloids, getting more intellectual, finishing with the *Guardian*. I top up the cups for the water filter and fluff up a vase of fresh flowers that she ordered in last week. They have a couple more days left in them yet. I am busying myself, trying to keep my mind off Ben. Also hoping that he will walk past and see how irresistible I look in my new clothes. Suddenly the lift door pings open.

'Where is he?' says a woman with blonde hair and tired eyes, who is suddenly standing in front of me. She's wearing a torn T-shirt and jeans. Her hair is a mess, and her face is very red with black make-up under her eyes.

'Who?' I ask, wearily. Is she a crazy person off the street? She looks like it.

'Please, get him for me,' she says, crying, falling to her knees. She is holding her mobile phone and has no bag.

'Get who?' I ask, keeping back.

She screeches in a frustrated way, gets up, and storms past me. She is really crying now; she seems to know where she's going. I follow her into the office and try to warn everyone that she's coming. 'Guys, I tried to stop her,' I say. They all look up and their expressions change, they seem to know who she is. People look back and forth at each other, but no one looks afraid.

'WHERE IS HE?' the woman shouts.

'It's OK Penny, he's here. He's in the kitchen. I'll get him,' says Georgina, sweetly. Who does she mean? Which 'he' is she talking about?

'You left me,' she cries, running to Ben as he comes out of the kitchen. 'I was all alone and I couldn't find you. You left me.' She is becoming inconsolable. Ben is trying to hold onto her arms to keep her still. He is saying, 'Penny, Penny, look at me. It's OK, I'm here. I just told you on the phone to go home, that I was leaving now. I told you to go home. I didn't leave you. I'm right here. I've got you. I've got you.'

Everyone is standing now. No one knows what to do, or how to react. I can't take my eyes off Ben. He is so focused on her. It's as if this has happened before. He knows what to do to calm her down. He looks into her eyes. 'Breathe with me,' he says, taking in huge deep breaths, blowing them out for six, until eventually her panting slows down, and her breathing falls in time with his. She's still crying though, not able to control the hiccups or the trembling. She whimpers like a little kid. Ben doesn't take his eyes off hers until she's calm. 'I'm here,' he says, over and over again. 'I am here. I am here.' He pulls her into his chest. He strokes her back. She holds on to him like her life depends on it.

After a few moments, he encourages her to move with him. They walk straight past me, and out of reception. As they wait for the lift, our lift, she is still crying. He holds her as close to him as he can. He never even looks back at me. I stand staring at the lift door as it closes.

'Poor Penny,' says Georgina, coming up behind me. 'She got sober last year, she was doing really well. Obviously, her demons just won't go away.'

'Sober?' I ask, still staring at the lift door. 'She's an alcoholic?'

'Yup. Poor thing. She's struggled with it for years. Ben moved them all here thinking island life would help. It seems to have made it worse.'

'Yeah, poor thing,' I say, kind of to myself as Georgina goes back to her desk. Now I understand. It should make me feel better, but it doesn't. I feel like the worst person alive.

Ben has been off for three days now. People in the office have been talking, of course. As they do when something like that happens. I've learned that Ben and Penny have been together nearly fifteen years, Georgina has known Ben since way back and was at the wedding. Apparently it was beautiful. Penny's problem with alcohol started soon after, although she'd always loved a night out. She's been sober a few times since, but always fallen off the wagon again. Ben is amazing with her, apparently. Loving, patient and understanding. Of course he is. If only they knew he'd screwed his receptionist.

It sounds so awful, and yet it isn't. Ben isn't a bad person. Perhaps just desperate for love, desperate for what we had. I searched on the internet for what kinds of people have affairs. Sociopaths, narcissists, and lonely people. Lonely people? I think it would feel really lonely being in a marriage with someone whose behaviour is that erratic. I've had a dose of that with Flo. I can imagine if she was like that all the time, the way she can be when she's drunk, that I would feel very lonely in our flat. But you can manage that with friendships, get some distance. With marriage, you have to be all in. You can be abandoned in so many ways. You can be hurt, sad, abused, have your dreams shattered, have your promises that you meant to keep made impossible to live by. But morally you have to stay loyal, cope with the grief of the happiness you thought you would feel. And if you don't, you're terrible. You don't deserve to feel love, kindness, affection from someone else, because you made a promise, and you broke it. Even though everything you hoped for didn't happen because somebody else changed. And so there must be so many people in a trap, whose partners didn't end up being who they thought they would be. People who are either miserable and lonely, or unfaithful and guilty. It makes you wonder how many people are actually happy.

I stand by my belief that if that lift hadn't broken down, Ben would not have had an affair. I refuse to believe he is a sociopath or a narcissist. He is lonely, he craves love. He deserves love. But even with knowing all that, I am what I am in all of this. An extra thing for him on the side. A soft, cuddly, calm way for him to feel loved. I might as well be a cat. It's such a bizarre feeling, to have been so intimate with him, but to be ignorant of this enormous detail of his life. That he was living with such pain. I really don't know him at all. He feels like a stranger now. A beautiful, elusive stranger who brushed passed me and left magic dust on my body that I'll never, ever be able to shake off.

HONEYBEE

He is off again today. The atmosphere in the office is calm and gentle. Everyone cares that Ben is OK. I put the phones on 'out-of-office' mode and go to the toilet. No period yet. My boobs are so sore, I wish it would just come. When I return, there is an email to us all from Ben.

> *I just wanted to acknowledge what happened the other day. Penny struggles with alcohol and is going through it pretty badly at the moment. I'm doing everything I can to help her, and I'll keep doing that until she's better. Her coming here and behaving like that was unacceptable and I'm really sorry if it made any of you feel uncomfortable. Penny wants me to apologise on her behalf, and she wanted me to tell you that it won't happen again. I'm sorry too. I'll be working from home for the rest of the week, but I'm available to you all as usual. Renée, please email on details of anyone who calls, and I will get back to them. Thanks for your understanding, I'll see you all Monday. Ben.*

'I'm available to you all'. If only that were true. I am the receptionist, of course he said my name specifically, and yet I wonder if he's trying to send me a message. He said my name to let me know he is thinking of me. He *is* thinking of me, like people do when they know you are grieving.

Georgina said that Penny had demons. I feel like I'm one of them. I have to be brave now, I have to do what is right. As much as it hurts, Ben can't be mine. Not now. Maybe one day, but this affair, it can't happen. It isn't the way it should be. None of us deserves the agony that it will bring, especially Penny. I think maybe it's not the married man who is having the affair who's the narcissist, but the woman he is sleeping with who is able to do that to another woman without the guilt crushing them to death. I reply to his email, hoping that I can relieve him of at least one trouble.

Ben, I'm so sorry about Penny. If I had known, I would have resisted more. I know you're not a bad person, and I know you didn't go looking for this. I laid myself on a piece of rice for you, I should have been more respectful of your marriage. But, as it stands, we did what we did and I am in love with you. I think it is important that I tell you that.

I didn't do this by myself, I know you felt it too. I will never forget our night in London. The way your body tastes, the way you feel inside of me. All of it, it's life-changing, life-affirming. I will never just be Renée again.

We both know this, but I still think it's important that one of us says it. Our affair must end now. I'll miss kissing you in the kitchen and the way you brush past me in the hall. Those tiny moments have been some of the biggest in my life. I'm trying hard to feel lucky for having you at all.

I'll call the agency and say I need a new job, it's not fair for me to stay. Go be a dad and husband, you're really good at it. I'm sorry for being so damn irresistible, Renée.

HONEYBEE

I read it through a thousand times. Have I taken too much of the blame? A little, but Ben doesn't deserve a guilt trip, he knows what he has done. This is what it feels like to have an affair with someone who isn't a sociopath or a narcissist. It's important to be kind.

SEND.

I immediately run to the bathroom to cry.

Flo

No. No way. Nope. No, this didn't just happen. I look around the office, everyone is stunned.

'WHAT THE FUCKING FUCK?' Matt shouts, standing up. Chloe is just staring at her screen. Georgina has stood up and is shaking her hands saying, 'Woah, woah, WOAH.' Phil's head is on his desk. What the hell did she just do?

'This must be a mistake,' I say, standing up. Covering for her. 'A joke, you know Renée, she's funny. I mean, this joke isn't funny, and I don't get it, but it's clearly a joke. Right? I mean, hahahaha, HAHAHAHAHA.' I have to stop talking. They're all looking at me like I am mad. I see Renée come out of the toilets and walk back into reception. She has no idea what she's done. When she sits down, I will tell her. I'll walk slowly, just to give her a few more seconds of life before she finds out. But she doesn't sit, she comes into the office to go to the kitchen. When she walks in, everyone stands up. It's a crazy act of awkwardness. No one knew everyone was going to stand up, but it's what we all do. Like she is the queen, and there will be a ceremony.

'What?' she says, confused. 'It's not my birthday.'

No one sits down. We can't. We're all frozen, no one knows what to do. She needs to know; she needs to understand. 'Renée,' I say, nervously. 'Did you press Reply All again by accident?'

At first, she has no idea what I'm talking about, but it slowly dawns on her and we watch as the colour drains from her face. Pure fear, like a terrified child. She turns from side to side, as if there should be someone there to hug her, to save her, to make her feel better. But there is no one there. I hate that she was screwing Ben, I hate it. But this, this is horrible. So embarrassing, so shameful. She doesn't deserve this.

'I sent that to you all?' she says, sheepishly.

Everyone nods. Matt looks angry, then upset, then angry. No one is saying anything. He takes it upon himself to go first. 'So, what, you like just get off with all the guys you work with?'

Ooof, that was mean. Too mean. Georgina walks over to her. 'Are you OK?' she asks. 'Things happen, it sounds to me like you're trying to do the right thing now.'

'His wife, she can't know, it will kill her,' Renée says. 'I didn't know she was like that, I just . . .'

'Oh diddums,' Matt says, and this seems to really rile Georgina.

'Oh give it a rest, Matt. People fuck. It happens. You fuck, Renée fucks, I fuck. We ALL fuck.'

This is a new Georgina. I like it. Matt doesn't like being challenged though; he is getting cocky. 'Oh, you fuck, do you? Who do you fuck?' Poor Georgina, what a horrible thing to be asked. Especially if she isn't really getting fucked by anyone, and then—

'She fucks me. Most days, actually,' Chloe says, going over and putting her arm around Georgina.

'Yes, I fuck Chloe every single day in those toilets and I fucking LOVE it.'

Renée's head shoots up, we all make an audible gasp. That was a shock and a half.

'Wow, so everyone fucks. OK, I get it now. Before we close this therapy session, has anyone else got a confession for the group?' Matt says, laughing now. Phil and I can't look at each other. I want to run out of the room. Surely we don't have to admit to anything just because everyone else does. Luckily he says nothing and neither do I. Georgina defuses the situation.

'It sounds to me like we need to work together on this, and that we all have a reason to keep our mouths shut, don't you think? I'm not sure any of us are squeaky clean. Matt, are we good? This is Operation Don't Make Penny Worse. And also, a lesson that humans do bad things, but we can be sorry. And also, that if anyone mentions this to anyone else, they will be fired. So, are we good?'

'We're good,' says Matt, stepping down from his pedestal. Between this and not being able to tell anyone who's at

AA, it's a good job I'm not drinking any more because I'd definitely let one of these secrets slip after a few wines. Phil makes a really strange noise. Like he wants to be in on this mass confession session but also can't bring himself to do it. Which makes me even more paranoid that the thing I did to him after our date is shocking; even more shocking than Renée talking about the taste of Ben's skin. He really looks like he's going to burst. Oh God, I think he's going to speak.

'Can I just tell my Mum?' he asks.

'NO PHIL,' we all say in chorus, even Matt, which is a good sign.

'When you tell someone, anyone, a secret, you have to trust that they won't tell a soul. And seeing as no one, not even your mum, has stakes in this like we do, it goes no further than this room. OK? Any of it?' Georgina is a force; I love this version of her. It's way better than the oversharing girl chat she's usually all about. 'Renée, why don't you go home for the rest of the day. There are no meetings, we can all handle the phones. Go and have a break,' Georgina says.

I go over to Renée and put my arms around her. 'Come on, I'll help you get your things.' I walk her out of the office and steer her towards the lift. 'Get home, get into bed. This is heartache, it will pass. OK?'

'OK,' she says. Childlike, again. She acts so big and tough, but no one feels pain like Renée.

'Flo?' she says, before she walks away. 'It's all such a mess, I think I . . .'

'No, don't think right now. Just rest, let today sink in, and then we will work out what to do, OK?'

'No, Flo. My period. I did the maths. I'm five days late.'

When I get back upstairs, my mouth wide open from horror and shock for a situation that I thought peaked an hour ago but just escalated to the totally unimaginable, Phil is waiting for me.

'Flo, can we talk?' I stop in front of him and realise my breathing is short. 'Are you OK?' he asks. 'I don't mean to sound rude, but you always seem to be on the edge of a panic attack. Do you get panic attacks? I do.'

'None of your business,' I say. 'What is it?' That was rude. 'Sorry, I just, you know, Renée, that was a lot.'

'Yeah, but while we're all being open, I thought maybe we could talk about us?'

'Us?'

'Yes. I like you Flo, I think I've made that obvious.' I mean, he sort of has. Apart from the bit where he stormed out of my flat and then hardly spoke to me for a week. 'I was so worried about you in London. It made me realise that I care about you, a lot. It's not often I meet someone who's lost their dad like me, I guess it makes me feel close to you, in a way.' It's like he's turning me off slowly, like a dimmer switch. I realise Renée and I came together through our shared experiences of grief, but do I want to go through my life gathering people because our parents died? Not really.

'I was wondering, and I know this is very old-fashioned, but I'm actually quite an old-fashioned person. Would you consider being my girlfriend? I think maybe it would be all right, with work, seeing that almost everyone has had sex with each other?'

'Oh,' I say, which is not the response he was looking for. 'Your girlfriend?'

He stands waiting for my answer. I am quite confused. 'But Phil, I thought you were angry with me, for doing something that you didn't like. You seemed really mad, and now you want to be my boyfriend?'

'Yeah, I mean, it wasn't that bad. Just don't do it again.'

'Wasn't that bad? How could it not have been that bad? You stormed out of my flat!'

'I'm just really ticklish, that's all.'

'Ticklish?' I'm sorry, what? 'Phil, what are you talking about? What was I doing?'

He looks around, lowers his voice. 'You were tickling my balls.'

'TICKLING YOUR BALLS,' I shout, not giving a shit about who in the office hears me. I'm sure everyone's tolerance for outrageous things is quite high after Renée's email. 'Phil, I have been going through hell trying to work out what I did. I thought I'd put my finger in your arse.'

'What? God, no. No you didn't, but I wouldn't mi—'

'Don't say that. Whatever you're about to say, please don't tell me that.' Oh my God, weeks of mental turmoil for tickling some balls. 'Phil. No, I don't want to be your girlfriend, but thank you. You've been incredibly kind to me, and I think you'd be a wonderful boyfriend to someone, but I'm not looking for a relationship right now,' I say, wanting to be nice and suddenly not fancying him at all.

I go back to my desk, a spring in my step. I need to get my shit together. I should be grabbing life by the balls, not just tickling them.

23

Renée

As I reach the front door, Lillian is coming out. She's wearing black for the first time that I've ever seen. 'Lillian, are you OK?'

'Oh Renée. My husband died a few days ago, at around 8.45 a.m.,' she says, gently. 'Isn't it strange. When I was tending to your sting, he must have been dead, and I didn't even know. They went to take him tea at 9.15, and he was gone. I got the call just after you left. I'd have come up to tell you but, well, I needed a moment alone. And I didn't want to upset you even more before you went to work.'

'Upset me? Lillian, I'd have taken the day off to be with you. I'm so sorry.'

'Thank you. I know a funeral director; I've adjusted his

suits for nearly thirty years. I called him right away. I said I'd rather not do a funeral and for him to just take care of things for me. He invited me to his offices today, for a committal, and then he will take care of the rest. He's already picked him up from the care home. It all goes so slowly and then it happens so fast.'

'Lillian, please, let me come with you.'

'No Renée, I'd rather go alone, but thank you.'

Such strength. I hug her really tightly. Her little body, more fragile than it looks.

'You know, love can be the most wonderful thing on earth, it can fill you up and lift you up and make you feel things that we all deserve to feel. But it can also be a trap. Something that holds you down, stops you flying away. Sometimes when it ends, you're not destroyed, you're set free. I'm free now, Renée. For the first time in years.' A tear and a smile appear at exactly the same time on Lillian's face, capturing the essence of everything love can be. She turns to walk up Mill Street.

'Lillian?' I say, calling her back. 'Don't fart during the committal.'

She guffaws so loudly it echoes off the buildings around us. As she disappears up the street, I hear her laughing the entire way.

Upstairs in the flat, the body of the dead bee lies lifeless on the living-room floor. I pick it up with my fingers. 'So strong, but so fragile. I'm sorry little bee.' I hold my palm up to the window and blow it outside. It wafts gently down onto the street below. Then I text Aunty Jo because some things are easier said written down.

I've been having an affair with my boss. I've wanted to tell you, I didn't know how. I think I lost my job. I think I'm pregnant. I'm sorry.

She replies straightaway: *Go buy a test and come here immediately. We will do it together. You're going to be OK. Never be sorry x*

I get two tests in Boots, in case one is faulty. I don't even care if anyone sees me buying them. As I'm walking down the high street towards the bus station, I get a text from Ben: *Renée, I saw your email. Can we talk? Georgina said you'd gone home, I could come to you?*

Should I turn around and go home, meet him there? I can't, being in my flat with him is too much. We'd end up in bed, I'm sure of it. I want that, I want to end up in bed. But I have to stay strong.

Can you meet me at Jerbourg Point in 30 minutes?

Perfect, I'll leave now x

The bus ride there is horrible. I am weepy, my boobs are sore, and I can't get a grip of myself at all. We need to close this out, but I don't want to. There is still this idea in my head that he is going to tell me he loves me, that he will leave his wife. That I am the one he wants. Just the thought of it makes my heart race, dries the tears, hurries me to the cliff where he is sitting on a bench, looking out to sea. He's wearing shorts and a T-shirt. It's strange to see him in casual clothes.

'Hi,' I say, behind him.

'Hi,' he says, turning around. 'Wow, you look great, new clothes? I love them.'

'Ben, I don't want to talk about my clothes.' He looks sweaty, maybe he is as nervous as me. I sit down next to him, making sure the Boots bag is wrapped up well so he doesn't see what's inside. 'I emailed everyone in the office and told them about our affair,' I say with a hint of humour, because it's so unbelievable there is no other way to say it.

'Yeah, I know. Saw that.'

'I'm really sorry, Ben. I was trying to do the right thing. I'm an idiot. I should have called you, not left a paper trail for everyone to see. I don't know what I was thinking.'

'You're a writer, you write stuff down. It's OK, what will be will be. Renée, I have to . . .' He starts to cry. Actual crying. Like this is hard for him, like he feels the same way I do. Gutted. Hard done by. In love.

'Ben, it's OK. I understand, I do. You have to be there for Penny and your kids. I don't want to be the reason you don't do that.'

'It's really important for me to tell you that everything you felt between us was real. It is real. I don't know how two people can come together the way we did and not be able to stay that way, but it's how it is. I don't get to have what I want here, I have to do the right thing.'

'I know.'

'You're very special Renée. You have something about you

that radiates. It shines. And you're talented. I think you'll do really well when you go to London, you'll take them by storm. And at some point, you'll meet the luckiest guy alive who gets to have you all to himself. I'll read about it in the papers one day, how Renée Sargent is madly in love with some brilliant guy. It's what you deserve. Come here.'

He stands up and offers me his hand. We hug, as tightly as we can. In broad daylight, for anyone to see. It has to end today, and that's it. Suddenly there's a gust of wind, it blows the Boots bag away. He runs after it; the tests fall out. He picks them up and just stares at them. 'Renée, are these for you?' I walk towards him.

'Yes, Ben, I . . .' And just at that moment, like a sign from Mother Nature that all of this is exactly as it should be, I feel a giant avalanche of blood come out of me like a warm blob of honey.

'Are you OK?' Ben asks, realising something has happened. My face must be a picture.

'Yeah,' I say, laughing.

'It's funny?' he asks, confused. 'I don't know if this is funny?'

'Ben, I got the tests because I am five days late. I mean, I was. But Ben, I'm about to bleed through these trousers, I just felt it start. Shit, I don't have anything.' I start looking around on the ground for something to put in my pants. There's nothing in my bag, just my phone and a lip gloss. 'Do you have anything, a tissue, anything?'

Ben turns out his pockets, just a phone and a credit card. He starts taking off his shoes.

'What are you doing?' I ask.

'You can have one of my socks?'

'Ben, I am not putting your sweaty sock in my knickers,' I say, laughing. This is funny but laughing is making the blood ooze out quicker.

'OK, well.' He sits down and pulls down his shorts.

'Ben, what the fuck?'

'Well, if you won't put my sock in your pants, you'll have to put my pants in your pants.'

'Ben, no!' But it's too late, he's whipped them off and he is handing them to me.

'A memento of all the good times,' he says. I'm reluctant, but the fear of destroying the gorgeous pink trousers that Lillian gave me makes me abandon all sense. I take the pants and stuff them into my knickers. 'This is ridiculous,' I say, laughing.

'I was not looking around to see if anyone was watching while I did that.'

'Neither was I.' I can see it now, front page of the *Globe* tomorrow. 'CLIFF DRAMA: Man stuffs pants in woman's knickers to stop her ruining new trousers.' It all seems so funny, until it doesn't. 'I'll miss you forever,' I tell him, pressing my forehead into his chest. His eyes fill up and he breaks away.

'It makes no sense, does it? Some people spend a lifetime searching for something like this and here we are, both wanting it but can't have it. It doesn't seem fair.' He sits down on the bench, he rests his elbows on his thighs and drops his head into his hands. I don't like to see him in pain but there is something very validating about how hard this is for him. I wasn't just a bit on the side. What we had was real. He stands up, pulling himself together. I try to ignore the ghost of my dad's abandonment tapping me on the shoulder, telling me I don't deserve the love of a man like Ben.

'I'd better get back,' he says, stepping away from me. 'I told Penny I was going for a run, she'll be worried.'

'You ran here?'

'Yes.'

'From Vale?'

'Yes, all along the coast. It's going to be a much bouncier run home now.' Funny. He's always funny, even when the air feels heavy. 'It's not that far. I'll miss it.'

'You'll miss what?'

'Yeah, Renée, there is one more thing. I'm moving the family back to London. I thought island life would be better for Penny but it's worse, she feels too isolated here. I can get her better help over there, and we will be near her mum and her friends . . . Also, another kid called Pandora the N word at school, and according to the Head Mistress it didn't even warrant a meeting with the other parents, so. I can't have my girls growing up in a world where no one looks like them, or where that kind of behaviour is tolerated. London is better for them too.'

'That's awful Ben, honestly, I'm so sorry.' A part of me wants to defend the island, but I know that would be wrong. Guernsey may be wonderful in many ways, but when it comes to diversity, we have a long way to go. I feel ashamed that his child was treated that way, and that he is everything that he is and still has to deal with that prejudice. 'You're doing the right thing, for the girls, and for Penny. Women need their women.'

'If you move there you can call me, I'll help you if I can.'

'I won't call you, Ben. You don't need to help me.' I feel proud of myself for saying that. And it's true, I need nothing from him other than a divorce and lifelong commitment to our love. But honestly, despite the fact I'm not sure my heart will ever recover from this, I don't want to be the reason someone else's life is destroyed. Ben can't be mine, and that's just that. He belongs to someone else.

He nods, grateful, I think. I suppose I could be demanding things of him, but what would be the point? We walk through the car park and stop at the bus stop. 'Aunty Jo doesn't live far from here, I'm going to walk there. You go.'

'OK. Renée, I meant everything I said. If things had been different.'

'I know.'

He kisses me on the cheek, we hug one last time. And then he turns and goes. Watching the one who got away literally run away from you while his underpants soak up your period is a whole new level of 'what the fuck' that I know will take me some time to process. I throw the Boots bag in the bin and waddle to Aunty Jo's.

EPILOGUE

Two weeks later

Flo

As the bus chugs happily across the island, from the depot in St Peter Port to the small roadside stop in Cobo, we both sit quietly and look out of the window once more.

'Your Fiat 126 broke down there, do you remember?' I say. 'We had to push it over the top of that hill so you could jump-start it down the other side.'

Memories, everywhere. We still have a story for every road. Chips in hand, the smell of vinegar wafting from the bag, we walk along the wall to the German bunker that overlooks the beach. It's a beautiful autumn evening, the sky blushing pink and orange.

'I know you don't want to hear this, Renée, but you suit Guernsey. You've got this earthy wholesomeness to you.

You get it from Aunty Jo.' I brace myself to be told to shut up. Renée has always seen herself as a future-big-city girl, but somehow that doesn't seem to work with who she actually is. Surprisingly, she doesn't say anything. She sort of smiles, like it was a compliment, then looks out to sea. Her hair is all tangled and she's stopped wearing make-up. She's got on a brilliantly casual green shirt with pedal pushers that used to belong to Lillian. It would look dated and unfashionable on anyone else, but on Renée it's adorable.

'I can't believe we thought you were pregnant,' I continue. 'Imagine if you were, I wonder how you'd be feeling right now.'

'Nervous but excited, probably. I wanted it. As soon as I thought it was happening, whether Ben was involved or not, I just knew without question that if I were pregnant, I'd keep it.'

'No way, you?'

'Yeah, me. I know. I think maybe you can kick about thinking you know yourself. Who you are, what you want, where you think you're going. But then something happens, like you think you're pregnant, and you get this really quick crash-course in everything you never knew you were. As it turns out, the idea of having a baby felt much more natural to me than most of the other things I've been hoping would happen.'

'I wasn't expecting you to say that, at all,' I say, shocked.

'Same. But what does it matter? I'm not pregnant and life goes on. But it's opened up a part of me I didn't know was there. Like in this weird way, thinking I was pregnant made my life feel bigger rather than smaller, if that makes any sense?'

'You mean, more purposeful?'

'Yeah, more purposeful, I suppose.'

We sit quietly for a while. Eating, looking at the horizon, taking long, deep breaths. I need to tell her, but I have to pick the right moment.

'Mad to think the Germans occupied the island, isn't it. They sat right here, pointing their guns out to sea, ready for battle. It wasn't even a hundred years ago,' Renée says, trying to imagine that scene. 'The Channel Islands are the only British territory that Hitler ever conquered, I remember learning that at school. I never quite realised the magnitude of it all. But Guernsey was totally under German rule for five years, there are bunkers and Martello Towers on almost every beach. Nazi Germans were sitting right here while their army committed the most heinous act of human violence in the history of the world and now you can come to this pretty island and do a walking tour of all their hangouts. Humans are so disappointing.'

There is another long pause. I just need to spit it out.

'Renée, I'm moving back to London. Guernsey just isn't the place for me, no matter how easy it is, how beautiful. I like the city. The way I can disappear there. I can't get my head around . . .'

'Flo, it's OK. I knew you would, I've just been waiting for you to tell me. It's better for you, I know.'

'Phew, yeah, and you'll find your way there too. It just

takes time, but you're Renée Sargent, London won't know what hit it.'

She puts a chip in her mouth and looks at what is left in the paper bag. 'I don't want to move to London, Flo. I hated it. I'm sure over time it would feel better, but for what? I want to write. I can do that here.'

'You can, but surely all the opportunities are there? How will you make any contacts?'

'I don't know. And I sort of don't care. All I know is that when I was there, I felt tiny, like one in a billion people who would have to fight so hard to get noticed. I get tired just thinking about it. I want to write a book, and until I've written it, I don't need to be there. Aunty Jo wants to take some time off, so she's asked me if I'd like to be manager of the garden centre and I'd actually really love that.'

'Wow, yes, this makes so much more sense than "office Renée".'

'Right? I mean, what maniac would let me loose on their phone lines?' She puts her head on my shoulder. 'I'll miss you,' she says.

'I'll miss you too.'

I never imagined that it would be Renée who would stay on the island, and me who moved to London. But maybe that's what adulting is, being honest with yourself about where you are supposed to be. I can't do AA here, it's too intimate for me. I'm going to rent a room from one of Mum's friends who lives in Chelsea and find a meeting in another borough so I don't bump into anyone I know. Unlike Renée, I want to go unnoticed. Guernsey doesn't afford me that luxury.

'I got a cheque in the post,' she says, a smile on her face.

'Wow, from your dad, how much?'

'No, from Magic Marketing. A thousand pounds. In the envelope was one of the cheese flyers, my logo written across it with a very happy teenager taking a big bite out of a lump of cheddar. Ben had written, "Congratulations, love Ben" on it. I keep it under my pillow. Pathetic, I know. I just . . .' Her eyes fill with tears. She loves him so much. Proper, grown-up love.

'Oh Renée, it will get easier.'

'It might, it might not. It's all material, right?'

'Yeah, it's all material for the brilliant books you'll write. But it's also OK if it isn't. You're allowed to find this really hard and you don't have to apply any kind of reasoning or meaning to it. It's heartbreak, no one ever said it was easy.'

'Love is like a disease. It will go away over time, and I'll be healthy again, but until then, I just have to suffer. It's so shit.'

'Ooh, that was good. You should put that in your book,' I say, genuinely impressed by her way with words.

'I've written three thousand words, you know. It's a book about a girl who falls in love with her boss and has to choose between him and her career. I've called it *Work/Love Balance*. It's just a working title. But it's good, I think, the story. And I'm good at it too. I enjoy it. So I'll plug away at it while helping people find the right soil for their gardens, and helping Aunty Jo with the bees, and I'll be fine. Possibly even happy, imagine that?'

'See, Guernsey suits you. It's weird, all these years I imagined you anywhere but here, but you weren't born to be lost among the millions, Renée. You're a . . .'

'Queen bee?'

'I mean no, that isn't what I was going to say. I meant you're supposed to be the big fish in a little pond but sure, Queen Bee, why not? So, is there a cool best friend in this book of yours? A darker, sultry type who returns from the big smoke and saves the day? Eye eye, wink wink.'

'No, but I've called my main character Flo, obviously.'

'Obviously,' I say, shuffling up to her. 'I'm honoured, thank you.'

'She smells of poo and never shaves her armpits.'

'Oi, watch it,' I say, picking up one of her chips and chucking it onto the sand below. A seagull swoops in and gobbles it up, then makes a horrible noise to let all his friends know that there are two humans sitting on the bunker throwing chips onto the beach. Soon we're surrounded. Renée throws a chip into the air and a seagull catches it mid-flight. This turns into an aggressive game of catch with the birds until all our chips are gone and the seagulls get bored and fly away.

'Promise you'll come back a lot?' she says, rolling her paper up into a ball.

'Promise.'

'This is your hive. You leave, but you can always come

back. Guernsey is nice when you think about it that way.'

There's a peacefulness about her; it's different from the way she has always been. Until now she's been consumed with a restlessness, a frustration. A feeling that she is running out of time, that nothing will ever be enough. Chasing something that isn't there, just to keep moving forward. But now she has found her purpose, she knows the role she wants to play in her own life. She is a creator, and she will build her own world here. It all makes perfect sense.

As for me, I am not my story's leading lady and I'm perfectly OK with that. I want to work for other people, sit on the sidelines and cheer other women on. I don't need limelight, I don't need power, I just want to feel peaceful. To keep that rat away. I feel that this time, with everything I've learned, London will do that for me. I'll commit to the grind and go to work. I'll hide in the anonymity of it all. I'll find people and things I love to cling on to, but I'll never need more than that. It's a very unimpressive thing to say out loud, but a very comforting thing to feel inside: that all you really want is to have enough to get by, enough to be happy, and enough to be healthy. Nothing more. Just . . . enough.

'I think you should have all of Lillian's suits for work,' Renée says, like a nana who is giving away her precious jewellery before she dies. 'I'll never get any use out of them here, and you'd look brilliant in them. I love all the casual stuff, and I'll keep the gowns, of course. And Lillian made me the most brilliant pair of dungarees covered in bees to wear at the garden centre. But take the suits. You'd have to promise me to wear them and ditch the black though. OK?'

'Wow, I'd love them. And yes, weirdly black hasn't been feeling right lately. Bright red trouser suits it is! Aren't we lucky?'

'We are. Let's swim,' she says, jumping up to her feet.

'No way, I'm wearing terrible knickers.'

'Well, I'm going in,' she says, running down the wall and onto the sand, tearing off her clothes and throwing them onto a rock. I sit back on the bench and take this spectacle in.

'One, two, three!' she shouts, running down the beach. I watch her bottom as it merges into the water, then bounces up as she dives and disappears. Like the true island girl that she is.

We're the same, but different.

Friends forever x

Author Note

Although there are similarities to my life in the Renée and Flo novels, all characters are entirely fictional. Guernsey is a real place, and many of the locations in the book are also real. But I made up lots of things about those too, so don't stress yourself with comparing it to the real thing. This is fiction. I hope you enjoy the contents of my head.

Dawn

x

Acknowledgements

This book has been in the making for many years. It's down to Emily Kent who emailed me one day, out of the blue, when my career was in the pan and I was on my knees. At the time, the only job I could get was doing a YouTube campaign for British potatoes. I had to eat potatoes every day for a month and make videos about it. At any other moment in my life, this might have been my dream job, but at the time it was extremely depressing. Emily emailed me to say she loved my weekly column in *Stylist* magazine (I'd just lost my column, thus being on my knees gorging on potatoes) and wondered if I'd ever considered writing fiction. I had but was way too scared to try. Emily gave me a two-book deal with Hot Key Books, and that was how Renée and Flo's story began. I'm honestly not sure what I would have done if I'd never got that call, it literally changed my life. A note to you all, if you're on your knees and feel like a total waste of space, eat some spuds and keep your head up. You never know what's around the corner. Maybe, just maybe, there is someone out there who thinks you're ace and the right opportunity is about to come knocking. Thanks, Emily, I'm so grateful for the opportunity you gave me. I owe you some potatoes.

Thanks endlessly to my agent of all agents, Adrian Sington, who I accidentally called my 'Adrient' on a call the other day. I think we can all agree that's how we should refer to him from now on. Over twenty years of working with each other and it just gets lovelier and lovelier. I adore you; you're brilliant and clever and kind and always make me feel so smart and funny, which is excellent Adrienting.

My team at HarperCollins, thank you so much, as always. Charlotte Brabbin, you are a brilliant editor. It's always such a thrill to get your notes back and work on these books with you. Liz in PR, thanks again for all the planning and bubbles. To everyone in Marketing and Design for the cover. Charlie for the support and absolutely everyone else who I don't work with often, but know you work so hard on my behalf. You're a brilliant team. Huge thanks, too, to Helen Gould for the sensitivity read and her insightful notes.

I must thank my school friend Sophie Riley who, back in 2018, spent hours on the phone with me answering many questions as I created the character of Flo. Your openness helped me draw Flo's experience and make what she was going through feel very real. Your honesty was so inspiring, and I'm sure many young women reading the book will find some comfort knowing they are not alone. The notes we sent each other at school gave me the original idea for *Paper Aeroplanes*. I keep them safe, a snapshot of who we were during a wild time in our lives, and which we would have forgotten had it not been for those epic notes we wrote. Thanks again, I owe you a lovely cup of tea.

My Aunty Jane and Uncle Tony, for all the animals you put into my life, including the bees and the countless moments of pride when I would give someone the gift of 'Aunty Jane's honey'. Thanks for making Guernsey more than just an island and making sure that Jane and I explored it. And for making home somewhere I still love to come.

I'd like to thank absolutely everyone who came to *Honeybee* because you'd read *Paper Aeroplanes* and *Goose*. This book really is for you. Since those books came out, we've shared so many beautiful moments at signings and events. You've told me your stories of friendship and loss, and I've taken them all in. I only get to do this because of you, so really, you're top of my list for thank yous. I've been so excited to give you this new instalment of Renée and Flo, I really hope you enjoy it.

My Patreon crew, you know I love you!

To Choose Love and Flackstock. I love being a part of both of you. Even though I wish there was no need for any of it, and that the world was a more gentle and kinder place, that is not reality. It is an honour to do what we do. I love you!

Eleanor Bergstein, my dear friend and oracle on love.

Thank you for creating the greatest love story of all time (*Dirty Dancing*) which inspires so much of my writing. I love you, and I'll come back to NYC for burgers and red wine really soon.

Thank you to Virginia Woolf for the words, 'A woman is to have money and a room of her own if she is to write fiction.' This year, I got the room. My studio is one of my favourite places to be. A room all of my own, to write my books and to hide all of my clothes from my husband.

Chris, Art, Valentine, Myrtle, Boo, Meatloaf, Puffin and Sandwich, I love you all. How lucky I am to go to my office then come home to you all.

I could go on… thanks for reading my book, I hope you enjoyed it. x